The Summer of 3

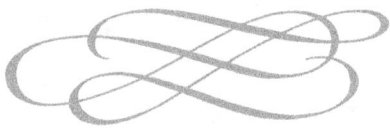

By

STEPHANIE CAPRINI

This book is dedicated to my aunt, Pam, and friend, Jeanne.
Thank you for all your wisdom and guidance.

Prologue

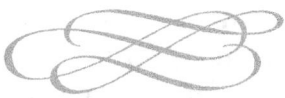

A bridal magazine lay open on the coffee table in the sun-filled, front room of Chelsea's small college apartment. Next to it scattered photos of tuxedos and flower arragements, cut outs of jewelry and beach-front hotels, and open notepads with perfectly written, detailed notes. Around the montage photo album in the making sat three good friends: Chelsea, Rachel, and Danielle. Chelsea and Rachel's friendship began in high school, and Danielle had rounded out the group ever since their freshman orientation at Boston College. Although Chelsea was the inarguable glue of the group – the one to whom the other two turned for advise and consolation – the three girls had grown to form strong friendships.

It was May, and they were all preparing for their graduation from Boston College. At twenty-two years old, life was yet uncharted, the vast open waters of the future promising glory, success, and blissfully happy lives. Therefore, it seemed the perfect time to be girly and ideal and fawn over marriages and what each saw as a fulfilled life. Albeit the reality that Danielle was the only one of the three who was currently "with boyfriend," the three friends scoured and cooed over wedding pictures and ideals. Weddings were every girl's dream and fantasy, and every detail needed to be discussed, perfected. The dress had to be pristine, the flowers bright and colorful, and the ring a reflection of the wearer's personality. Therefore, the girls had plenty to discuss.

Rachel took charge of the afternoon and the cutting, finding, and distributing of photos for all three of the girls. She sat on the sofa in a sky blue, summer sundress with her laptop open, magazines sprawled in front of her, her brown hair tied back, and her Tiffany pearls playing against her wrist as she flipped through different websites and magazine pages. Her personality was superfluous yet distinguished. She always wanted the biggest and the best of everything, basking in every part of being the center of attention at events and gatherings, yet she strove for the utmost refinement in decorum and presentation. To her, life was about having the best, one that echoed tastefulness and demanded jealousy. She was raised to believe that apprearances not only mattered, but got you where you wanted to go.

Her choice of photos, therefore, was a perfect mirror to her personality. Strewn around her lay pictures overflowing with tightly bound, full bouquets, princess dresses, tiaras, banquet halls, and glasses of champagne. Although recently split from her two year college sweetheart, Rachel, as of late, erred on the side of optimism. She believed that life outside of college held the man of her dreams, one who was already working to accumulate wealth and a lifestyle in which she could share. She wanted to be married, but she would not settle for anything less than everything. Although she wanted to be married in a timely manner and prior to her entering her late twenties, she felt she could wait just a little longer if needed, especially if it was for Mr. Right and With Money.

Danielle sat opposite her friends, at the other end of the coffee table, perusing aimlessly through the photos Rachel kept tossing her way. She wore short black shorts and a snap-up summer blouse over her bikini top. She seemed more distant than overtly involved in the wedding gossip. Although she made it a point to actively participate, she found her mind distracted by thoughts of Paul, even when she tried to focus them on the matter at hand.

Only in the last few weeks had Danielle started dating Paul, another senior at Boston University. Paul had sparked a passion in her that ran fast and deep. The two spent almost every free moment together biking and seeing the sights around Boston because after graduation they would both go their separate ways. When Rachel asked Danielle if the two were yet in love, Danielle hesitated. That hesitation in answering was enough to send Rachel into a whirlwind of wedding planning for Danielle and Paul's future wedding. To Rachel, Danielle's hesitation meant the possibility of a "yes" answer and future wedding bells. Thus, Rachel had insisted on today's get together as a way to start preparing for the inevitable.

Althogh Danielle saw the entire ordeal of wedding speculation as superfluous, she indulged her friend and now sat crosslegged on the floor of the TV room, surrounded by an array of photos that did not necessarily have any cohesive theme. Danielle was still trying to grasp the notion that she might have actually fallen in love with a boy she would have to say good-bye to in under one week. Wedding planning, therefore, did not even have enough persuasion to hold rental space in her brain let alone take up permanent residence. However, if this was what girl-time today included, then she would at least entertain her friends. Being together was always enjoyable, even if the topic at hand was not on Danielle's list of top things that needed to be accomplished immediately.

Danielle laughed at Rachel's ooing and aahing over different pictures and destinations, as Danielle herself had never given much serious thought to her own wedding. She had other things on her mind, like law school. She dreamt of law school often but had recently come to terms with the fact that the dream would have to hold off for another year as she needed to increase her LSAT score in order to attend a good school in the Boston area. It was not the ideal situation, but having wanted to be a lawyer since high school, she had deemed the wait as necessary. It was her first and most important goal at the moment.

Her future wedding, on the other hand, was more of a blur. She had always assumed it would be there, but the specifics were not necessarily ascertainable at the moment. She was the type of girl who could only truly dream of something when it had the actual potential for being a reality and was something she wanted for herself without question. Right now, that something was law school, not a wedding, but she chose to stay seated and laugh along with her friends, knowing these moments would dissipate quickly with next week's graduation.

Between the two friends and curled-up on the floor in a Boston College t-shirt and khaki shorts, Chelsea found herself simply enjoying the afternoon. It was a Saturday; it was sunny; and she was with her two best friends. Wedding browsing was always an exciting activity, and she anticipated her own would occur in the "sooner rather than later" future as well. Therefore, it was always important to stay on top of the latest trends. Plus, real life would be occupying her time soon enough, so imagining herself in gowns and on exotic beaches was clearly the more enjoyable, and therefore winning, option.

Still, it was not as though she was without post-graduation thoughts. Chelsea had already enumerated the lifestyle changes that would be occuring in her own, very near future. She was moving home with the parents again, looking for a job in Boston and the surrounding areas as she still had not found one, and doing that long-dreaded thing called being a grown-up. She had always envisioned herself moving out of the house after college, yet the reality of the economy and her own job situation – or lack thereof – proved that leaving home would have to wait. However, with Danielle moving an hour outside of Boston and Rachel moving into the heart of Boston, Chelsea wanted to immerse herself in all of the time she had left with her friends. Right now that meant looking through wedding websites and magazines.

Unfortunately for Chelsea, wedding planning was still more aspirational play than serious detailing. She had grown up dreaming of her own wedding and had attended plenty in the process. Her steadfast Italian upbringing drove the certainty of the event into her as deeply as the necessity for air. A wedding was not a question of "if" for her, but rather a "when." Her mother had disappointingly made note that she was graduating "senza boyfriend" and that unless she found a job quickly, her prospects would be less than optimal. Initially Chelsea's mother's words had scared Chelsea into feeling like maybe she had done something wrong by not finding "Mr. Right" already. However, with Rachel also being in the same non-husband boat, she somehow felt a little more confident and assured that things would happen in their own time. Fate, as her mother had put it, sometimes needed a push every now and again but often knew exactly what it was doing. So, Chelsea chalked up her current relationship status to Fate and determined it would push her in the wedding direction when it was actually the right time for her.

Right now, however, Chelsea dedicated herself whole-heartedly to enjoying her friends and their wedding magazine afternoon. They only had a matter of hours together before they were pulled in other, pressing directions. Danielle was scheduled to have dinner with Paul and his family in a few hours, Rachel was running off to have her hair highlighted before graduation, and Chelsea had more job applications to complete. Life was happening whether they wanted to face it or not, and the blissful display of dresses and laughing and smiling women all resonated with each girl in a different way. In each's mind, the pictures represented a type of certainty or inevitable future. For Rachel, it was just a question of who would win her heart. For Danielle, it was more of a potential idea than steadfast certainty, and for Chelsea it was a matter of timing and Fate. All three, however, knew it would be an occasion to celebrate, in time. They all just had to deal with the real-world first.

Five
Years
Later

Chapter 1 - Chelsea

"What do you mean he's not coming in today?" Chelsea bellowed into the phone, the annoyance of her phone conversation overcoming any leftover Friday morning sleepiness she may have felt. "Does he have any idea how many accounts we have to process?"

A silence passed through the room as she listened angrily to her boss on the other end of the phone. Her boss, Patrick Whitesman, had been out of the office all week, and every bit of business that had gone on in the bank had been conducted over the phone. Now, though, instead of dryly catching him up on daily figures and occurrences, she found herself arguing with her boss over the competency, or lack thereof, of her co-worker, David Garoff.

Finally, Chelsea hung up the phone, annoyed. "Well that's just brilliant."

Chelsea Farrera was twenty-seven years-old and a bank employee. She lived in the suburbs of Boston and went to work like every other twenty-something year-old college graduate, working jobs they did not necessarily picture themselves doing forever but kept in hopes of staying afloat while trying to forge ahead in life.

She had been with Hobson Bank & Trust for a year, although recently it had started to seem like a year too long. She was not completely unhappy but not necessarily happy either, which left her somewhere stalely in the middle. Lately, she felt the staleness starting to gain speed.

Sighing aloud in early morning annoyance, she combed her thick, wavy brown hair off her face with her fingers and rested momentarily in the curve of her hand.

Danny Fieldman knocked on her cubicle half-wall. "Everything all right in here?"

Shaking herself upright, not expecting someone to be standing behind her, she replied, "Yeah, it's fine. David is just not coming in today, *again*. This is the second week in a row he's called off last minute on a Friday. I just don't understand why Pat can't see through his bullshit. Who calls off two Fridays in a row because he's 'sick'?" she added, including air quotes on the last word. "He just doesn't want to work, and he ends up leaving all these accounts on me."

Danny leaned his hip against the wall of her cubicle, crossing one foot over the other and asked, "So then, I take it you can't come to lunch with Stacy and me in an hour?" He had noticed her frustration.

She looked at him as he stood in his business attire and steel rimmed glasses, contemplating the state of her soon-to-be hunger.

"Oh, right, lunch."

"It's cool. I understand if you can't make it," he offered.

"No, I want to go, it's just…" she shuffled a handful of papers around her desk. "Okay. Here's the deal. If I can close out these three accounts here before noon and double check something with the mortgage department on this one, then I'll come."

Danny nodded. "Sounds good. We'll stop by on our way out."

"Thanks, Danny. I'll see you both in a bit."

Chelsea shifted herself back behind her desk and grabbed the first account file. Bouquet's R Us was a relatively new, local, flower company whose owner needed more hand holding and account updates than any other start-up she'd handled to date. In fact, she had hoped to give the account over to David since start-ups were his specialty. However, since he was not coming in today, she had to figure out the logistics herself. Unfortunately, her year-long career at Hobson Bank and Trust had not provided her with much practice in this area. Now this one account alone would probably take her three times as long as it would have taken David. Additionally, she had a stack of eight accounts on her desk already, and it was only 10:30 a.m. Days like today made her wonder how much longer she would last at this job. Yes she had majored in Management, but she had also minored in English, really wanting to use her degree in some writing capacity. She knowingly admitted she had no connections with any magazines or newspapers to help her get her foot in the door, but she just did not see herself writing bank jargon for much longer. And on days like today, when David stuck her with double her workload, she would have rather written him a few choice memos than file and fix clients' paperwork.

Still, she opened the file and started making phone calls. The sooner she finished this work the better. Lunch with Danny and Stacy had been planned all week. They tried to do something at least once a week to stay in touch, since it was so easy to fall into the routine of eating at one's desk to finish early on Fridays. Technically no one was allowed to leave early, but having the work done early occasionally made it worth forgoing lunch. However, as of two months ago, the three had discovered their lunch outings proved more enticing than the extra break at the end of the day, and Chelsea did not want to miss out on today's lunch for anything. She already had a hectic weekend planned and could use some much-needed socializing. Rachel, her best friend from high school, needed help bridal dress shopping. They had already allocated the entire weekend to hunting for the perfect dress. Plus, with Rachel, nothing was ever a small endeavor. Even if wedding dress shopping finished early, they would still find something to do. As a result, Chelsea had made a point of marking off the entire weekend as unavailable. Therefore, she neither wanted to have any accounts lingering in her mind over the weekend nor have to stay late to finish things. She needed to work quickly and diligently.

Chelsea glanced at the clock on the wall. It was 11:32 a.m., and she knew Danny and Stacy would be showing up any minute to see if she would be joining them for lunch. In the last hour she had completed two accounts and found herself currently on hold on the phone with the third. She had not even tried to reach the mortgage department because she thought they would probably be out to lunch around this time, so there was no point in trying to reach them until after one 'o clock. That meant she could squeeze in lunch with her co-workers once she finished her phone call, a reality which brought with it a sense of welcomed relief.

"Hey girl," Stacy beamed, finishing off the last bit of her coffee and walking into Chelsea's cubicle. "How's the work coming?"

Chelsea waved to Stacy and then signaled to the phone. She held up one finger, and Stacy seemed to understand Chelsea's message. Stacy mouthed to Chelsea that they would wait and bowed out, allowing Chelsea another five minutes to wrap up the call.

Stacy Branson was Chelsea's co-worker and also worked in account management like Chelsea. She was a cute, five-foot-three, box-assisted strawberry blond, and had sprung back to normal quickly after having her first child nine months prior. She and Chelsea sparked an easy work friendship and could talk about most things, save conversations revolving around children as Chelsea had little experience in that area.

Chelsea was still single and had moved back in with her parents after a bad breakup with her now ex-boyfriend. It was not the ideal situation, but it worked for now. She had initially felt this job to be a good thing, since she had been out of a job when her relationship ended. Her life was still not perfect, and Chelsea chalked up her current relationship status to Fate, making mental note that this now made the score Fate: 2, Chelsea: 0. However, she was determined to come out of everything somehow better off than before her failed relationship. It was just that her family and current lifestyle did not necessarily make that easy for her, but it was a work in progress.

Chelsea came from a large Italian family, had wavy, dark chocolate hair, rich, mocha colored eyes, and a light, glowing, year-round tan. She was almost five-foot-six, generally wore nothing less than three-inch heels to work, and always donned sparkling silver jewelry. To Chelsea, bank life was fine but monotonous. The work, though, was at least constant and kept her busy. Therefore, for now, she could not really complain. She was always hopeful there might be something else in the future, though, and days like today increased the need for such hope. She was just relieved to be heading to lunch with friends.

When Chelsea, Danny, and Stacy arrived at the diner down the street, sitting outside seemed the best option. It was the first day of warm weather since the snow had melted. Sunny and sixty-five degrees for the beginning of May in Boston warranted praise.

"Long morning, huh?" Danny asked, taking a seat in the wrought-iron chair.

"I seriously don't even want to talk about it," Chelsea answered, taking a seat herself. "David left me in the same position last week, and I just don't have the mental space to deal with it right now. I have so much on my mind already with this upcoming weekend," she finished, half-laughing in disbelief.

"You're bridal dress shopping aren't you?" Stacy inquired.

"Yeah. This is our last hope at trying to find her a dress. Actually, Rachel and I were supposed to do it last weekend but she came down with a cold and we moved it. It is like do or die time, though. Her wedding is Labor Day Weekend and it's already May! We have to find something pronto because it takes time for the order to arrive, and we want alterations to be completed in time. We are so down to the wire!"

Stacy asked, "Why so late?"

"Well," Chelsea explained laughing almost to herself, "Rachel wanted every dress at first and refused to buy one until she had scoured multiple stores. When the end of March finally arrived, she freaked out because she realized she not only *hadn't* decided on a dress but *couldn't* decide. We started going back to places she'd already been, but, so far we've had no luck. Now we are down to like our last stores. Keep your fingers crossed. She has to find one soon or she'll be a bride in nothing but jewelry and an incredible pair of shoes!"

"That sounds hectic, but it should be fun!" Stacy started. "That was one of my favorite parts about getting married. I loved trying on all those gowns."

"Yeah, it should be a lot of fun," Chelsea agreed, and then she laughed. "Danny, feel free to jump in whenever."

Danny turned to Chelsea and smiled. His wide grin offset his green eyes and steel-framed glasses. He looked thoughtful even when he wasn't sitting over his computer analyzing data.

"You girls and your bridal stuff," he stated. "My older sister was the same way the first time she got married, and if she gets married again, I can't imagine her being any different. Personally, I just don't understand any of it."

"You mean you don't dream about your wedding?" Stacy jokingly asked, pretending to be offended by his lack of interest. The two of them had been working together for three years now, and their rapport was obvious. They had sparked a close friendship, although strictly platonic. Stacy was happily married, and Danny dabbled in relationships. He said he just didn't wear them well, at least not yet. Their friendship, instead, was solidified by their love of movies and the ever-changing events of the Boston suburbs. Chelsea found herself floating in the middle, trying to feel out where exactly she fit into this friendship, but she knew the three of them fit together well enough, at least, for work.

"Oh, constantly. I kiss my glass slipper every night before I fall asleep," he chided.

"Hmm, good to know," Chelsea joked back, taking another sip of water.

"Well, go have fun," Stacy said happily to Chelsea.

"Yeah. I love shopping, and it has been two weeks since Rachel and I last had a chance to really see one another, which is when we last went shopping, so this will be good."

"Plus, you can get good ideas for when it's your turn to go shopping!" Stacy added eagerly.

Chelsea half-laughed, noting Stacy's need to idealize marriage and Chelsea's own need to avoid a conversation about her non-existent relationship status.

"Right," Chelsea said and then picked up the menu quickly to change the subject. "What are you guys going to order?"

Chapter 2 - Rachel

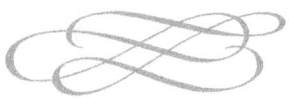

Rachel Rosen sped around the corner onto Mulville Street. She had been to Chelsea's parents' house so often that driving there was as natural as breathing. In fact, she had eleven years of auto-pilot working in her favor. She had picked up Chelsea so many Saturday mornings to save her from her parent's arguments that she almost felt the drive to Chelsea's bordered on heroic. Chelsea had always watched out for her in school, as Rachel's middle school years had not favored her. Before she met Chelsea, she was harrassed constantly for always being taller and earlier to fully develop than the other girls. Her height became a reason for self-doubt until high school, when the boys started paying attenditon to her, albeit for other reasons. Chelsea, during middle school, had always stood in Rachel's corner, defending her no matter what. Rachel couldn't have asked for a better friend, then or now. Now, though, she laughed, wondering if today she would, again, be the one who needed a little bit of rescuing and guidance to make it through the wedding dress shopping successfully.

She continued driving. The music boomed through the speakers, the windows were rolled down, and Rachel's long, honey brown hair blew in the wind. She was so thankful to have such a great friend in Chelsea.

It was ten in the morning, and Rachel's first bridal appointment was scheduled for ten-thirty. She had an incessant need to arrive at these appointments early, always figuring the earlier the better. If she was able to start into her appointment early, it would allow her more time to try on more dresses. Plus, this was her last-ditch bridal gown shopping effort. She needed a gown, and she needed to make today as efficient and productive as possible. However, she still wanted to grab coffee and a bagel before heading over to the bridal store. To make the most of today's bridal dress hunt, she needed to be fully charged with food, coffee, bridal accessories, and best friend support.

Chelsea, unlike Rachel, always seemed to be running about five minutes late, and Rachel worried this morning would be no exception. In fact, she already had her cash and credit card out and ready to go so there would be no time wasted when they arrived at the bagel shop. Much to her surprise, though, Chelsea was already waiting on the front porch of her parents' house when Rachel pulled into the driveway.

"You're ready!" Rachel chimed.

"I tried," Chelsea laughed, closing the car door behind her. "Mom knew you were coming, and she gave me so much grief about it this morning that I got ready faster just so I could leave the house!"

Rachel backed out of the driveway and began the first leg of the journey – the bagel shop.

"Still pressuring you about marriage?" Rachel wondered.

"Duh. I wouldn't be surprised if she asked to adopt you just so she could have the pleasure of saying one of her daughters was married off."

Rachel threw Chelsea a sideways sympathy glance.

"It's fine, but you would think I would be used to it by now. It's just that it gets old really fast."

Chelsea had grown-up with the assumption that she would be swept-off her feet and married by the time college was finished. She had even thought she had found her prince in her most recent ex-boyfriend, until that relationship took a nose-dive last summer right around the time she started toying with the idea of attending graduate school to enhance her writing. As a result, she was just now becoming accustomed to the idea of pursuing something in her life that did not also involve a relationship, but her mother seemed hard-pressed to change Chelsea's ideals back towards the more traditional mindset of marriage and family.

"Isn't your cousin getting married or something?" Rachel asked.

"Vince? Yeah."

"You would think your mom would be preoccupied with that," Rachel offered.

"Oh she can't get enough of it! She loves it, but Vince is a guy, and it's different with guys. Guys can get married whenever they want, and everyone thinks it's wonderful. Girls, on the other hand, need to start producing babies by the time they're twenty or something's wrong with them, and they'll die old maids."

Rachel laughed, "Oh, come on, Chelsea. It's not that bad."

"I know, I know. I'm exaggerating. Sorry."

"What did she say to you this morning?"

Chelsea laughed, "What didn't she say to me this morning?" Then Chelsea shook her head, "But really, let's not even start down that road. Today's about you and your wedding, and I'd rather like to keep it that way."

"Fair enough," Rachel said pulling into the parking lot. "But first we need breakfast. I'm buying."

When Rachel and Chelsea finally pulled up to Clara's Bridal Shoppe, the clock flashed 10:18 a.m. Rachel eagerly bounced her way into the store toting two bridal magazines and an oversized purse with two different pairs of heels inside. She wanted to be sure she was completely prepared for everything, because she was determined to find something at this store, even at the expense of blisters, arguments, and messed-up makeup by the time she finished. It was "go" time.

Chelsea followed her in with an extra-large, iced mocha knowing full well this would be a day-long affair. Rachel's appointment was technically only scheduled until noon, but, from experience, Chelsea knew Rachel did not work on time limits. She worked on Rachel-time, and if Rachel had not found a dress by noon, they were not leaving the store. Therefore, Chelsea determined the more caffeine the better. Plus, with all the bridal magazines Rachel had brought, and the ones the store was bound to have, Chelsea was certain she would have plenty to occupy her time.

A short woman named Marianna greeted the two girls upon entering. Chelsea deduced that she could not have been more than five-feet tall, even with heels on, and her short hair-cut radiated a dyed purple-red in the store's lighting. Her makeup was fully applied, and she dressed in black from head to toe with a tape measure hanging around her neck. She told the girls it would just be a few moments before someone would take care of them and asked for Rachel's name and appointment time before leaving.

Once Marianna left the lobby, Rachel scrunched her face and said, "A few moments? There's no one else in the store! What are they waiting for? I have to be their first appointment. This is dumb. She didn't even ask us if we wanted something to drink!"

"Maybe she saw we already had some?" Chelsea offered.

"Still. That's not the point. I could potentially be spending thousands of dollars here. She could at least have offered us something while we wait."

"Well, they probably can't offer coffee because of all the white dresses they work with. Could you imagine if someone spilled?"

"We're in the lobby, Chelsea, not trying on dresses right now."

Chelsea decidedly switched subjects as she could see Rachel's temper was short. "Ok. Fine. Well, while we're waiting, what have you decided on, dress wise? Have you been able to narrow it down any more?"

Rachel perked up slightly. "Okay, see, here's what I've been thinking." She grabbed one of the bridal magazines and flipped open to a page that had been folded. "I really like the mermaid style, like this one. From what I've already tried on, I think it shows off my curves really nicely, and Charles totally loves my curves, so it's kind of like a bonus for him. But, I don't know if I'll be able to dance in it well, so," she paused, turning to another folded page, "I was thinking I would also try on something more ballroom styled. The puffiness would allow me to move more."

Rachel then paused and turned to another page, adding, "But I could always go with something slinkier for the reception and change after the wedding. Something like this would let me move for sure."

Chelsea leaned over to look at the long, straight, silk dress more closely. The one Rachel had picked from the magazine had invisibly thin straps, a low "V" neckline in the front and back, and hung more willowy than fitted on the model. It was simple but with some very pretty overlay work along the base of the dress and the neckline on the left side.

"It's pretty. Do you want two dresses, now?" Chelsea asked. "I thought you had originally wanted the perfect *one*, which was part of why this whole process has been so difficult."

"Well, originally I had wanted *the one*, you know? That was until, like you said, we spent so much time looking. Then I started to realize that maybe I don't need to have just one, which is why I wasn't finding it. Maybe two dresses could still be perfect, so I revisited all the pictures and things I had set aside and came up with what I just showed you based on what we've seen and tried on. I have to find something today! Plus, please, I didn't spend all this time looking to walk away with only one semi-okay dress. I need my dress, or *dresses*, to make a statement and allow me to move!"

Chelsea pointed to the slinky, simple dress Rachel had just turned to and asked, "Why not this dress for the whole wedding? It's pretty. I can't imagine why you would need another."

Rachel looked at Chelsea, stunned. "Chelsea, I'm not getting *married* in this. It's too simple. There's no wow factor, and I need the wow factor. I just thought it'd be simple and easy for the reception, and if I had to get two dresses I wouldn't mind the second one being less flashy than the first. The first one I'd take all my pictures in. That's the one that needs to be wow-worthy. This one wouldn't hold up well enough in pictures," Rachel declared.

"Got it. Well, hopefully they'll have a lot here for you to try on."

"I know. I'm excited. But, okay, you have to promise me you'll be honest with me."

"About?" Chelsea wondered.

"The dress! I refuse to go down the aisle in something atrocious, so no holding back. If you don't like something, let me know. There is zero time for you to pretend to be nice."

Chelsea laughed, "I think I can handle that."

"Good."

Marianna walked in behind Rachel. "Hello girls. I will be helping you today. Rachel, come with me, and we'll get started. I'll show you to your room, and we can talk about what you had in mind for your dress."

"Perfect," Rachel responded, picking up her bags and magazines. Then she turned to Chelsea and whispered, "I don't know how she's going to be able to carry all the dresses I need! She's so small; the dresses might topple her over!"

Chelsea laughed and pushed Rachel towards the room. Rachel explained the criteria to Marianna on the way to the room and, once in the dressing room, proceeded to pull out the two pairs of shoes she had in her bag. Marianna went to pull the first few dresses while Chelsea sat in the dressing room lounge chairs with bridal magazines and iced mocha in tow, ready for the show to begin.

Rachel prepared herself while Marianna was out pulling dress options. She changed into her strapless bra, knowing full well she'd never buy a dress with straps thick enough with which to wear a regular bra. Her neck and shoulders were too toned to cover up. In fact, she had worked out regularly for the last five months to get herself into shape for this wedding. Her waist had whittled back down to a size six, her 34C breasts were toned and perky, and her legs were finally and once again defined when she strutted around in heels. In fact, she had not felt this healthy or this in-shape since her days as a high school swimmer. She was so proud of her hard work that she wanted to flaunt it on her wedding day.

Charles, her fiancé, had even agreed to undergo diet revamping for the six months prior to their wedding, at her behest. His condo in the city had a gym in the building, which they both frequented on weekdays, and Charles even argued that summer golfing would help keep him in shape for their early fall wedding. Rachel deemed golfing as an excuse to get away more during the summer, but he had compromised on other things, so she decided to let him have his summer golf-outings. He had agreed to cut back on drinking, and together they had given up fast food and soda. Charles had even bought a new gas grill a month ago in April, deciding to remove it from the wedding registry so they could grill out all summer. As far as she was concerned, there was no reason she could not keep this body in shape over the next three months, so the fit of the dress was crucial.

When Marianna returned, Rachel slipped into the first dress – a mermaid Caroline DeVillo dress. The design looked much like the reception dress Rachel had shown Chelsea: skinny straps, beaded bust with a high waistline and flowing bottom. The material hugged her hips in all the right places, and her breasts sat high and round against the beadwork. Rachel turned around in the dress three times to see how much she could move in it. It moved with her flawlessly, and she stood up an inch straighter before leaving the dressing room to show Chelsea.

Chelsea looked up from her magazine. "Oh wow, Rachel."

Rachel stood on the platform in front of the three-paneled mirror. "Wow, right?"

"It is beautiful. You look stunning."

"Thanks," she beamed. "I feel stunning. And it's not the princess dress or the tight mermaid I had envisioned. It's like the reception dress I showed you in the magazine."

"It is, isn't it?"

"So are you still considering two different dresses?" Marianna asked. Rachel ignored her.

"Well I think it's great," Chelsea offered. "Charles will love it."

"Won't he though?" Rachel echoed, imagining Charles' face when he saw her in this dress.

"Is this the one or are you going to try on more?" Chelsea wondered.

"Oh, please. I didn't come here to leave after just one dress! Of course I am trying on more. You're okay to stick around, right?" Rachel asked.

"I wouldn't be anywhere else today," responded Chelsea.

Rachel picked up the dress and stepped off the platform as she headed back into the room, Marianna at her heels.

Chelsea picked up the wedding magazine again, flipping through more Vera Wang and Christian Lacroix photos. She sipped on her iced mocha and passed nonchalantly over the pages, stopping briefly to glance more closely at the dresses Rachel had earmarked. She thought about all the wedding magazines they had glanced over that one day in college, planning dream weddings and jaw-dropping receptions. Today suddenly seemed like déjà vu. They had imagined themselves married by the time they were twenty-three, twenty-five at the latest, because anything older just seemed so…*old*.

Chelsea shook her head at that thought. She had turned twenty-seven three months prior and was currently boyfriend-less.

Wonderful. I'm old *and* not married, she thought. Awesome.

"Okay, what about this one?" Rachel asked, finally deciding to come back out of the dressing room after trying on dresses that she refused to leave the room in. The question shook Chelsea back to the present.

Chelsea looked up and saw Rachel in the strapless, mermaid dress she had talked about for so long. The dress had a soft champagne tint in the lighting, which made the ruching, gathered at the smallest part of the waist, more dramatic. Then, from the mid-thigh down, the dress flowed into the style of a large ball gown with pick-ups, tiers, and a long train. It captured the drama and extravagance that Rachel had always envisioned, and Chelsea could see Rachel radiating from the podium. In fact, Chelsea found herself suddenly speechless.

"You don't like it," Rachel started, taking Chelsea's silence as a negative.

"What?" Chelsea returned, collecting herself quickly, "No! I love it. I'm just speechless."

"Speechless, like good speechless?" Rachel inquired.

Chelsea nodded. "Really good speechless. Rachel, this is incredible. I feel like this is what you've been trying to find for the last two months. I'm just … speechless."

"So you like it?" Rachel squealed.

"I think you just found your dress," Chelsea replied.

"I do too! But I want to see it with a tiara, veil, and some big jewelry," Rachel added, motioning for Marianna to find her something amazing. Marianna took the cue and left.

"And it's literally the perfect length. That's incredible."

"I know! Now all I have to do is find some killer four-inch heels."

"You're wearing four-inch heels?" Chelsea asked, stunned. "You really want to wear four-inch heels on your wedding day?"

"Why not? It's only for the ceremony. I can change into those cute flip flops or something for the reception."

"So, then you'll take the dress up a few inches?"

"No, this dress is perfect."

"Okay…" Chelsea started. She had no idea where exactly Rachel was in Rachel-land and was not about to try to catch up on her own, so she waited.

"Well, this one's only $3,300, and I had given myself an $8,000 budget for the dress and accessories. I could buy the two and just take the other one up if there's time, because it fits pretty well otherwise," Rachel announced, very matter-of-factly.

"You could, but did you include alterations in that budget? Or a veil and jewelry for that matter?"

"Alterations, smalterations. I'm sure my parents or Charles can help me take care of anything over that amount, especially because it will have to be rushed. We just don't have time otherwise. Besides, it's not every day your only daughter gets married. Dad said he'd pitch in for whatever I needed, since Charles and the Waterfords are paying for the reception."

"Oh, right, it's at the Langham Boston, isn't it?"

"Yup. We're getting a really good deal because the Waterfords have stayed at that hotel so many times they are practically like VIP. They're helping Dad save a bundle on the wedding already, so a few extra thousand for dress stuff won't matter."

A few extra thousand? Chelsea thought, gasping to herself. A few extra thousand would have been a welcomed addition to her bank account or the help she needed to start looking into leaving her parents' place. The thought of a "few extra thousand" as something to just throw around on a dress worn once made Chelsea shake her head. However, this was Rachel, and what Rachel wanted, Rachel got.

"Rachel," Chelsea said, "you like literally have it made. I don't know how you got so lucky."

"I know, right?" she smiled, excitedly. "Me either. Okay, but we really like this one?"

"Yes, I absolutely love this one. I love it enough to say you should wear it for both the wedding and the reception, personally. However, I also know you, and you seem to have your mind made up about the whole two-dress thing, so I say both of these are really nice. They're two totally different looks, too–"

"Which I think is perfect!" Rachel interjected, cutting off Chelsea. "People get to see me in two looks. Pictures will have me in two looks, and the second one is still gorgeous enough to warrant photos, which I'll probably insist on, because it is so pretty. But that will just mean two wow-factors, and I can afford both, so, why not?"

"Right, why not?" Chelsea chimed in agreement. "If you had planned on spending the money, I guess I say go for it. However, just to play devil's advocate, you could always just buy the one and put the money towards the honeymoon."

"True. Could. Probably won't."

Chelsea laughed, "Well, then, in that case, I think they're both great. And, they will both go really well with the bridesmaids' dresses, so no worries there."

"Good point. Okay, I'm totally getting both. We'll see if we can negotiate the price a bit. I'm not paying full price if I can help it."

"Maybe we can get them to throw in the accessories for free, if she brings back some good ones."

"Oh! Good idea."

Rachel turned away from the mirror and looked at Chelsea, a thankful expression overcoming her face. "Thanks again so much for being here. It really means a lot."

"Of course, Rach. I wouldn't have missed it for the world. After all the dress shopping we've already been through, I'm just glad we found you something!"

"And I promise I'll repay the favor when it's your turn," Rachel added.

"Well, I think you have a while before that even comes onto the table," Chelsea responded quickly.

Marianna returned with three tiaras, four veils, and a box of jewelry options. Rachel's eyes lit up as she tried on varying combinations, making faces that denoted clearly unacceptable candidates. Finally, a small, bedazzled tiara with a cascading veil and a big, brocade, costume-sized, diamond necklace met Rachel's standards. Additionally, after much finagling and hard-pressed faces between Rachel, Chelsea, Marianna, and the manager, it was agreed to drop the price on the total sale 10% and throw in the veil for free. It was not exactly what Rachel had envisioned, but it was enough to entice her into buying everything she wanted.

Chapter 3 - Danielle

Friday afternoon arrived. The sun was high in the afternoon sky, and the clock on the wall of Danielle Sutterton's office showed it to be almost 3:15 pm. She glanced out the window and then back to a picture sitting on her desk of Paul and her and smiled as her conversation came to a close.

"Sounds perfect," Danielle chimed. "Tell me where we're going? Okay fine, you win. See you then. Love you, too."

She hung up the phone giddily and returned to her laptop. She liked surprises and felt certain she would love whatever was in store for her tonight.

Today, May 15, marked her five-year anniversary with her boyfriend, Paul Gracin. They had started dating at the conclusion of their senior year of college, making their relationship official the day of graduation. They had fallen fast and hard for one another, agreeing to try to make their long-distance relationship work once school ended and they both returned home to separate states.

During that first year apart, they made frequent visits to see one another, trying to determine what lay ahead for both in regards to life and their relationship.

Danielle, immediately following graduation, moved in with her parents who lived an hour outside Bostom, Massachusetts. She worked temp-jobs so she could study to retake the LSAT. She also worked to complete her application to Boston University School of Law. Ever since she was sixteen she had wanted to attend law school there. The studying was tiresome, but the reward, she knew, would be worth it in the end.

Paul had always been supportive of Danielle's drive and ambition because it matched his. He spent the year after college at home in Buffalo, New York. He went on to obtain his CPA while working for a small accounting firm in the city. His hard work and ambition paid off, and he managed to make the most money of all the new hires for the firm that first year. They offered him a hefty raise and promotion, which he graciously accepted while deciding how to handle his next relationship move with Danielle.

Over the course of that year, the two of them made an effort to visit as often as possible. The drive between the two cities was long and draining, but spending a weekend with each other always made it worthwhile. That year, when Danielle finally received her acceptance letter to Boston University School of Law, she was beside herself, and Paul initially worried how their relationship would handle his newfound promotion and another move on Danielle's part.

After much debate and input from both of their parents, it was agreed that Danielle would start law school, and they would see if their relationship could survive the distance and the change. Danielle found herself buried so far in stacks of books and homework that first year that she almost never had time to travel up to Buffalo to see Paul. It became increasingly apparent that Paul had to do all the traveling. He finally concluded that it was time to find a job in Boston if the relationship were to survive.

Luckily, Paul was able to find one and moved to Boston in January.

Initially the move had seemed exciting, but their relationship wavered once Paul finally made it out to Boston. They had idealistically envisioned his move to mean more time together. However, Paul's new job at Thomas Cane and Associates, CPA, kept him traveling to see clients the first four months of the year. That meant they communicated through email and phone calls most of the time. When he returned in May, Danielle's finals had started.

Following finals she began her summer internship with Hobbs Allester and Thorton which required her to be at the office daily from eight to five-thirty. There she completed a variety of tasks that kept her running around all day and occasionally trekking documents home at night. Those first six months were not easy and made them question their relationship. In fact, they found themselves on the verge of breaking up on three different occasions.

Since that first year in law school, things had sorted themselves out on their own. Both Paul and she lowered ideologies and focused on realities and goals. So long as their goals were the same – to make something of their lives and enjoy each other's company – their lives and their relationship continued without fail. Sure, they had their spats and low points, but none so low as the three breaking points those first six months. In fact, since deciding that they loved each other, wanted to be together, and were determined to support one another, everything else just fell into place. There were no hopes to make something more out of it, no attempts to rush something that was not there, and no ideals of married life yet. Married or not, they were together, and that was all they wanted and needed at the moment.

Now after having graduated and successfully passing the Bar, Danielle had finished her first year as an associate with Hobbs Allester and Thorton, specializing in administrative and employment law. It was hard to balance the two. She bounced between both types of cases as the work came into the office, working alongside more experienced attorneys. However, she loved the job and looked forward to building a resume there before eventually branching out on her own. Paul continued to be supportive and backed her completely. It was hard to believe that five years of their lives had passed and their relationship had survived. She could not wait for what was in store tonight.

Wrapped in excitement, she picked up the phone and called her best friend.

"Hello?"

"Chelsea!" Danielle beamed. "How are you?"

"Danielle! Oh it's so good to hear from you! It's been forever. I'm wonderful, how are you?"

"Great. How is everything?"

"Good. Busy. I actually just finished wedding dress shopping with Rachel this past weekend. It was fun. She finally found a gorgeous dress, or, well, two dresses, but they're both beautiful."

"Two dresses?" Danielle laughed. "Sounds like Rachel. She was always very extravagant."

"Was?" Chelsea joked. "Not a whole lot has changed since college. She still *is* very extravagant, but she's also lucky. You know Charles. Between him, his family, and her family, she can afford it, so, you know, why not?"

"True. Good for her."

"Right? And she and Charles are wedding cake shopping next weekend, so the final touches are wrapping themselves up, which is great."

Then Chelsea promptly switched subjects, "But what about you? What's going on with you?"

"I'm still at work writing a brief."

"Sounds fun."

Danielle chuckled, "Almost, but I'm trying to finish as much as I can in the next hour. Paul just called. He says he's planning a surprise dinner and evening for our anniversary!"

"Oh how fun! That's so sweet of him. Where are you guys going?"

"I have no idea, actually, but it's like date-night all over again!"

"That's so cute. Glad to see he's still good at surprising you. Listen to how excited you are!"

"I know! I really am excited. We've been downplaying our anniversary these last few weeks because he just finished tax season and this case I'm working on has been crazy, so I feel like this surprise came out of the blue."

"That's a good thing, though, right?" Chelsea wondered.

"Oh definitely. I just have no idea what he has planned."

Chelsea started slowly and suggestively, "Well, you guys have been together for *five years* now."

"Oh, Chelsea, please. He's not going to propose if that's what you're getting at."

"How do you know?"

"We haven't talked about marriage, like seriously talked about marriage, in a long time. I'm not ready. He knows that. I'm just starting my career and couldn't imagine trying to plan a wedding on top of it. After five years of everything we've been through and all the non-marriage conversations we've had, he wouldn't just suddenly surprise me with an engagement ring without discussing it with me first."

"If you say so. I'm just saying, it has been five years," Chelsea defended. "However, I'm still excited for you. Tonight should be exceedingly fun."

"Thanks! I'm excited too," Danielle replied, suddenly tapping her keyboard. "However, I have to go and try to finish more of this brief before I have to leave."

"Okay! Thanks for calling, and have a wonderful time tonight!"

"Thanks! I will! And tell Rachel to have fun next weekend going cake shopping."

"Will do. Have a great night."

"I will. Talk to you soon," Danielle responded and hung up the phone. She suddenly felt a worried pang rising in her chest, disturbing the excitement she had initially felt. What if he did propose? She had not considered that even for a moment, but Chelsea was right, it had been five years, and according to most normal social standards, five years screamed, "It's time to get married." She just could not imagine it, though. She and Paul had been so honest with one another about their relationship and what they wanted. They had not even talked about marriage since she could remember. Maybe last year they brought it up briefly, but that was it. There had not been any discussions as of late. He would not just randomly pop the question, would he? Would he just assume that now that she was done with school she was ready to get married?

She did not know, and not knowing worried her. She tapped the keys and glanced at the clock. Forty-five minutes. She had forty-five minutes before he would call her back with the name of the restaurant. Forty-five minutes for the thought to fester, or she could attempt to finish more of the brief. She was hoping for the latter.

Paul sat waiting at a booth in the back of the restaurant when Danielle arrived. His brown, slicked back hair gave way to his tanned cheeks. The dark grey blazer he wore contrasted strongly with the dark jeans and white pinstriped shirt beneath, the top button undone in a hastily yet lazy fashion. He looked suddenly grown-up, almost sophisticated, in a way Danielle had not noticed before now. She had just always seen him as Paul – crazy, loving, adventurous, twenty-two year-old Paul – the boy who had stolen her heart in college, and the man she had grown to love. From here, though, as she watched him spin his wine glass aimlessly, he looked like any other young man working to forge his way in the adult world. It caused her to smile automatically.

How far we've come, she thought.

"Hi," she cooed, standing at the edge of the table, her black pants skimming the corner.

"You made it!" he replied, standing. He took a step forward, wrapped his arms around her lower back, and kissed her. "Happy Anniversary."

She hugged him tighter, felt his hands play with the seams of her back pockets, and allowed his words to echo in her head as she took a seat across from him. He watched her sit, noticing the silk chiffon, light blue blouse hug the curves of her bra. Her waist was still the same as it had been the day he met her in the library in college, toned and seductive. Her long blond hair reflected the light, and her hazel eyes smiled back at his. He was as much in love with her at this moment as he had ever been.

Danielle broke the silence, "This place is wonderful! I've been wanting to try it since it opened last year."

"That's what you kept saying, so I thought tonight would be the perfect excuse to finally give it a try."

"Thanks for remembering," she smiled, reaching out to squeeze his hand in gratitude. "You always do a great job of surprising me. This is perfect."

"I'm glad you're happy," he said, smiling proudly at his accomplishment. He knew how much she loved seafood, and the restaurant had received rave reviews since it opened. He had even made the reservation a month in advance, just to ensure they had a table. It had been hard keeping this secret from her that long, but seeing her radiating happiness now made it worthwhile. He just hoped what he had to tell her later would not change things, but he was determined to wait until after the gallery-show he had planned for after dinner tonight to discuss it.

Danielle sensed a hesitation in Paul. Was it just lingering post-work stress or was something else on his mind? Chelsea's comment about an engagement still played in her head, and she wondered if his hesitation wasn't nervousness.

"Is everything all right?" she questioned.

"All right?" he looked surprised. "Of course. I'm here with you. Why wouldn't it be?"

"You just seemed a little …" she paused, searching for the best word, "preoccupied."

"Not at all." He smiled and fixed his napkin in his lap. "Like you, just a long day at work. I didn't realize I was still thinking about it. Sorry."

"Anything you want to talk about?"

"Not now. Let's just enjoy dinner. We can talk about work later."

Paul filled her wine glass, and they toasted to the last five years and the many more to come. He told her about the gallery show after dinner and watched her smile even brighter. She was in awe of how much thought he had put into tonight, and he felt relieved everything was working smoothly thus far. He just hoped the conversation later that night went equally as well.

"Oh, Paul, thank you so much for tonight," Danielle said, kissing her boyfriend on the cheek as they walked up to their apartment, her arm wrapped around his.

"I'm glad you enjoyed yourself," he responded, placing his hand over hers.

"The gallery show was wonderful. I can't believe how talented Dale Chihuly is! No wonder his glass pieces are in places like the Bellagio and Atlantis. I've never seen anything more beautiful. I can't believe that gallery has his pieces on loan for the time being. They were beautiful."

"He is incredibly talented, that's for sure."

Paul opened the door to their apartment and took off his jacket for the first time all day. There was a certain sense of relief in returning home and finally unwinding, but a ball of tension still sat inside him. He knew he would not be able to relax until they had finally discussed the matter eating away at him.

"Danielle?" he began. She turned and looked at him lovingly, joy from the evening still flowing through her.

"Yes?" she responded, watching him move towards the wine cabinet suddenly.

"Uh," he hesitated, "more wine?"

She smirked, coyly, "More wine? Are you trying to get me drunk, Mr. Gracin?"

He looked at her and then closed his eyes. This was not going to work.

Bite the bullet, he thought. You have to tell her sometime.

"Actually, Danielle, there's something I need to tell you."

Oh, shit, she thought. She tried to keep her face unchanged, but the thoughts sped through her mind anyways. Is this the proposal? Why does he seem so distraught?

"What is it, Paul?" she asked as lightly as possible.

He took her hand, guided her to the table, and the two of them slid slowly into the chairs. He took a deep breath in before continuing, "You know I love you. You are the love of my life, and we have been through so much together. These last five years have been the best five years because of you."

Danielle smiled, but inside she did not like where this was heading.

"Moving here to be with you was the best decision I ever made. I know we fought a lot at first, and it was a rocky start, but if I had it to do all over again I wouldn't change a single moment of it."

Danielle tried to continue smiling as she felt Paul grasp her hand more tightly, but she could not bring herself to say anything.

"I don't know what I would do without you," he continued. "And I feel that if we can get through everything we have gotten through in the last five years, dealing with growing up and moves and school and starting careers, then we can make it through anything."

Paul dropped his head, as though he were worried. "At least, that's what I hope."

Hope? Danielle thought. This no longer savored of a proposal. Now she just found herself confused.

"Hunny, what's wrong?" she finally asked.

Paul looked up at Danielle and could see the confused worry in her face. She had been so elated all night that to see her mood change so quickly hurt him inside, and he did not want to drag this out any longer. He bit the bullet.

"I'm being transferred to Albany, New York."

Chapter 4 - Rachel and Charles - The Cracks

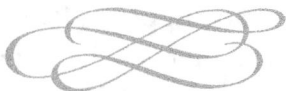

That same Friday, Rachel walked through the door to Charles and her place after work, tired, exhausted, and ready for a long-awaited night with her fiancé. She felt as though it had been weeks since she last saw him. He spent the weekend she had gone dress shopping with Chelsea playing golf in North Carolina with some college buddies. That North Carolina trip marked the third weekend in a row that he had left Boston without her to play golf. He and his friends had started a "Tour de Golf," as he put it, meeting in different cities to play, and it was starting to annoy her. There were plenty of golf courses around Boston, and only a handful of his close buddies lived out of state, so why they all insisted on making a weekend out if it was beyond her. All she knew was that he had not mentioned golf all week, and that alone made her excited for tonight. He would be home for the weekend. Finally.

Charles had beaten her home, his black Audi TT sitting quietly in the building's garage when she had pulled in. Her 2000 Volkswagon Passat looked humbled next to his beautiful car, and she could not wait until the day she received the new, white, Lexus ISC with beige interior he had promised her once they were married. She had already waited longer than she had anticipated waiting to be married that any and all perks that came along with the title were happily coveted.

Once in the condo, she put down her purse and keys and headed to the kitchen for a drink of water. It was only the middle of May, but the weather was already getting hotter by the day. Only three more months, she thought, and I will be Mrs. Charles Waterford II.

"Hi hunny," she called loudly as she walked into the kitchen, still smiling from the thoughts of becoming a Mrs. and finally having her new car. She was not sure quite where Charles was in the apartment, but she knew he was home.

Glancing through the mail on the counter, she finished the rest of the ice-cold water she had just poured. In her mind raced ideas of where they would go for dinner, images of them going cake tasting tomorrow at the hotel where the reception was to be held, and lust for a night filled with wine and the new lace négligé she had just purchased. She felt excitement build in her chest, and she found herself on the brink of dashing off to look for Charles when she heard the sound of footsteps approaching. A smile brushed across her face, but just as suddenly as it had arrived, it disappeared. It was not only footsteps she heard but also wheels, wheels to a suitcase she already knew the sound of too well.

"Charles?" she nearly wailed, racing out to the hallway. There he stood in his khakis, loafers, and long sleeve, button-up, Ralph Lauren shirt. His chestnut hair was gelled lightly, and his hazel eyes sat behind lightly tinted shades, which he pushed back atop his head upon seeing Rachel come at him, looking distraught. Behind him rolled the black Tumi suitcase, the same suitcase he had used on the last three trips.

Rachel felt pains of loneliness and anger stab at her heart.

"Where are you going?" she demanded helplessly.

"I have to go to New York City for work this weekend," he responded.

"Work? What are you talking about?" Rachel shook her head, confused. "You never mentioned anything about working this weekend."

"It just came up today. We have a meeting back here with clients first thing Monday morning, and Tom and I have to finish analyzing these portfolios from New York before that."

Rachel stared blankly, still clearly confused. "So you're leaving? Why can't you have the information faxed or shipped here? I don't understand why you have to go."

"Because the company is sending us today," Charles responded very matter-of-factly.

"I just don't understand –"

"There's nothing to understand," he interrupted. In his mind, this was a very simple situation. "We're being sent to New York City today, so I'm leaving today. I'll probably be back Sunday night depending on when the flights are and how quickly we finish going over these portfolios this weekend."

"But the cake," she protested. "You said –"

"I said I would try," he interrupted again, "but I can't. This isn't up to me."

Rachel's anger turned into sudden loss. She tried to hold the tears back, knowing full well they would not do her any good at the moment. Charles was already packed and ready to leave, and it did not sound like he could change a work appointment.

"I know it's not. I just," she sniffled trying to compose herself, "I just haven't seen you for the past three weekends, and now this will be number four. I feel like I never see you, like we never have 'us' time anymore."

"What do you mean? What about last night? That was 'us' time, wasn't it?" he asked.

Rachel stood, baffled. "Last night? We had sex last night and then you got up to finish work. I didn't see what time you came back to bed, and by this morning you had already left for work when I awoke at six-thirty."

"And that work is now taking me to New York," he explained.

"Charles, I just don't get it. We're getting married in a little over three months, and I feel like I haven't seen my fiancé in weeks!"

Charles stepped closer to her. "Rachel, now you're being ridiculous. I see you every day when I come home from work." He put his hand on her arm. "We live together. I don't think you get much closer than that. I have work, and it's requiring me to leave town for the weekend. There isn't much I can do about that. I need to make money, so I need to go."

"I know, I know," Rachel responded, eyes glancing downwards. Even though she knew she could do nothing to change the situation, she was still upset and could not bear to look at him. His weekend absenses were really starting to crack the picture she'd held of what their pre-wedding relationship would look like. It was not supposed to include this many weekends without him.

"I was just so looking forward to seeing you," she whined. "It's not fair. I don't understand."

"Rachel, stop."

"But what about the cake?" she began again. She could not help it. She felt herself falling apart involuntarily, all the ideas for the weekend scattering just out of her reach. "What about –"

"Get whatever cake you want," he responded, not allowing her to finish. "I will like whatever you pick. Cake is cake. Get Chelsea to go. Ask her opinion."

Rachel's frustration increased. "Chelsea's not you!" she cried. "I wanted you to be there. I wanted to spend the day with you, the night with you – an actual night where you weren't working or golfing the next morning with your buddies. I don't ever see you anymore!"

Charles took hold of Rachel's other arm and stared into her eyes, "Rachel, now stop. You're making yourself crazy. This wedding is making you crazy. You will see me in a few days. I will be back."

He dropped his hands and stepped back to his suitcase. "Now, my ride should be downstairs waiting outside the building's lobby for me. I love you and will see you in a few days."

Rachel could not even muster an, "I love you." She diverted her gaze away from his, sniffled back the tears that pushed at her throat and her eyes, and just nodded. She did not even see him leave; she only heard the clicking of the condo's door close behind him. She flinched at the sound and then stood until there was silence, a hollow silence that echoed somewhere between the walls of their home and her heart.

Chapter 5 – Saturday Arguments

Chelsea sat upstairs in her room listening to her parents argue below her in the kitchen. Saturday morning should be a quiet, peaceful time in a house as it is the first day of the weekend and most people are not working. This, however, was not a normal house. This was the Farerra house, and nothing was ever peaceful or easy in the Farrera house. In fact, Chelsea noted that her parents always seemed to make a point of fighting on Saturdays, as though they are trying to get it all out of the way before Sunday came, like they wanted to arrive at church cleansed or something. This morning followed tradition.

Chelsea closed the door in hopes of muffling the sounds, but her parents usually argued so loudly the neighbors had to turn up their music to drown them out. Agitation bubbled up her spine. How was it a twenty-seven year old still had to be at home listening to her parents argue? The thought made her queasy.

Just over a year ago her boyfriend of two years, Terry, had ended their relationship. Honestly, looking back, she had seen it coming, but that had not made the break-up any easier. They had even been living together in his condo in Boston for over a year, so when they split, she moved back home to save money. Although she loved the city, she did not want to spend her entire paycheck on rent. She had been able to afford bills while she lived with Terry, but on her own, rent was not even a fleeting possibility. Her job at the bank now paid a fair amount, but since she eventually wanted to be able to buy her own place, she decided living at home was the most reasonable option.

Now, she wondered if the reasonable option had been the best option. On mornings like this one, she could not help but feel like a teenager again, stuck in the house instead of voluntarily living in it. Luckily, Rachel was due to arrive in the next ten minutes, so she would not have to deal with the bickering much longer.

And man did they bicker. This morning's argument revolved around her cousin's wedding. Vince had asked Elena to marry him only four months ago, and Chelsea's mom, Tina, had been in wedding-mode ever since. Vince's mother, Tina's sister, was a horrible planner and terrible at organizing anything, so Tina had jumped at the opportunity to help plan a family wedding. Tony, Chelsea's father, had played along at first, but with Tina's incessant involvement, he quickly fell out of favor with all such discussions, and they tried his patience. It was known that Tony had a temper with a short fuse and, not enjoying the ongoing saga regarding a wedding that was neither his nor his daughter's, he reddened faster than a summer turnip at Tina's constant mention of it. Since it was all she ever had on her mind, the arguments were plentiful.

Chelsea sympathized with her father. She was tired of hearing about weddings too. She was already her best friend's maid-of-honor and did not want more wedding talk at home. When her relationship with Terry had ended, her dreams of a wedding had faded as well. It was not that she minded, per se, that she was a big part of Rachel's, but the whole scenario stabbed at her more consistently now. Some days she felt fine, but more often than not she just felt old, like she had missed her moment and was going to be an old maid before she ever found someone. She, therefore, didn't want to be reminded of weddings any more than necessary, and, in her mind, being part of Vince's planning did not fall under the "necessary" category.

Chelsea's mom failed to understand this and unknowingly slashed Chelsea's heart every time she said things like, "That was almost you," or "Hadn't you thought about those for your wedding?" or "It'll happen, we just need to help Fate a little and find you another man." The closer it came to Rachel or Vince's weddings, the more comments Chelsea's mother made. It was hurtful and annoying, and Chelsea did not want to be around her mother as a result.

Chelsea's phone beeped. Rachel was outside.

Running downstairs, hoping to quickly escape unseen, Chelsea silently cursed herself for leaving her purse in the kitchen. Unnoticeably entering and leaving the kitchen was not a possibility, so, instead, she simply hoped to grab her purse quickly enough that her parents would not have time to pause their arguing.

"Stop talking about the wedding, Tina. Find something else to do."

"I don't understand why you're not excited. It's Vince after all."

"Yes, it is, but it's not my wedding. It's his, and I'm invited to enjoy it, not plan it. Keep it that way."

"I know, but," Tina said, turning her head when she noticed her daughter, "but just like Chelsea's helping her friend plan, I'm helping my family plan."

"You shouldn't be planning it! The bride should!" Tony nodded to Chelsea, "Hi, Chels."

"Hi," she replied quickly, trying to convey her sense of urgency. "Just grabbing my purse. Bye!"

"Are you going out with Rachel?" Tina wondered.

"Yup, she's waiting. Gotta go."

"Well, where are you going?" she asked.

"Cake tasting."

"Oh! You guys should try that cute little bakery in Medford, or the great cupcake one in the city. Vince is using –"

"Leave her alone!" Tony roared. "Jesus Christ woman. You're like a vulture."

"I am not," she bellowed back. "So sue me for trying to help her out. That's what families do: help each other out. You know, when we had talked about the possibility of Chelsea getting married, you were all about having people help."

"But she's not close to getting married anymore!"

Chelsea felt her heart and stomach fall straight to the floor. Her brain shook with anger.

"Bye!" she yelled above the screaming and bolted for the front door. She threw her head back once outside, relieved to feel the non-toxic, non-wedding air fill her lungs even if only for the brief moment she had between the house and Rachel's car.

"Coffee?" Rachel asked as Chelsea slammed the car door shut. She could see her friend was riled up over something. She handed Chelsea an iced mocha.

"You're a saint."

"They're fighting again." It wasn't a question. Rachel knew Chelsea's parents.

"How did you guess?" Chelsea sarcastically replied, taking a long gulp of her iced mocha.

"It's Saturday," Rachel smiled. "When aren't they fighting on a Saturday?"

"Right?"

"That bad, huh?"

"My mom just always finds a way to put a dagger through me every time she can. She's either dumb enough to not know she's doing it or thoroughly enjoys seeing me writhe in pain."

"What was it this time? Finding life's direction or relationships?"

"Weddings."

"Ouch."

"Yup. And Dad didn't help either. He was trying, granted, but in trying to stop my mom from talking about the wedding that they had semi-started planning for me last year, he shouted 'but she's not close to getting married, anymore'."

Rachel cringed, "Double ouch."

"Yeah, well, if you have any whiskey or Bailey's that I can add to my coffee, I'll take some now," Chelsea jokingly offered as she leaned back in her seat and momentarily closed her eyes.

"Are you okay to come with me today?" Rachel asked, her tone falling towards sadness.

"Oh, oh my God, yes, of course. I'm sorry. I'm really excited to go cake tasting at the Langham today. I'm just … venting."

"No, it's okay. I just…" Rachel did not finish her statement, but she could not stop the hurt from seeping into her voice. She was still broken from Charles' leaving the night before, and she really needed her friend to support her today.

Chelsea noticed the downward turn in Rachel's words, and it shook her out of her argument-ridden morning and back to focusing on her friend.

"What's wrong, Rachel?" she questioned lightly.

Rachel shook her head after taking a breath, like she wanted to say something and then thought better of it. She just half-smiled instead. "Nothing."

Chelsea, refocused on her purpose as a friend with maid-of-honor duties, stirred her iced mocha and smiled to herself. "You know I know you better than that. Something's bugging you. What is it?"

"It's nothing. I'm just frustrated."

"Charles couldn't make today because he's gallivanting around another golf course this morning?" Chelsea half-laughed, remembering the trips he had taken these last three weekends. Rachel had sounded so happy about him finally being home for a change this weekend that she laughed at the thought that an 18-hole golf course might have pulled him away again. It baffled Chelsea how strongly his indifference to the whole wedding process screamed through his actions. She wondered how Rachel handled it sometimes, but she seemed happy, and that was Chelsea's greatest concern. Right now, however, she realized her comment was met with silence, and a friendship-based pang of fear and empathy instantly cursed through her veins like electricity.

Chelsea turned to Rachel involuntarily, blurting out, "Oh my God. He left again, didn't he?"

Rachel just kept driving. She could not respond. The emotions flooded her throat, and she felt choked-up. Instead of using words, she simply rubbed her newly rouged lips together and nodded.

39

"Oh, Rachel," Chelsea began, her heart breaking for her friend. Admittedly, Chelsea had not really seen Rachel this vulnerable in a while, and that, more than anything, shocked her. Rachel was normally very composed and very aware of the image she presented to others, so upset like this did not normally occur outside her home. In fact, the shock of Rachel's demeanor caught Chelsea more off guard than the actual comment of Charles' not being home.

"I'm so sorry," Chelsea continued. "I had no idea. I wouldn't have said anything if I – what happened? Where is he?"

"Work," Rachel responded. "He said he had work in New York City all weekend and that he had to leave right away. I was barely home ten minutes, and he left," she finished, but not before adding in an "again" at the end of the statement.

"Oh, Rach."

"That's four weekends, Chelsea. Four. Four weekends of him leaving and me being all by myself to do just … everything. I'm tired of him being gone, and I'm so annoyed that he pulled this one on me last minute." Rachel's distaste for her fiancé's move showed clearly in her voice.

"Ew. He didn't even let you know?"

"No! I walked in from work, and he walked out with that stupid-ass, black suitcase," Rachel started, and then sighed. "I don't know, Chelsea. I just don't remember him being gone this much before all the wedding stuff started. I feel like things are changing, and I don't know why."

Chelsea tried to find an explanation to calm her friend, as she could see Rachel needed reassuring, but her certainty in what to say was fleeting. "Well, maybe it only seems that way because you're life has been so crazy since the wedding planning schedule became busier."

Rachel shrugged at the remark. There was no real response, so Chelsea tried a different angle, hoping to make light of the situation. "Plus, I mean, it is summer, and you did give him permission to go golfing with his buddies."

"Yeah, but every weekend? And, suddenly they all have to be somewhere other than in Boston?" Rachel retorted.

Chelsea's attempt clearly failed.

"I just don't get it," Rachel continued. "I feel like I'm ..." but she could not find the right words to finish that statement. She didn't even know if she wanted to finish that statement. If the answer led everything back to her in any way, then she definitely did not want to know the answer. Instead, Rachel simply ran her left hand halfway through her hair, rested her elbow on the door's window-ledge, and shook her head.

"You're probably just stressed," Chelsea said. "I mean, we had a big weekend last weekend with the dresses, and now we're going to do the cake. It's a lot, and it's stressful, and with Charles not being much help, you're probably just overwhelmed."

Rachel let out a long sigh, because she knew her friend was more than likely right. Rachel just wanted Charles to be more involved, and he wasn't.

Chelsea also reminded Rachel that Charles was a guy, and most guys did not get overly excited about wedding planning in general, let alone to Rachel's extent. When Rachel heard that, she had to laugh lightly, remembering the wedding dress experience from the previous weekend and failing to see Charles fussing over anything wedding related the way she had. Maybe Chelsea had a point.

Still, though, Rachel wished Charles cared just a little more about the whole thing. To her, a wedding and marriage were huge deals, and he just was not being as active of a participant as she had hoped. Admittedly, she did know girls did more work for the weddings. Obviously. She had organized the college wedding day and spent months finding a dress! Still, she expected her wedding to be a great success, but in her mind that included a cooperative and participatory fiancé.

She took in a deep sigh. At least she had Chelsea with her today to help make cake decisions, and that was another very important decision she was going to have to make. A cake helped set the tone for the reception, and she was determined to have the wedding of her dreams, regardless of Charles' involvement, or lack thereof.

Rachel and Chelsea arrived at the bakery and headed inside to see the decorators. Rachel smiled as she and Chelsea entered, and Chelsea was hopeful that Rachel had put her worries behind her. Unfortunately, although outwardly Rachel seemed as put-together as any self-respecting bride should be when hunting for the wedding cake of her dreams, inside she still struggled with the events of the previous night. She could not seem to shake them, no matter how big she tried to make her smile or how much she tried to tell the story in a way that made sense. It all felt forced and fake, a fact that did not go unnoticed by Chelsea.

Chapter 6 - Issues & Obstacles

C helsea arrived at work on Monday, exhausted. The long and trying weekend took a toll on her, pushing her brain and emotions to the limit. In fact, the weekend had been so involved she almost hated admitting she looked forward to work. She knew exactly what to expect at work, and working meant eight hours of things that did not involve weddings, relationship problems, or arguments with her parents.

Work, however, did mean dealing with her unfortunate, waste-of-human-space co-worker, David. He had shown up to work on Friday for a change and pulled his weight, which had been a relief. It had been refreshing to Chelsea to actually leave for the weekend feeling like she was not going to have to play catch-up on Monday.

As luck would have it, though, this Monday morning his eyes were wide and bloodshot, and he walked around in a sort of light delirium. Chelsea rolled her eyes and cursed under her breath when she saw him. He was high on whatever drug it was he smoked, and he was therefore piling her with work. The whole situation grated on her nerves so much so that she could have smacked his head into his cubicle wall for being an idiot. How her boss could not see through all of his bullshit was a mystery even to the banking gods. Anyone with half a brain, she imagined, could see that David was undeserving of his job and needed replacing, but apparently her boss disagreed. David had been here almost three years now, and from what she gathered, he had always been this way.

And yet another reason I need to find a different job, she thought.

"Morning sunshine," Stacy said, leaning against Chelsea's cube, sipping her vat of coffee. Stacy never walked around with anything other than a full cup of coffee lately, and her coffee mug rivaled a baby's face in size. Stacy had laughed the day Chelsea commented on the behemoth nature of that mug, returning with a statement about how a new mother needed all the extra help she could get.

Last fall, about the end of September, Stacy and her husband Mark had had their first baby. The boy, Marcus Jacob, had been a welcomed addition to their young family. She and Mark had been married for nearly five years, yet Stacy was only twenty-five years-old and Mark twenty-seven – a young couple by most social standards. However, as Stacy had continually pointed out, she and Mark needed to have children, because that was just what people did after being married for as long as they were. She felt like it was the natural next step.

Chelsea had not known Stacy long, but from everything Stacy had always said about her marriage, the beginning of the marriage had been easy. It was with time that things had become increasingly more difficult. At first they had had nothing over which to quarrel and were so infatuated with each other that all they wanted to do was roll around in bed whenever they could. Stacy said she felt more like she had been playing house than actually living the married life when things began. Now, though, as they tried to stand on their own two feet, things progressed from feeling like a honeymoon to feeling like an icy mountainside.

Just like for everyone else, the year of the economic collapse had been a year of suffocation. Mark had been laid off, and Stacy had taken a pay cut to stay at Hobson Bank and Trust but had been given more work. Their bills overflowed with the drastic change in income, and they had had to trade in her car for an older one, amongst other things, just to stay afloat. In fact, money became such a reason for arguing that friends of theirs had suggested divorce. Stacy, refusing to think she could be divorced by twenty-three, decided to wait it out. She said that, with time, life would work itself out, and they would have a family instead.

After a year of being out of work, Mark finally found a job in a packaging plant and, working as a manager, had a secure enough position that he and Stacy finally started paying off their debt and talking children. Within four months, Stacy was pregnant, and her life was "back on track," as she put it. Marcus Jacob arrived nine months later, and she was busy being super mom, wife, and bank employee.

And all that simply meant was that she needed as much coffee in the morning as possible, this morning being a prime example.

"Morning, Stacy. Long night?" Chelsea asked, motioning to the coffee mug.

"Oh, yeah, this is water now. I feel like I already had two kegs of coffee this morning, so I figured I should probably re-hydrate before starting up again on the caffeine."

"Yikes," Chelsea laughed, "but yeah, good idea."

"I know. Marcus has just been sick and not sleeping. I feel like a zombie half the time."

"I can only imagine."

"But it's good. That's why God invented coffee," she responded, smiling and lifting her mug in an honorary toasting motion.

"Or water," Chelsea laughed, "but whatever works."

Stacy looked sheepishly down at her cup. "Oh, I guess you're probably right."

"No, it's fine," Chelsea reassured, denoting that she was only kidding. "How is everything on the home front, anyways, aside from the sickly baby?"

"Oh, yeah, um, it's fine," Stacy managed. "Yeah, fine. No, it's good."

Chelsea glanced sideways at Stacy. "What's going on?"

Stacy shook her head. "No, it's fine. I'm probably just overtired and overreacting."

Chelsea put her pen down and swiveled her chair around to face Stacy, now completely fixated on the conversation and not the stack of papers David had brought over moments before Stacy arrived.

"Overreacting to…" Chelsea questioned.

Stacy slumped against the cubicle, succumbing to her frustration and the reality of having someone to whom she could vent.

"Mark and I got into a fight last night," she admitted, playing with the giant brown mug in her hand.

"Oh, boy," Chelsea started. "About what? The baby?"

"Kinda, but I don't know. It was stupid stuff, but apparently it's been building. Mark feels like I've been too obsessed with 'family perfection,' as he puts it," she stated, adding emphasis with air quotes, "and not enough with us as people and the family we are. He says I make him out to be some bad guy who isn't home enough or helping with the baby at night. I've just been frustrated because I feel like everything falls on me, you know? He's a dad. He should help, too. I mean, it's not the 1950s anymore where the woman's supposed to do all the work and stay home all day long. He should be around too. I just told him I don't think that Marcus and I see him enough because he's always working weird hours."

Stacy took a sip of her water and shook her head before continuing, "That's when he said I should be happy he's getting overtime at all, after he struggled without work for a year, that this should not even be an argument because we need the money. He keeps reminding me how we need the money, but I keep reminding him that I work too, you know? I make some money, which should be helping, but he says our bills are still so bad that we need all the help we can get. But how would I know? He never lets me see a bill and keeps saying everything is 'fine'. Well, clearly it's not, or we wouldn't be fighting. And then he threw in how I need to stop spending money on Marcus all the time or we really are going to be broke, but how do you not spend money on a baby? I mean, okay, maybe I could not buy *as* much, but that's what you do when you have a baby. You're supposed to spoil him and buy him things, right?

"And that's when we started talking about Marcus. It's like all he does at night is cry, and then Mark just expects me to take care of it. Don't I work, too? Don't I have a job to go to in the morning as well? Why am I the one getting up at night? I know his job is more labor intensive than mine, granted, but, my God, I just want to sleep, too. And then I'm tired from being up all the time, and he's tired from work and hearing the baby cry all night, even though he doesn't do anything about it, and it's just eating away at both of us, making last night an all-out, blowout argument."

Chelsea glanced at Stacy, who took yet another sip of water before continuing, "And then there's the fact that we have to find a nanny or day care or something. My mom's been nice enough to watch Marcus during the day because Mark's mom died four years ago, and his dad works during the day so he can't help. My mom, however, is not going to volunteer to do this forever. And, I mean, it's not her job either; it's not her baby, but if we're already fighting about money and everything, where are we going to find the money for a nanny or daycare? I just, I don't know what to do."

Stacy stopped talking and just looked at her mug. Chelsea waited until the air became quiet enough that it bordered on awkward before realizing Stacy was officially finished. Chelsea did not know what to say, but Stacy, although waiting in an awkward silence, felt lighter having released some of her frustration.

"I'm sorry," Chelsea finally managed. "That sounds really intense and like there are a lot of things going on between you two."

"There are!" Stacy returned. "Except, I didn't even know half of them were issues before yesterday."

"Right."

"Which is even more annoying. I feel like we talked about things so much more before the baby."

"Did you? I mean, maybe it just seems like it," Chelsea volunteered. "Or maybe you're both just busier now, you know?"

"No, we did," Stacy said with finality. "I mean, this isn't the way it's supposed to be. We're supposed to be happy. We have a family and a cute little baby. He's not supposed to cry this much, and we're not supposed to fight like this. It's exhausting! There is no way things were this bad when our parents had us."

Chelsea smiled at Stacy and laughed to herself.

"What?" Stacy asked, noticing Chelsea's smile.

"Nothing. It's just our parents didn't have us *that* long ago. I mean, granted my mom didn't work, but a lot of moms and dads both worked. They obviously figured it out somehow. I mean, we're here aren't we?" Chelsea finished, not sure if she was trying to make a point or just make light of the situation.

Stacy stared at Chelsea for a few moments before responding, "But it's totally different. I mean, yeah, we're here, but things are different now after the recession."

"Granted."

"But I don't want them to be. I still want to be there for my baby without killing myself! I would totally rather stay home with Marcus if I could, but I can't, and that's part of the problem. Mark and I always wanted to have a family, start young, and have it go perfectly, but it's not. He works too much. I can't be home with Marcus, and the affect that has on our finances is kicking our butts. I just don't know what to do or how to fix it, and I just really wasn't prepared for our fight last night."

Chelsea, again, sat silently. She had no idea what to say. She felt like she could not relate at all. When she was twenty-five, she and her ex-boyfriend, Terry, had been together a year and had only just started talking marriage. They had had an apartment in Boston and absolutely no plans for kids or a family or anything that remotely resembled settling-down.

Chelsea wanted to find something comforting to say to Stacy, but she did not know how. The only thing she could offer was an "I'm sorry," but that was not enough, and Stacy's fallen face echoed Chelsea's intuition.

Standing up, Stacy apologized for venting and told Chelsea she'd leave her to her stack of papers and talk to her later. Chelsea truly did not mind the visit, apologized herself for not having better advice, and told Stacy to stop by whenever. However, both of them knew another visit would not happen today. Stacy was too overwhelmed and Chelsea too unknowledgeable in the area of family life to truly be much help. Their two realities were separated by the waters of parenthood, and someone had yet to build a bridge. It seemed, for today at least, their chats would be restricted to work.

Chelsea turned back to the stack of papers David had left her. She cursed David for being stoned and for his pitiful excuse for a work ethic. Then she opened the first file wondering if she, herself, couldn't get high off bank jargon.

Chelsea's purse vibrated. She looked at her phone: Danielle.

Chelsea had not spoken to Danielle since Friday afternoon, which had been Danielle's five-year anniversary celebration with Paul. Having not heard back from Danielle all weekend, she was not sure what to think, so the phone call made her jumpy, although she could not decipher if it was nervousness or excitement.

"Hi," Chelsea greeted.

"Oh, good! You're not busy!" Danielle exclaimed. "How are you?"

"Great, just finishing up lunch. You?"

"Good. Working through lunch, sadly. We have a deposition later this week, and I feel so far behind, but I wanted to call. I feel so bad for not having called you back this weekend! I wanted to tell you what was going on with everything."

"Oh it's okay, but I'm glad you called. I was almost worried when the phone rang because I wasn't sure if the lack of a phone call this weekend was a good thing or not."

"I know. I'm sorry."

"No, it's totally fine!" Chelsea began. "So, what happened on Friday?"

"Oh my gosh, Friday. Okay, I have so much to tell you," Danielle started, and then proceeded to retell the events of Friday night, everything from dinner to the Dale Chihuly exhibit. Chelsea listened intently, enjoying the seemingly good-natured air of the evening.

Finally, Danielle arrived at the part of the night back at their apartment where things turned serious.

"So, Paul opened a bottle of wine and sat me down on the couch," she explained. "He seemed jumpy and nervous, but I was already tipsy and found him utterly adorable in his nervousness."

"Aw, he was nervous?" Chelsea replied.

"Yeah, and he gets awkward when he's nervous. It's endearing, really. But, then, once I sat next to him, you know, I started noticing it wasn't just jitters but like utter nervousness, and then I started worrying."

"Why was he nervous?"

"Well, he started stuttering and everything, saying how these last few years have been the best, and he loves being with me. Seriously, Chels, I suddenly panicked. All I could think about was your comment about how he was going to propose."

"Oh, no! He didn't!" Chelsea quickly inserted. "I'm so sorry!"

"No it's fine! I'm not finished!" Danielle returned.

"Okay. Continue. So he's nervous –"

"Yeah, okay, so he's getting really nervous, and I'm starting to get nervous, and it's just bad. He keeps going on about how great everything's been and how he loves me so much and how he doesn't know what he would do without me." Danielle's tone started to savor of seriousness, which did not go unnoticed by Chelsea.

"And that's when he said it," Danielle stated.

"What?" Chelsea could not stop herself from asking. It was almost an involuntary response.

"He wasn't proposing, Chels," Danielle explained, pausing to catch her breath before continuing, "He's being transferred."

Chelsea gasped, "Transferred? To where?"

"Albany, New York!" Danielle wailed.

"*What?*" Chelsea exclaimed. "Oh my God, Danielle. Why?"

Danielle allowed the frustration and sadness to fully overtake her voice. "I don't know. I don't know what to do. Paul said that because he's been doing so well with the firm that they want to send him to the Albany office to help expand it. It's only been open for a few years, and they think he'd be great at building the business out there. They see this as a promotion!" she cried. "A *promotion!*"

"Oh Danielle," Chelsea consoled. "Oh hunny. I'm so, *so* sorry. I had no idea."

"I didn't either. And now I don't know what to do. What am I supposed to do, Chelsea? I can't just leave my job. I just landed this job, and I actually like it here. I like Boston, and I like being close to you and Rachel. But even more than that, it's not like I can just find a job anywhere. I don't have any experience, really; this is only my first year, and, do you know how hard it is for new law school graduates to find a job anymore? It's like in the sixty-percent range! At least I *have* a job. I don't want to give that up yet, and I really can't either, with loans coming due soon. I don't know. I don't know what to do!"

"Well, what does Paul say?" Chelsea offered, hoping that maybe he had introduced a plan.

"He feels the same way. He doesn't know what to do, but he knows how fortunate we are to both have jobs. It's just that this is such a great promotion and an increase in pay for him that he can't see passing it up. I don't know what we're going to do, and neither does he. He's just as upset about this whole thing as I am."

"Oh my God. I would be upset, too. I don't even know what to tell you right now. I'm shocked. I can't believe they want him to transfer. You would think that because he was doing so well here that they wouldn't want to lose him."

"Right? So did I, but the problem is they don't see it as losing him. They see it as having him help them expand, and having him benefit from the process is what they want to offer him. I understand it from their perspective, I do, but that doesn't make figuring out what we should do any easier."

"Right, I mean, how do you just give up your job? Like you said, it's not like you can just pick up and find a job anywhere anymore. Maybe they have jobs in Albany, but Albany isn't Boston."

"Exactly! This sucks so much, and all weekend I've just been fretting about the whole thing."

"Oh, Danielle! Why didn't you call me?"

"I didn't want to interrupt, and, honestly, I didn't even know what to say. I feel like I need to really talk this out with you guys, you know?"

"Well, why don't we?" Chelsea offered. "I'm busy this weekend, but we could get together a week from Sunday? Maybe by then you'll have more information, too, so we'll be able to talk about it more?"

"Yeah, that might work," Danielle said, tapping the base of her pen against the desk, thinking. She decided she needed some outside opinions because she was starting to get lost in her own head.

"And I'll call Rachel and see what she's doing. I can't imagine she'd be busy or, well, at least too busy to have lunch with her two best college friends!"

"Oh, that would be great. I'll write it on my calendar right now. Are you sure you wouldn't mind?"

"Absolutely not. Don't even think twice about it. Plus, it would be great to see you."

"I know. I feel like we've all just been so busy," Danielle replied. "Okay. The date is blocked off for lunch with you guys. Why don't you come into the city and we can go get lunch on the water. It'll be perfect for the end of May."

"Love it. I'll call Rachel, and we'll see you next weekend."

"Okay! Thanks again, Chelsea."

"Don't mention it. See you soon."

"Absolutely! Have a good day at work."

"You too! Good luck with your depositions. Bye, Danielle."

Chelsea sat back in her chair and glanced out the doorway of the break room while somewhere on the other side of Boston Danielle rubbed her face with her hands. This was proving to be a very complicated summer.

Chapter 7 - Missing

R achel agreed to lunch the following weekend, however, upon hanging up the phone, she was back to worrying. No matter how much coffee she drank nor how many different desk arrangements she made to refocus herself, she could not focus. Last night played over and over in her head.

Rachel had sat in the blue armchair in the living room of Charles and her condo. It was a plush, new, and plaid chair with piping along the seams. The high back curved into strong, rolling arms, and she had tucked herself into the corner and curled into a ball. The glass of red wine in her hand had remained untouched, but its presence alone had comforted her along with the hugging nature of the chair.

The still Sunday night had hung motionlessly outside the window. It had been late – quarter past ten to be exact – and Charles still had not come home from NYC. He had not called, and three hours had passed since the time she had expected him to come through the door. He had emailed her earlier that day to say he was almost certain he'd make the 6:00 p.m. flight home. Delays were often inevitable out of LaGuardia, but three hours was beyond any understandable delay. Plus, when she had called him, his phone had been dead. It could have been off, she'd admitted, but she had preferred to think it dead, which had been the entire reason he had not called.

She had swirled the wine in her hand, aggrevatingly. The motion was the manifestation of her frustration, but it also helped her focus her energy. She had something to hold onto and watch. She focused on the wine and how the deep crimson clung to the sides.

Good legs, she had thought. Good wine. She had wanted to sip it but could not bring herself to do so. Her stomach turned. The frustration from his sudden leaving on Friday, leaving her alone again, had bubbled and festered all weekend. She had already been stressed enough from his leaving, that his sudden and unexplained avoidance of home had pushed her stress levels over the edge. Thoughts raced through her head in fragments, flashing only momentarily before running into the next. Pictures of the weekend without him and his leaving had raced unchecked. Then, however, they were suddenly coupled by new thoughts. The legs of the wine transferred into legs of a woman, and the red coloring echoed of blood. The thoughts were unsettling yet vivid. Even though she had technically known the plane had landed safely, ruling out the possibility of a death by crash, the thoughts had still prevailed. However, she had not honestly thought him dead.

The notion of legs, on the other hand, had crept further towards the forefront of her mind. What if it were a woman and not an accident that had kept him? What if he had spent his late, Sunday night hours in Massachusetts with another woman instead of with her?

She had shuddered at the idea, but it wasn't the only one. Her thoughts had then skipped, uncensored, to an even more terrifying idea. What if it had not been golf that had taken him away all these weekends but a woman?

The notion alone had made her close her eyes and tremble inside. They were not even married and already she was entertaining the idea of the *other* woman. This was the thing of stories and older generations, petty relationships even, not of her life. This could not be part of her life. Sure, girls broke up with guys over affairs and cheating all the time, but not once they were at the point of being engaged and almost married. It just did not happen then.

Or did it?

Rachel sat at her office desk, grabbed onto the desk's edge and sighed aloud as the same thoughts raced again. She hated that she was even entertaining the idea.

No, she thought. It's not that. It can't be.

But she continued to stay stew over the events. Even though he had failed to return home before she had fallen asleep Sunday night, she had awakend to traces of his presence this morning, signaling to her that he had at least come home at some point. She saw his side of the bed crinkled, his toothbrush used, and shaving remnant in the sink. His suitcase was tucked away in the closet but still lay open, and when she ventured curiously into the kitchen, the blender pieces were laying out on the kitchen counter to dry. Clearly, he had returned, but she wondered how she had slept through it all.

When she had walked back to her room to check her cell phone, she noted that he had both texted and called her at 1:30 a.m. The messages had been apologetic but short, confessing to have gone drinking with his co-workers but nothing more. Again, she had sighed. She must have slept through the call, too, though it was odd she had missed it all. Still, she had wanted to believe him.

Now, she tapped the pen in her hand against the desk, channeling her nervousness. She tried to believe him – that he had just been drinking – and part of her did. However, emotions and frustration did not always work the way she wanted, and they wanted her to believe otherwise. Meeting with her friends next week, therefore, might be just what she needed to help her sort out her thoughts. However, that did not help her channel her worries right now. The steady echoes of Sunday night's fears overwhelmed her, and she could not seem to bring herself out of it enough to focus. The idea was absurd at best and probably completely unfounded. She was probably just blowing something out of proportion, but it did not asuage the fact that the thought was now lodged in her brain. It was like an annoying tick that would not cease.

She tried calming herself, reminding herself that he had just been drinking with the guys like he had said. He had just been drinking, and that was all.

But still, what if he hadn't been?

Chapter 8 – Battling Ideals

Late Wednesday evening, Chelsea pulled herself up to her desk in her room. Her latest encounter with her co-worker, David, had finally pushed her into realizing that she needed a change in her life, and it needed to occur now. Having sat herself down at her desk, Chelsea mentally prepped herself for a night of soul-searching when a knock resonated from her bedroom door.

"I want to talk to you," Chelsea's mom announced, knocking on Chelsea's door as a mere formality, inviting herself in. Her mother had taken note of Chelsea's demeanor these last few weekends and had decided to help. Unfortunatly, although she always meant well, often her idea of help came across as bossy and invasive. Barging into her room as she did, Chelsea already suspected this would not be a constructive use of her time.

"Mom, not right now," Chelsea returned, looking over her shoulder from her computer. "I'm in the middle of something."

"It'll only take a second," her mom insisted, sitting on the edge of Chelsea's bed.

Chelsea glanced longingly at her computer. There was no rush to finish the online applications to graduate school or for a new job, per se, but she had truly wanted to accomplish something tonight, and these applications had been that something. She had finally reached a point at work where she realized she either needed to find a new career or go back to school to get a degree in Journalism or English if she ever wanted to escape the seemingly dead-end job she currently held at the bank. These applications were the first step towards moving her life forward. However, she could feel from the tense air in the room after her mom entered, that it would just be easier to go along with whatever her mom wanted to talk about than to argue. The applications would still be there when the conversation with her mom finished, so she turned around fully in her desk chair until she faced her mom and tried to swallow her annoyance before speaking.

"What?" Chelsea asked.

"I just got off the phone with Vince's mother," her mom started, and Chelsea tried desperately to hide the aggravation that suddenly flowed through her veins from showing on her face while her mom continued. "They are going to be doing a Plus One invite on your wedding invitation in October. Now I know you're not taking anyone to Rachel's wedding because you're in the wedding and mentioned there's no one you care enough about to take with you, which I understand. However," she started, which made Chelsea's skin crawl, and then paused for a breath.

The pause Tina required before continuing her story was just barely long enough for Chelsea to butt in, "Mom. I don't know what you're going to say, but please just stop. I'm so tired of hearing about this wedding stuff! I can't handle it right now."

"Oh stop being dramatic, Chelsea. You make everything seem like a big to-do. I'm merely trying to help here," she explained in her overly motherly tone. "Besides, there is no reason you shouldn't go to these weddings without a date."

"Date?" Chelsea repeated, bewildered. "What are you talking about, Mom? You just said that you knew I wasn't taking a date to Rachel's wedding."

"Right. And I think that's a poor choice. It's a wedding, and you're of the age to be taking a date, so you should take one. People expect you to have a date at these sorts of things. Plus, Rachel already told you that there was room for a date for you if you wanted."

"But I told her I'm not taking one," Chelsea replied quickly, her tone laced with bitterness. "And what do you mean *supposed* to?"

"I'm merely saying it's not proper, is all. A girl your age should have a date, and I'll be dead before I see you go to a family wedding without a date."

"Family wedding?" Chelsea cried, completely lost. "What are you talking about, Mom? Rachel's not family." The connections her mother made on her own accord made Chelsea's head throb. She did not fully understand the way that woman's brain worked, but it always seemed to produce some idea that proved more condescending and invasive than helpful.

"No, but Vince's is, and their weddings are only a month apart. If you aren't taking a date to Rachel's wedding, how on Earth are you going to find one in the month between the two?"

Chelsea stared at her mother, shocked. "You're unbelievable. I can't believe we are having this discussion right now."

"Well, hold on now," her mom said in her self-assured manner, straightening up a little more on the bed before continuing. "I've figured out a solution."

Chelsea muttered under her breath, "Oh Jesus, Mom," which was either inaudible to her mother or something her mother just chose to ignore, because she continued as though Chelsea had said nothing.

"I spoke with Vince's mother. A woman Marie works with, Deb, has a nephew who's about your age. He sounds really nice: thirty-ish, works in banking like you so he has a steady job, and is apparently recently single. There was something with a crazy ex-girlfriend, but I don't remember. Either way, that's not important. She couldn't remember what Deb's nephew's name was, but she was going to ask Deb if this was something he might be up for. It would be perfect."

Chelsea found herself stupefied. She rested her head in her hands, her fingertips pushing against her temples just hard enough to both keep her from lashing out at her mother and remind her that she was, in fact, awake. Somewhere after "Vince's mother" life had taken a wrong turn, and Chelsea felt suddenly trapped in a "Twilight Zone" styled, parallel universe. Her mother was officially

61

crazy – loony, in fact. Sitting there like she did, Chelsea noted that her mother actually thought she was doing her a favor. What part of that last statement had made any sense, though? Did she not just say that this guy had a crazy ex-girlfriend? Was that not enough of a warning to say that maybe this guy was crazy himself? Like generally finds like, so why would her mother, even for a moment, consider this as someone Chelsea wanted to meet, let alone date?

She must have lost it. That had to be it. Tina Farrera was officially off her rocker.

"Mom," Chelsea started, almost feeling sorry for her mother, "I think you've officially become wedding obsessed, and I'm worried about you. I don't know what you're talking about. I don't want to be set up on a blind date. I don't want to take anyone as a date to these weddings, let alone some total stranger who recently broke up with some psycho, crazy person. None of that sounds like fun, and I can't believe you would even consider that as a viable option for anyone, let alone your own daughter!"

Tina sat back, instantly offended. Ungrateful was the word flashing through her mind, and that was exactly how she perceived her daughter at this moment. After all the work she had put into trying to find Chelsea a date so she would not be looked down upon at these weddings, this is the response she received? Yes, Chelsea was most certainly ungrateful.

Tina's tone was terse and her voice louder as a result. "That's exactly why I was considering it," she threw back, "because you *are* my daughter. I care about you, and I refuse to let you be embarrassed at these weddings by not having a date. Think of all the comments and the pity you'll get."

"Mom!" Chelsea cried, "You're being ridiculous. This isn't 1942! People go to weddings without dates all the time nowadays. You are making a bigger deal out of this than it needs to be. I think, actually, it's you who is afraid of some kind of gossip. That's all you seem to be concerned with these days – what people are saying and how you'll look."

Then Chelsea threw in a low-blow, "You're just mad it's not me getting married."

Her mom stared at her momentarily, and then she stood.

"How dare you!" she yelled, "You have no idea what I've been going through with these weddings, or what I've done to try to help you find a date."

"I never asked for you to find me one!" Chelsea yelled back, unable to control her own anger.

"You didn't have to! I see how you look when you come home from being out with Rachel all day. You don't say anything, but I know you. Your face and your tone say it all. You're upset and depressed, and I know it's because you have no one and your best friends are getting married or close to it."

The last sentence pierced Chelsea like a dagger. Although true, Chelsea's frustration and anger prevented her from acknowledging the truth in her mother's words, which was that she had been a little down lately. It was hard for her to constantly be around people who were so happy with their relationships, who had people to fall back on or with whom to spend their time. Chelsea sometimes found herself missing the idea of Terry more than she missed Terry himself. They had been wrong for each other, him highlighting that they wanted different things, and she knew she was better off without him, moving forward with her life and discovering who she was as a person. That did not, however, make the lonely, single moments any easier. Between the stress of work and Rachel's wedding, she would have loved to have had someone in whom to confide, with whom to spend time and just be there as support, but she did not have that right now. She had only herself, and despite being upset every now and then, she was trying her damnedest to stay above the stress. Apparently, though, it was not going as well as she had thought.

But that did not give her mother permission to butt-in, Chelsea reaffirmed for herself.

"So what, Mom? So what?" Chelsea replied, giving in. "Fine. Maybe I am. Maybe I am lonely and upset every now and then.

Maybe I miss having someone, and maybe it is hard for me to go through all this marriage stuff to some degree because a year or so ago I thought maybe Terry and I would be going down that road. But you know what? We didn't. I am working on getting over it, so why can't you? I'm not getting married, Mom. Not now, nor anytime soon. Why can't you understand that? Talking about weddings more, trying to constantly pull me into Vince's wedding or prying into Rachel's won't change that. It won't make me get married sooner."

"But you're not even trying," her mom started.

"Trying?" Chelsea cried, astounded at her mom's inability to even pretend to understand. "Trying to what, Mom? Get married? No, I'm not. These things don't happen overnight."

"But you haven't even really dated since your break up."

"Ouch," Chelsea responded. "Harsh."

"I'm just being honest. You need to move forward."

"I am."

Instantly her mother calmed down and perked up upon hearing that. She had no idea her daughter had actually been making plans to move her life forward, seeking dates and looking for someone new to help fill her life. All she had ever seen was her daughter leave too quickly with Rachel on the weekends, return tired and silent, and run straight back to her room or to the patio with her computer. She had not seen her leave on weekend evenings dressed up because she had plans, at least, not that she could remember. Maybe, though, she had been mistaken. Maybe her daughter had been meeting people, just quietly. If that were the case, maybe a date for the weddings would not be such a far stretch.

The thought soothed her, and she wanted to know more. "You are?"

"Yes, I am. I'm working on moving my life forward," Chelsea stated, and then pointed to her computer. She wanted to be sure her mother knew that her idea of moving forward revolved around her *life* and what she wanted to be doing with it, not just her relationship status.

"I'm looking into going back to school or finding a new job."

"What?" her mom shot back, the soothing feeling vanished. Job? School? She could not believe what she was hearing. None of those were going to land her a date to these weddings, and no date meant no prospects for a husband and marriage. It was not that Chelsea was old, exactly, but she was not the twenty-two year-old, care-free college girl she had been, and she wanted to see her daughter married and taken care of.

Chelsea smiled smugly at her mother. She knew exactly what her mother was thinking, and none of it revolved around being pleased with the news she just heard.

Waiting, Chelsea stared back at her mother wide-eyed, wondering when the silence would be broken, but her mom had lost. She did not know what to say. Anger had turned to disappointment and fear, hushed words of gossip running through her mind. She could already hear what all the relatives would be saying at the wedding about how unfortunate it was that her daughter was still single. Her heart broke even further seeing how Chelsea seemed so pleased with herself. Chelsea just did not understand how vital appearances were. People would talk when they saw her alone and not in a pleasant way. At least if she had a date they would overlook her or wonder momentarily about the boy, but ultimately they would leave her alone. Chelsea could do what she pleased with her date after the wedding – stay with him or find another man later – but at least she could survive the wedding unscathed. But how could she explain that to her daughter when Chelsea clearly did not understand?

But Chelsea saw it differently. Granted, Chelsea hated the idea of being alone and the questions she faced when with going to functions alone, but awkward relative questions were better than an awkward four-hour wedding date with someone she did not care for or did not know. Girls went to weddings solo now, anyway. They did not have to be "spoken for" like they did in the days when her mother was young; they could be single and have that be acceptable. Was it ideal to most people? No. Was it what Chelsea wanted forever?

No, but for Chelsea, a wedding was just one more day, not the end-all-be-all of her life. Plus, there would be some single men at the wedding and probably someone to hook up with that night if she really wanted to, so it was not like she was condemned for being twenty-seven and single. In fact, twenty-seven and moving forward with life was a perfectly acceptable way to be. She just had to actually get the "moving forward" part down, which she could do if her mother left her alone for half a second to fill out applications.

Chelsea stared at her mother, wanting her to leave. Both of them were angry, but both of them knew there was nothing else to be said at the moment. The silence said it all. There was an irresolvable distance between them, or at least it was irresolvable for now.

Tina stood to leave. Chelsea was thankful their crazy discussion was over. She did not want to have any more discussions about dates, and her mom knew discussing it further would only frustrate both of them. She just wanted what was best for her daughter, and Chelsea wanted her mother to drop the subject. It was just over two months until Rachel's wedding, and Chelsea's date status seemed to be solidified in both of their minds.

Chapter 9 – Worries

Two weeks later, when Rachel arrived at lunch on Sunday, Chelsea and Danielle were already seated and waiting anxiously. They sipped their iced teas and coffee, doting lightly on the bread and bubbling on about the weather and other surface topics. Underlying the niceties, however, pressed the real issues, the stress that consumed them all individually and brought them to today's much needed luncheon. It seemed everyone had imperative news to share, but none of it was uplifting. In fact, the relief they felt just by being around each other was met with equal amounts of exhaustion in trying to stay as upbeat as possible for as long as possible before finally succumbing to the reality of why they were there in the first place. It was just a matter of who wanted to break the ice first.

Midway into the starter salads, Danielle asked Rachel how the wedding plans were going and which cake she had chosen. Danielle had been asked to be in the wedding but initially had turned down the offer because of a court case she was overseeing. It had been set to go to court sometime in the fall, and she had not wanted to put Rachel through the agony of having to back out last minute if she had to leave town for the trial. As it turned out, the case looked like it would be settled out-of-court, so Danielle could have participated in Rachel's wedding. However it was too late now, seeing as how Rachel had already turned down one of Charles' college buddies just to ensure the numbers stayed even. Trying to find last minute groomsmen, Rachel had said, was too stressful, so Danielle agreed to help as needed, but she would only be a supporter at the wedding as opposed to a supporter in the wedding.

Bringing up the wedding in general, even though Danielle's only question had been regarding the cake, was enough to crack Rachel's upbeat exterior.

"I don't remember exactly, something with white icing and strawberries," she sighed, clearly upset but trying to pretend otherwise. She looked down at her plate and pushed around some grilled chicken while she said it.

Chelsea instantly intervened. "She picked a wonderful cake," she covered, looking at Danielle and grabbing Rachel's hand supportively. "It's going to be absolutely perfect, just what she wanted. It's vanilla cake with strawberries, whipped cream, and a white chocolate ganache filling. Then it has a beautiful white, black, and sky blue colored, five tiered set up. It's going to look just perfect with the dresses and the decorations at the reception."

Danielle had noticed the sideways glance Chelsea had thrown her prior to responding. Clearly, there was a deeper issue than just something being wrong with the cake.

Uncertain how to proceed, Danielle simply said, "That sounds lovely. Did you and Charles come up with the theme together?"

Immediately Rachel started crying. Danielle knew that her safe question had been anything but. It was not the cake that was upsetting her.

"Rachel, what is it?" Danielle asked. "Did I say something wrong?"

Rachel shook her head and tried to stop her tears from cascading down her face and ruining her makeup.

"No, no," she replied. "You didn't say anything. It's fine, but I knew this was going to come out sometime today."

"Obviously it's not fine," Danielle cautiously stated. "You're crying."

Rachel continued to dab the tears off her carefully painted face while continuing, "No, I'm fine, really. I'm sorry. I didn't think I would get this emotional, you know?"

"Rach, it's okay," Chelsea consoled. "What is it? You can tell us. Did something happen with Charles?"

Rachel tilted her head back and shook it slightly, like she was saying "no" to her entire reality. She had already started crying, so now proved as good a time as any to confide in her two best friends. Danielle and Chelsea sat patiently, though worried and confused, waiting for Rachel to say something. Neither of them wanted to butt-in when it appeared clear to both of them that Rachel just needed a moment.

Rachel took in an audible breath before starting, returning the napkin to her lap and readjusting her short sleeved, light blue camisole. "It's just been piling up, I guess. All the little things have just been adding and adding, and with the wedding in two months, I just can't handle it all."

"What's been piling up?" Danielle asked.

"Just everything," Rachel admitted while trying to maintain composure. She was, after all, in a restaurant, and a restaurant was no place for hysterics. It had become grounded in her beliefs that appearances were everything, and allowing people to only see what you want them to see is of the utmost importance. Granted, if it had just been her friends seeing her cry, she would have been less concerned. After all, that's what friends are for, but it wasn't just her friends. It was strangers. It was an entire restaurant, and that was no place for tears.

"The wedding alone has been stressing me out because it's so much work, but everything with Charles is just making it so much more upsetting. I'm not supposed to be upset when I'm about to get married, and all I can think about is how –" and then she paused, catching herself, "– why –"

She stopped and looked down, pressing her lips together, as though she were subconsciously trying to keep herself from continuing.

"How or why what?" Chelsea prodded gently.

Rachel lowered her voice both in tone and volume. She did not look at either of her friends, "He's never home."

"What do you mean he's never home?" Danielle returned, hoping clarification might sway the worse case scenarios running through her head.

"Just that," Rachel stated, then continued poignantly, careful to separate each of the words. "He's never home."

"Well, where does he go?" Danielle needed to know before she said anything else. She felt questions were the only safe seg-way for the conversation. She had looked to Chelsea for a hint, but judging by Chelsea's startled and confused look, she was clearly just as unsure of what to say.

"I don't know," Rachel admitted. "But this is the first time after five weeks that he's been home for a weekend. His parents came into town to see the church and the hotel's reception hall, and I don't think that was a coincidence, nor do I get the feeling he would have stayed in town if his parents had not arranged a visit."

"You don't know that," Danielle tried.

"Don't I?" Rachel snapped back, looking at Danielle for the first time. "For the last month and a half I have been doing absolutely all of the wedding stuff by myself or with Chelsea because she's been nice enough to tag along and at least be around. He doesn't care. He jets off every weekend to a new place with his buddies to play golf or catch up with the guys, and he's gone *all* weekend. He leaves the minute he's out of work on Friday and then comes back late Sunday night when he knows I'm already tired and probably sleeping because I have to leave for work at seven-fifteen in the morning.

"Then, two weekends ago he said he was on a business trip, so, yet again, where was he? Gone. All weekend. I saw him for thirty seconds maybe on Friday before he sped out the door again. And then I don't know when he came home Sunday night. Do you know when he came home at a time when I could actually see him?"

She was asking a rhetorical question and did not wait to hear an answer.

"Monday. Monday night," she said, throwing her voice angrily at the air. Then her eyes burned and filled with water as her breathing failed, and she broke composure.

"He was supposed to come home Sunday, but he didn't, at least not until after I had already fallen asleep. He didn't call, he didn't text, he didn't ... anything. Nothing. Nothing until 1:30 in the morning. Who the hell is up at 1:30 on a Sunday night? His phone had been dead when I had called, but at 1:30 a.m. he was going to try to call me? What is that? I was so worried initially, too, thinking maybe something had happened with the plane, that I called the airport just to find out he had arrived safely and on time. On time! It was ten p.m. when I had called, and he was three hours late at that point.

"And that's when it hit me," she sniffled. No longer angry, her demeanor and words turned sad and broken. "What if he's not ... with friends every weekend? What if his phone's not dead? What if the golf outings are just a lie and he's really ..."

Rachel could not even say the words, but Danielle and Chelsea both knew what they would have been. Cheating. What if he's cheating? The pits in both of their stomachs tightened but for different reasons. Chelsea had secretly wondered for the last few weeks if there was not something seriously wrong with Rachel and Charles' supposedly perfect relationship. Rachel had talked about him a lot, almost too much, during the cake tasting, like she was trying to convince herself he was around more than he actually was. Plus, when they had gone cake shopping, Rachel's mood had been different – distant almost. Yes, she had explained that Charles' absense had been due to a business trip, but it was more than that. She had been incredibly indecisive that afternoon, which was uncharacteristic of her. Rachel had chosen two wedding dresses, decided on flower arrangements in an hour, and booked the band with full music selections four months ago. Having to watch her friend struggle with making cake decisions had rattled Chelsea.

Plus, again, Rachel had not shut up about Charles during the whole cake appointment. It was almost as though a different Rachel had taken over. She had described his weekend business trip in details only reserved for a personal assistant, talking at length about how worried he seemed to be about work, constantly putting it first as of late, which she explained as a way to help pay for the wedding and honeymoon. She had even talked about his rushed exit, but that was solely mentioned because she extensively explained how she had kept him from his plane by insisting they discuss the wedding and his workday. She had said he had been so nice humoring her by allowing her to rant that she completely lost track of how long she had been talking, which is why his hurried exit was necessary.

Now Chelsea wondered if all the discussion that day about Charles had not been a self-defense mechanism Rachel had used to deflect her worry and pain over his absence. She wondered if she should make note of that to Rachel, but when Chelsea glanced over at her friend, she thought better of it. Now just did not seem like the most appropriate time to bring it up. Rachel was already distraught and Chelsea didn't think adding more distress would help. Then again, Chelsea thought maybe it would never be an appropriate time to discuss her concern. Rachel wanted relationships to be rosy-colored so badly that saying any of this might have an adverse affect, especially this close to the wedding.

Plus, since this was the first time that Chelsea was hearing about Charles going missing after his NYC trip, she wondered if Rachel had wanted to hide the event completely. Sometimes Rachel's reality was a lie by omission. She kept things to herself as long as possible if she feared that discussing them would alter others' perceptions of her appeared perfection. Then issues only surfaced if she couldn't file them away in good conscience. The more Chelsea soaked in what Rachel said, the more she could hear the defensiveness in Rachel's voice. It was as though she were still fighting the reality she had tried to keep hidden, and Chelsea just could not bring herself to mention what was truly on her mind.

Instead, Chelsea tried to dance around the topic, trying simply to cheer up her friend.

"Oh Rach," Chelsea began soothingly, "No. You can't think that way. I mean, maybe he just really is busy, you know? Then there's the fact that you have the big account at work ending in a few days, so maybe you just feel like he's gone more often because you know you'll start to be home more once you finish the account. Plus, he's always traveled for work, ever since I've known him at least. I mean, remember all the times we loved getting together and touring Boston when he'd be gone? We had some of the best girl's weekends because he was out of town!"

Chelsea smiled at Rachel. Her upbeat voice and talk of memories made the left corner of Rachel's mouth turn up, but Rachel returned immediately to being upset once she realized she had started to smile. She needed her friends and their advice, but she was not ready to stop being upset.

Chelsea continued, "You know, I mean, this wedding has been so crazy, and you have been like seriously so on top of your game with the whole thing that it boggles my mind. I don't know how you do it. And maybe, I mean, you haven't seemed overly stressed, but I know it has to be stressful, so maybe you're just focusing your stress back into your relationship and worrying about something that really isn't even there, you know?"

"Well, maybe," Rachel returned, "but what about the fact that his phone was off that whole time?"

Chelsea shook her head. Her being at a total loss for how to answer that question was obvious, but she tried anyway. "Maybe he really did go out for drinks that night and got drunker than he anticipated, just like he said. I mean, I don't understand it, but maybe in his mind he was afraid you'd be upset that he came home wasted because of the deal you had made with him about not drinking so much before the wedding, so he just waited it out.

And, if he was on the plane that day, there's really a good chance he didn't turn the phone back on. I mean, there have been plenty of times where I'm in the middle of talking to someone as I exit a plane, and I just forget to turn my phone back on."

Rachel shook her head and looked down at the table. "Maybe," was all she said. She knew Chelsea was trying, and it warmed Rachel's heart to know her friends were at least making an effort to cheer her up, even if Chelsea's voice gave away her doubts. However, it still did not sway Rachel's worry. She still had shadowy thoughts of another woman running frustratingly through her head.

In the meantime, and on the other side of the table, Danielle also worried about Rachel. However, she worried that Rachel's predicament might be a projection of her own life. The notion of cheating, the notion that someone in a seemingly happy and committed relationship could potentially cheat made Danielle's heart race. Charles and Rachel were almost married. She wondered how someone could cheat on someone they were supposedly in love with enough to marry. Not all marriages are perfect, granted, but to go into a marriage already worrying about cheating? Danielle was flabbergasted. Plus, where did that leave her? What would happen to her relationship if Paul moved to Albany? Sure they'd been together for five years now, but she did not feel ready to be on any "marriage" track. They discussed it occasionally, but discussing it was one thing. Acting on it was another, and he had agreed that, given the reality of their situations with work and finances, a wedding just did not fit until Danielle felt more ready. It was not like they had not talked about it before, but it was not something she was ready to commit to just yet, and he had agreed to wait.

But now Paul might be leaving, and that meant less time together and more time for them to possibly want someone to fill the void. She loved him enough to believe she would not cheat, and she knew he loved her, but love alone did not always keep people from acting impulsively. Paul had always seemed a little needier than Danielle. It was not that Danielle did not equally want to be with Paul, but

Danielle seemed to feel she was always the one putting the breaks on milestones. She had pushed back their buying a place in Boston three years ago until after the six month breakup threat passed as to ensure they made it through that fiasco before fully committing to something so monumental and concrete. Then she had always been the one saying she wanted to settle into a career and pay off some law school debt before ever discussing marriage. She knew how much weddings cost. Her parents had paid $46,000 for her older sister's wedding four years ago, and that was money neither she nor Paul had right now. Would her parents help? Sure, but with the recession hitting everyone a few years back, everything now was just a little different. Money was a little tighter, and Danielle was trying to be smart about it all. Why start off a marriage in debt? That seemed irrational, so she had pushed the idea of marriage back every time it had come up in conversation.

But what if Paul was ready and she was unknowingly pushing him away? Would moving away mean the end of their relationship or cause unforeseen cheating?

It was a frightening thought but one now playing loosely in Danielle's mind. She still had yet to tell Rachel about Paul's job offer in Albany, and now she wondered what her reaction would be. Would Rachel turn pessimistic because of what she was going through or would she insight hope inside Danielle like she always seemed to do whenever there were problems between Paul and her?

"Hunny, I don't know what to tell you either," Danielle began, sympathetically. "I think I would feel just as confused if I were in your shoes, but, you know, Chelsea has a point. You guys have always seemed like the perfect couple, so maybe it is just stress or a rough patch and nothing more. I know Paul and I can have those, but we get through them."

"You do?" Rachel asked.

"Oh of course," Danielle replied. "I mean, we practically broke up three and a half years ago, and we've had our ups and downs since. We're even going through one right now. It's not like we planned for it; life just brings different challenges, and we have to work through them."

"You two are fighting?" Rachel returned, surprised. The surprise was almost enough to snap her out of her funk and back to normal Rachel levels. Rachel may have relished in having all the attention on her in most scenarios, but when she was in a bad mood, she knew the fastest way to remedy that was by focusing her energy on helping her friends. That sort of service almost always lifted her spirits.

Rachel wondered, "Oh my God, what happened?"

Danielle waved her hand dismissively, trying to lighten the heaviness of her last comment. "We're not like 'fighting' fighting, but it's been a really tough couple of weeks."

Chelsea intervened, "Is this about the moving thing?"

"Moving thing?" Rachel sputtered, shocked. She officially had moved past her problems with Charles. She figured Charles was at least living with her, even if sometimes it felt more like a technicality. If Paul was moving, then he and Danielle would not be living together, and, to Rachel, that was like a relationship death sentence.

"It's complicated," Danielle sighed, "and totally sucks."

"Dish," Rachel insisted.

Danielle straightened up in her chair, fixing the napkin in her lap as she did so. Sipping her water, she mentally prepared herself to rapid-fire the details of her life since the anniversary. "Okay, so, our five year anniversary was the other weekend. It was wonderful, and he did a fabulous job surprising me, and so on and so forth. In short, it was great. That night, however, when we arrived home he started stuttering about how much he loved me."

"Aw that's cute," Rachel hummed, like she was playing with a newborn puppy.

"Oh, it gets better," Chelsea assured.

"I thought it was cute, too, until he got really awkward and started talking about how I'm the best thing in his life, how he wouldn't know what to do if he lost me, and how he can't imagine his life without me. It legitimately started worrying me, you know?

I momentarily thought he might propose, which I totally wouldn't have been ready for, so thankfully he didn't," Danielle said, tilting her head towards Rachel to keep her from getting overly excited about an engagement that did not happen.

"Anyway," Danielle continued, "he sat me down on the couch and told me that he's being transferred to Albany, New York for work. Indefinitely."

"*What?*" Rachel roared. Her roller coaster of emotions had just hit another turn. "What do you mean *indefinitely?*"

"Just what I said. Indefinitely. We don't know when exactly he's being transferred, other than before the end of the fourth quarter which gives us somewhere between one and six months, and we don't know how long he'll be there. It could be a temporary move, or it could really be a permanent one. It's technically a promotion, according to his company. Paul's been doing such a stellar job at work that they're sending him off to build up the branch in Albany, which, honestly, is super exciting. How many twenty-seven year olds can say that? So, I mean, I'm excited for him. It's a great opportunity and a pay raise, and it's just a really great thing," she rattled, and then she sighed, "except that we have no idea what to do about *us.*"

"Well what have you guys discussed?" Rachel inquired.

"Nothing," Danielle interjected, "because I haven't wanted to deal with it, to be totally honest. All we ever do is talk in circles or act like it never came up in the first place. It's exhausting. I hate not knowing, and I hate not having an answer. I mean, we've considered everything. We've talked about him moving out there and me staying here to build my career a little more first, since it's only a three-hour drive, but still. When do either of us have a free enough weekend to spend six hours round-trip in the car? Plus, then that just means we could potentially go weeks without seeing one another if one of us can't make the trip.

"Then, we thought maybe I could try to find a job out there. I'm fresh out of school and haven't officially built roots anywhere yet, so I could move. The only problem with that is that it is so hard to find a job right now for a new lawyer. I mean, it's just like any other job. It's nearly impossible, so why would I give up a job with a law firm I love, where I get to do work I love, and where I've been working and interning for nearly four years already to move somewhere without a job? Granted, I could probably look or ask if someone in the firm has connections, but it's not a guarantee and that freaks me out. Plus, Paul alone doesn't make enough money here, nor will he in Albany, to pay for both of us, a place for us to live, and my loan payments.

"But then, if he stays here he passes up a really great opportunity. He has worked so hard to get where he is with that company, and he loves it. I can't ask him to give that up. He's moving forward in his career. Why would I want to stop him from doing that? For what? So we can stay in Boston? I mean, I love Boston, but that just seems selfish."

"But you have your job here," Chelsea said. "I mean, it's not like you're a stay-at-home wife who's asking him to stay in Boston just because she likes it. You are actually making a living here."

"And he's trying to do the same. I can't ask him to give up this opportunity," Danielle responded.

"I don't know, Danielle," Chelsea began. "I mean, yeah, I think that's great for him, and a raise is a raise –"

"– a twelve thousand dollar raise," Danielle interjected. Rachel's eyes widened in surprise and she looked at Danielle in a way that said the answer was obvious. Clearly, her new vote was for the move.

"Okay, so, that's a big raise," Chelsea redirected, but not before getting right back to her point. "But still, Danielle, I mean, you could be making ten grand more at your job in a few years or so if you keep up your work. You've been there for almost four years already. They know how well you work. They know what you can do, and you keep telling me they put you on cases constantly. Clearly you're doing something right, so it's not like you're not capable of moving up the ranks there. I don't know, but I feel like if you're so willing to compromise then he should be, too."

"Oh, he is," Danielle insisted. "He is. But I just feel like I'm only one year into my job, officially, so it's still 'new', and a new job is a new job regardless if I'm here or in Albany. With him, though, he's already moving up at his job, but, for me, I'm just worried about being able to *find* a job in Albany and one I actually like."

"Okay, so you split for a while, and then when you find a job, join him out there." That seemed like a very obvious answer to Chelsea.

Danielle sighed, "You make it sound so easy. It probably would be, too, if I didn't love it here in Boston. I mean I love it here. You guys are here, I love living close to the ocean, and I've literally just fallen in love with Boston since I moved into the city four years ago. I don't know what to do. Why can't things just be easy? I feel like life just keeps getting more complicated."

Chelsea looked at Rachel while Danielle pushed food around her plate. Everyone was at a loss for what to say.

"What would you do, Chelsea?" Danielle asked.

Chelsea shook her head. "I don't know, Danielle. Normally I would say to do whatever you think is right and what your gut tells you, but that's not always the easy answer nor the one other people like best."

Chelsea scoffed at that last statement, thoughts of her mother's anger passing through her head.

"But you have to do what's best for you," she continued. "If you don't have a clear head right now, then wait. It's only been two weeks. Give it some time, and maybe things will make more sense in a few weeks or so."

"Yeah, sleep on it," Rachel interjected. "You and Paul have always been so rational and steadfast in your relationship. Don't go getting all emotionally responsive now. I mean," she joked, "that's how I work, but you've always been much more level headed than me, especially when it comes to you and Paul. I agree with Chelsea. Just wait. Something'll make sense soon."

Danielle shook her head. "You're probably right. It just sucks in the meantime. I hate feeling 'in limbo', you know?"

The other girls nodded in agreement, and the waitress came by and laid the check on the table.

"Okay, so that's clearly enough about me," Danielle said, glancing over the bill and reaching for her purse. "What about you, Chelsea? What was the big thing you wanted to talk to us about?"

Chelsea inhaled deeply and rolled her eyes at the thought of her mother. She, too, grabbed her purse and took out her cash to help pay for lunch.

"Let's head out for ice cream or coffee or something quickly, and I'll fill you both in on the latest fight with my mother."

Chapter 10 – Back Home

Lunch left all the girls overwhelmed and exhausted, yet somehow a little more comforted and confident. No one knew how to solve the others' problems, but knowing they had each other for support left them feeling less boxed-in and suffocated.

Around three-thirty they said good-bye and headed their separate ways. Chelsea returned home to work on graduate school and job applications, Danielle went home to spend the rest of the sunny afternoon with Paul, and Rachel left to straighten the house before Charles was set to return home from lunch with his parents. It was not that life was easier, but the three friends had managed to shed light onto what were probably just molehills and not mountains, making the challenges they each faced feel more manageable and conquerable.

Chelsea's house was quiet when she returned. Her mom and dad were nowhere to be found, and Chelsea breathed easier upon entering the house simply because she did not have to deal with her mother. She carried her laptop outside along with a freshly made margarita on the rocks and lounged in the patio chair on the back porch. She had changed into shorts and a halter-top to catch maximum rays, thrown on a sun hat so that she could still see the computer when she worked, and looked forward to an afternoon of sun and the accomplishment of small goals. The annoyance towards her mother's persistence regarding her date-status for the wedding and overall love life still resonated, but, for the time being, it was quieter.

Settling into the lounge chair, Chelsea turned on the computer. It hummed as it started, and she turned on her music to set the tone for the afternoon. She would finish some of her applications, and she would finally start moving herself in the direction she was meant to go. Forward. Maybe it meant school, or maybe it just meant a new job. Either way, she hoped it would be the start that would move her away from the situation in which she currently found herself: at home, in a job she did not enjoy, alone, and wanting something else for herself. She knew enough to know that it only took one small change to enable bigger changes down the road, and she could think of no better time to work on making that change possible. And, considering the house was finally quiet, which was itself a rarity, now seemed the perfect time to start.

She sipped her drink, made herself comfortable, and prepared for an afternoon of questions and applications.

Yes, she thought, a change is exactly what I need.

Browsing over applications and school curricula, she spent the afternoon applying to the CUNY Graduate School of Journalism, the University of Baltimore's M.F.A. in Creative Writing & Publishing Arts program, and the UMASS M.F.A in Creative Writing program. Additionally, her resume now found itself electronically shipped to over twenty different companies or general online "position available" postings ranging in everything from magazine and print services to hotels and PR firms. Chelsea figured that the worst she could hear was "no," so there was nothing to lose in trying. To her, this was a start, an effort to get out of her current dead-end situation, and there was nothing wrong with that. In fact, she even found herself feeling a small bubble of hope welling up somewhere inside, and that was something she realized she had not had in a really long time.

Across town, Danielle returned home to find Paul watching the end of the Boston Red Sox game against Texas. He was hunched forward on the couch and sipping a beer, which could only mean they were losing. He had not heard her enter, as he had not turned around to say hello, so she went to surprise him. As Danielle moved closer, she could see that the Red Sox were, in fact, losing 3-6 in the eighth inning. She came up behind him on the couch and wrapped her arms around his neck, kissing his check.

"Losing, huh?" she offered.

"Ugh," he growled. "They're playing like shit."

"I'm sorry."

"Whatever. Can't win them all, I guess."

Paul was frustrated but could feel Danielle smile next to him. He turned to kiss her hello and then asked, "How was lunch with the girls?"

"Needed," she offered, standing up and walking around to join him on the couch. "I missed them. I've been so busy with this case, I feel like I haven't seen them in forever, and it was just nice."

"You seem a little happier," he noted but wasn't sure why.

"Better," she returned. "I'm confused still, but I feel better about things. Plus, I just know I'm lucky to have you."

She kissed him again, starting to realize that although they did not know what to do regarding his move, she was happy to have him. He was not running off every weekend nor nagging her to figure out her life's direction. She may not be problem free, but her problems seemed at least a little more relative for now.

Paul handed her a fresh beer, and she waited for a commercial to explain what was going on with Chelsea and Rachel and Charles. Paul did not seem too surprised by the idea of Charles cheating, but he explained it was simply because he did not know the guy very well. As a result, he could not know what he was capable of or how it would look if he were cheating. He also agreed that it was good that Chelsea was looking to move in a new direction if that was what she wanted. Really, though, he was just relieved to see Danielle in such a good mood. It was a clear change from when she had left that morning, and anything that made her happy made him happy.

"So what are your plans for after the game?" Danielle asked, smiling and rubbing the back of Paul's neck.

Paul just shook his head and pointed at the TV with his beer, annoyed that his team was losing.

"Well," Danielle cooed, moving her hand down a little to play with the collar of his shirt, "I can think of something that will cheer you up."

Paul glanced sideways at her, and she put her beer on the coffee table.

"And we don't even have to leave the house to do it," Danielle finished, leaning in to kiss the exposed part of Paul's neck, her left hand moving up the inside of his thigh. "Let me know when the game's over."

She stood up and left him alone on the couch to finish the last inning of the game. She knew better than to try to distract him during a game, unless he initiated the distraction. She also knew he would come to find her as soon as the game ended. In the meantime, therefore, she headed to the bedroom to change. This morning, sex had been the last thing on her mind. Now, however, after talking to the girls, she realized things on her end were not as broken as they had seemed. In response to her better mood, she wanted to be with Paul, and she wanted to make sure she looked as good for him as she felt inside.

She found the red slip he liked and changed into it, fixing her long, blond hair in the mirror. She smiled. Five years and she still found herself incredibly turned on by Paul. She felt lucky, and although the idea of cheating had surfaced during lunch, she knew she had a good man in Paul. She loved him, and he loved her. That was all she needed, at least for now. They could worry about how to fix the future and what to do about their jobs later, but she was not going to allow something so up-in-the-air ruin the rest of the day she had with him.

She sprayed a dash of perfume onto her clavicle bone, eyed herself over once more in the mirror, smiled, and then left the bedroom. As she walked down the hall she could hear Paul yell at the TV, which meant the Red Sox had not come back from their three-run deficit yet, and she knew he would be annoyed when the game ended in the next few minutes. Instead of bothering him, she sauntered into the kitchen, poured herself a glass of cold white wine, and passed over a few magazines while sitting on one of the island's stools.

Barely ten minutes had passed when she heard the TV click off and footsteps move behind her. He grumbled about something, and then all the noises stopped. She felt a sly grin pass unchecked across her face, and she pretended to not notice the sound of footsteps start up again and move closer to her.

Within moments she felt a hand slide along her right shoulder and another run its fingers through her hair. The smile still lingered on her face as the hand in her hair tilted her head slightly to the left, exposing the right side of her neck. She felt the sensation of warm lips press against the delicate skin at the base of her neck. She let out a sigh that hummed wantonly.

"You're bad," Paul whispered, pretending to be surprised. From her comment on the couch, he had expected sex was following shortly, but the red slip was a welcomed and enticing surprise.

"Me?" she played, the smile still playing along her lips.

"Looking so seductive in red," he continued. "It's distracting." He moved his lips lower to kiss the part of her body where her neck met her shoulder.

"I have no idea what you're talking about," she responded as he swiveled the island stool around so she faced him. Her eyes teased as they reflected his, and he laid his lips heavily against hers, running his hands along her shoulder blades, pulling her off the stool and into him. She moaned acceptingly and followed his lead. Her hands trickled along his waistband near the small of his back until they found their way under his shirt. Her palms moved up his back with a pressure and eagerness equaling his excitement for her and her desire for him.

His hand moved down her body, over the hard nipples of her breasts to her waist, which he squeezed into him. Continuing to move, his hands found their way under the red silk and along the lacy part of her thong, where her lower back met the curve of her butt. He squeezed again and she moaned in response, biting gently on his earlobe and pulling against his strong back. There was no point in moving, no sense in delaying what they both wanted by taking the time to walk down the hallway to the bedroom. Instead, Paul, with his hands still grasping her from behind, switched their two positions, pushed her into the kitchen counter's edge, and ran his hands under the slip in its entirety.

She echoed his moves, starting with his belt and making her way to the zipper of his pants, until she felt him bare in her hands, ready and desiring her. At that moment she gave into him, her body braced against the counter and wrapped around his. She could feel him inside her, the two of them moving together passionately, and she no longer cared about their past fights or the fear of things to come. She was his and he hers, and that was all she wanted. The rest, their future, would sort itself out in time.

Rachel was the only one of the three who returned home still confused. Chelsea had ascertained a solution on how to move her life forward, Danielle had decided she and Paul still wanted to be together and could settle career moves with time, but Rachel had left with nothing.

Well, she thought, that was not entirely true. Both girls had insisted her fear about Charles having an affair was unfounded, which had calmed her, but her mind was still not quieted. She was working to convince herself, though, that all her stress was nothing more than pre-wedding jitters, that her friends truly did believe what they had told her about the potential affair, that it really was not a possibility, and that she was being crazy.

Charles would be home from lunch with his parents shortly, she assumed, so she wanted to straighten up the condo a little more. His parents had seen the condo the previous night before dinner, but she still wanted it to be clean. She hardly expected them to come back up to the condo after lunch just to see it again, but with Charles' parents, she could never be sure. Just in case, therefore, she needed everything to be presentable and acceptable, maybe moreso as a result of the previous night.

The four of them had spent dinner on Saturday night at Parker's Restaurant in downtown Boston, a more upscale, American style restaurant. They discussed wedding plans and honeymoon arrangements, work and other daily happenings, and had had a generally enjoyable time. Rachel liked Charles' parents for the most part, but sometimes she felt they did not fully approve of her marrying into the family. Although Rachel had also come from money, her mother a pediatrician and her father a criminal attorney, Charles' family was "old money." There just seemed to be a barrier she could not overcome with them, like they were expecting her to slip up in some way – say something vulgar or show up discheveled – as though to prove she had not yet "arrived" at their level of social standing. She may have conjured that entire delusion herself, granted, out of some old self-doubt of not being good enough, but that was how it sometimes felt. Last night the dinner air had held what Rachel had perceived as tension, yet she could not put her finger on the exact reason why.

Shaking her head, Rachel forced herself back to the present with a good scrub of the counter. What was she saying? Of course they liked her. They were actually helping to pay for the wedding. They did not have a daughter of their own, only three boys with Charles being the youngest, and they seemed as excited about this wedding as she was, so of course they liked her. They would not be willing to help finance this wedding otherwise. Right?

Stop worrying, Rachel, she reminded herself. You're lucky to have what you have.

Around four-thirty Charles came walking through the door. His baritone, business mode voice echoed through the halls, and Rachel removed a glass from the cupboard suddenly to appear busy. Moments later two more voices carried through the halls, and when Rachel turned around she saw Charles entering the kitchen followed by his parents, Claire and Charles. She breathed a sigh of quick relief internally, thankful she had decided to clean upon returning.

Without missing a beat, Rachel offered both her guests something to drink. Charles simply shook his head "no" and continued speaking with his son. He was slightly shorter than his son, still in shape but with age starting to show around his midsection. His once chestnut hair was speckled with grey, but he wore it well, and it was always styled neatly. He wore a pair of khaki chinos, white Lacoste boat shoes, and a full, button-down, white-collared shirt.

Claire turned to address Rachel, responding with a quick "No, thank you," and an explanation that they were not staying long. She held up her hand as she did so, reinforcing her response, and Rachel dually noted her future mother-in-law's demeanor as well as her attire. Claire wore a double-strand pearl bracelet, which fell along her arm towards the elbow when she raised her hand. She wore a crisp, light green, summer dress, a matching pearl necklace and earring set, and simple, camel colored, peep-toe heels with toe nails painted a summer mango color that matched her fingernails.

Rachel determined the three of them must have lunched somewhere expensive and was suddenly glad to have not changed out of her light blue cardigan. Although she always preferred to look put-together and classic, the importance seemed to double whenever she found herself in the presence of her future in-laws, despite having known them for over three years.

"No, that should be fine," Charles replied to his son. "Just call me at the end of the week and give me an update so I can forward it to the attorney. No rush, but like everything else, stay on top of it."

"Will do," Charles responded. He nodded once to his father in a manner that seemed to suggest he wanted the conversation to finish.

"Attorney? Is everything alright?" Rachel inquired as lightly as possible. No talk of attorneys had even surfaced during Saturday night's dinner conversation, yet, despite being confused, Rachel tried to maintain an air of friendly concern.

Claire stepped in as though on cue. "Nothing to worry about, dear. It's just a few formalities that need addressing is all. I'm certain everything will be just fine." She smiled at Chelsea warmly and then removed a manila envelope from her Louis Vuitton handbag. After handing it off to her son, who laid it on the counter under his hand, Claire stepped lightly over the Chelsea to say a quick goodbye. Chelsea hugged Claire lightly in return, smiled brightly as she hugged Charles, too, and expressed her appreciation for their weekend visit. Charles walked his parents to the door, and Rachel simply waved her final goodbye from the kitchen, eyeing the envelope on the counter once they had moved out of sight.

As far as she could remember, Charles had never mentioned the need for an attorney, let alone an intervention on behalf of his parents, so the envelope teased her brain annoyingly. The only feasible solution would be a change in his parents' wills or some stipulation on the money he had in his trusts, but he had had access to those accounts ever since turning twenty-five. Maybe it was something related to his father's business, but Charles had no immediate hand in the business, so that did not seem plausible either.

Confused, Rachel decided to wait until Charles returned to ask for more details. When Charles re-entered the kitchen, he seemed exhausted and ready to be done with the day. He did not bother coming over to kiss Rachel hello, which also annoyed her. Instead, he grabbed the envelope, unhinged the clasp, and quickly checked the contents inside. Unaware of how to react, Rachel awkwardly stood in place, waiting. She was not sure what she was waiting for exactly, and she deduced from Charles' lack of communication that she was probably the only one feeling awkward at the moment anyways, so she tried to ignore it and continued waiting.

Charles reclasped the envelope and pushed away from the counter, walking over to Rachel.

"Here," he said, handing her the envelope and kissing her quickly on the temple. "These are for you."

"For me?" she returned, her face blank and scrunched in clear confusion. She went to say something further but the words never formed. Why would his parents have brought legal papers for her?

"Yeah, for you," he answered, and then nonchalantly added, "You don't have to worry about it now. Put it away and look at it tomorrow." He guided her hand to the counter to lay down the envelope and then asked about her lunch date with the girls and what she wanted to do for dinner. She tried to focus on the moment, catching him up on lunch and the girls. Then they discussed if they wanted take out or leftovers from the night before, but part of her remained fixated on the envelope. Every time she went for it, Charles found a distraction or a way to momentarily satiate her need to see what was inside by either moving it or negating its seemingly important nature. He said if it had been a big deal he would have shown her the first time he opened it, so she let it slide for the following few hours, enough to make him think she had forgotten about it.

Charles called it a night around nine-thirty. He retreated into their room to read a few documents before bed, and Rachel knew he would be sleeping within an hour. She, too, changed, kissed him goodnight, and then said she was going back to the main room to watch a movie while he worked. Whether easily convinced or generally indifferent Rachel was uncertain, but Charles remained in their room while Rachel went to turn on the television. After about fifteen minutes had passed and Rachel was certain Charles was not coming out of the bedroom, Rachel moved quietly across the kitchen to the mail pile on the counter, where the envelope sat.

She stood over the envelope, thinking. Charles had seemed so indifferent about the whole situation that she wondered if maybe there really wasn't anything over which to worry and that she was making a much bigger deal out of a packet of papers than she needed. However, Rachel's curiosity was not easily assuaged, and she grabbed the envelope from the bottom of the mail pile, all the while keeping one eye on the bedroom door and an ear turned up in case Charles started moving.

As quietly as she could, she unhinged the back of the manila envelope and slid out the stapled pile of papers. Rachel quickly noted the legal format of the papers, glancing over the middle of the first page. Her heart pounded against her chest in a way that made her feel like a twelve-year-old doing something she knew she should not be doing. The only problem with this was that she technically had no reason to fear, as these were her papers to look at, so she had a right to look at them. Still, that failed to calm her nerves. Something just felt off.

Glancing over the papers again, she noticed the bold print on the top of the first page. It was not in forty-point font, but it was clearly discernable, and Rachel's heart stopped. It did not thud in fear. It did not quicken with nervousness or skip a beat in shock. It just stopped. Instantly. She stared at the black words on the page, the black words of death, words that she had never expected to see, not at least in a manner referring to her and her life.

Prenuptial agreement.

Rachel turned cold. She could not breathe. She could not collect her thoughts nor could she think. She felt completely removed from reality, as though she were only floating in her current body instead of actively and consciously attached to it. She heard nothing and saw nothing, and yet the ringing in her head and the blur of the world in front of her refused to go away. Unconsciously she raised her head to look at Charles, as though she could see him through the closed bedroom door. Her feelings rendered her unable to form a cohesive thought, yet she knew she felt angry and betrayed, even downright hurt. She stared at the door, imagining Charles on the other side reading his documents and working out his agenda for Monday.

How could he? she thought. How could he have known about these papers and not discussed them with her? This was her life, their life, their *future*, and he had acted as though it was nothing more than a mail order receipt for new cookware or something, something that could easily be dismissed and forgotten.

How could he?

She did not remember opening the door and calling out his name sternly. The only thing she knew was that she was suddenly standing in their bedroom, looking at him and holding up the papers, watching him stare back at her blankly, like he was waiting for her to stop being childish.

"What do you want me to say, Rachel?" Charles asked. "I don't see what the big deal is. There's no reason for you to be so angry. They're just papers."

"*Pre-nup*," Rachel stressed in return, shaking herself and the papers quickly. "When exactly were you going to tell me about this, Charles? On our wedding day?"

"Rachel, that's months away."

"That's not the point! You waited until the last minute to throw something like a pre-nup at me and never even warned me about something like this. We've been dating for more than three years, engaged for over a year, and I'm just *now* finding out about the fine print of this marriage?"

"Calm down, Rachel," Charles said, finally putting aside his paperwork and straightening up against the headboard. "My God. I just found out about this too, you know, which is why I wasn't going to make a big deal out of it. That's what Mom and Dad were discussing with me at lunch today, which is why I came home so late. I probably would have beaten you home otherwise, but they insisted."

"You're parents came up with this idea?" Rachel asked, making a point of showing she did not believe a word of this.

It's always something, she thought, first I'm worrying about an affair and now a fucking pre-nup. Unbelieveable.

"Yes, my parents," he retorted, "which is why you *hadn't* heard about it until now."

"Then why are these even here?" she asked, matching the sternness and annoyance in his voice. "If this wasn't your idea, then how the hell did it end up on my counter?"

Charles looked at her like he expected her to drop it, and when he realized she was going to be a permanent statue in their doorway until he talked to her, he let out a deep sigh before beginning.

"Because of Peter, that's why," Charles began, a slightly patronizing tone resonating in the aftertaste of his words. "My parents are still so distraught over Peter's divorce two years ago that they insist on some kind of protection for us should we ever get divorced."

"We're not even married and your parents are talking divorce?"

"Well, Peter and Michelle never talked divorce either, and look how their marriage ended. My parents expect us to learn from their mistakes."

Rachel thought about what Charles had just told her. Peter was Charles' oldest brother, and his twelve-year marriage had ended abruptly two years ago, the couple insisting they simply had irresolvable issues. Based on what she had heard, Rachel understood the divorce to be messy, complicated, detrimental to Peter's inheritance, and an overall disaster. The specifics were never something the Waterfords discussed, at least not in the presence of Rachel, so beyond the basic gossip, Rachel knew very little of the ins and outs of the divorce. However, Rachel knew it was messy, so she could partially understand from where the prenuptial agreement might have originated, yet it did not completely quiet her newfound discomfort.

"God damnit," she finally responded, weakly.

Charles simply stared at her, waiting for her to stop being childish.

Finally Rachel was able to calm herself down enough to form a coherent sentence. "I'm still really thrown by this whole thing, but fine. I mean, I don't know why we couldn't have just discussed it right when your parents left and you opened the envelope. I just still don't really like it."

"Well there's not a whole lot I can do about that."

Charles waited, expecting the conversation to be over and Rachel to leave, but when she did not move and stared at him angrily, Charles asked, "What is it?"

"Well, you don't have to be an ass about it."

"What do you want me to say, Rachel?"

Rachel asked herself the same question before giving an answer. "I don't know. Like I said, I just really didn't see this coming. There have been so many other things on my mind lately, this just never even entered, to be honest. I love you and was just looking forward to marrying you. I never in a million years thought I'd have a pre-nup to deal with, and I just don't like you acting like this isn't a big deal."

"I love you, too, and we are still getting married. This is just the business of marriage."

Rachel nodded, although mostly as a questionable nod to herself before turning and walking out of the bedroom.

The business of marriage? she thought. That was certainly not the way she had ever pictured marriage. Was that all marriage was now to them, a simple business transaction? She headed past the kitchen straight to the liquor cabinet. She needed something strong to calm her nerves and settle her suddenly upset stomach.

Chapter 11 - Dinner Guest

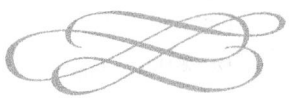

June and July passed quickly and rather uneventfully. Except to gather for a quick Fourth of July drink, the girls really did not see one another. Summer trips, family gatherings, and general work demands overtook everyone's schedule. Even their drink-date had been cut short so Rachel and Charles could leave to be at his family's home in the Hamptons by morning. Life was a whirlwind.

Chelsea had made minimal progress in regards to any of her applications, and she dealt with work as best she could. David was still regularly high, Stacy always had stories about baby Marcus' summer playground adventures, and Candice, the owner of Bouquets R Us, made regular phone calls for account updates. Overall, it was just a little numbing.

Chelsea also hadn't heard much from Danielle other than nothing had changed in the Paul-getting-transferred department. Things were still very up-in-the-air, and Danielle had no desire to bother with hypothetical scenarios. Therefore, there was never much to discuss.

Both of them, though, had been made aware of Rachel's prenuptial papers. "Fiasco" was the word Rachel had used. When they had tried to learn more or even just discuss how Rachel was handling it, Rachel had become extremely defensive and as tight-lipped as a fortress. She not only refused to have any of Danielle or Chelsea's thoughts on the matter, but she also refused to entertain any discussions that weren't a positive reflection of her wedding.

As a result, the summer had passed quietly and without much new news between any of the girls.

Now it was August and business for Chelsea was crazy. She determined that summer was the time when stupid people came out to ask to start businesses and get loans. In the last month alone she had turned down fifty-four different business loan applications because of poor credit or because customers simply did not know how to fill out a step-by-step application form. She had also denied twenty-eight applications for private school loans. At the same time, thirty-eight loans had been approved and she was now the liaison for some of them because her oh-so-reliable co-worker, David, could not handle them on his own. That, however, had not negated all of the other companies and customers she still had in her normal circulation. Work was just becoming crazy.

In fact, life in general was becoming crazy. Dinner the other weekend with her cousin, Vince, his fiancé, and the family had turned into a nightmare. Chelsea's mom had recently seen all the information from different colleges come through the mail and proceeded to pull out one of Chelsea's applications during dinner. She showed her sister, Vince's mother, and then proceeded to whine about how she did not understand why Chelsea never talked to her anymore.

"Why do I have to find out about what's going on in my daughter's life by way of mail?" she asked her sister, literally shaking the information packet inches away from her sister's face. They went on to discuss how children are so much more distant now than they used to be, how they have phases and maybe this was just one of the phases Chelsea would outgrow, and how the concept of family just was not the same as it used to be.

That was when Chelsea heard her mother say, "Well at least you have Vince's wedding to look forward to."

Hook, line, and dagger straight through Chelsea's heart. She knew her mother would have preferred that she marry rather than think about going back to school and possibly moving away. However,

Tina clearly never stopped to consider that her very insistent attitude might be the exact reason for the recent "distance" she felt between her daughter and her.

Chelsea saw her father start to intervene, but Vince knowingly and discretely shook his head to signify that it was wasted effort, and it was. Once Tina was on a topic, she was on a topic, and one just had to wait it out until it was over, almost like a storm. Chelsea found it amazing that even her twenty-seven-year-old cousin saw the futility of trying to stop her. Chelsea silently thanked her father for even considering trying. It had been an honest gesture. Futile, but honest. It reiterated to Chelsea one more reason why she needed to find something else to do with her life. If she did not, this ongoing spiral would only continue.

Right now, though, Chelsea found herself buried elbow deep in the middle of a different spiral, one involving ringing phone lines and stacks of client paperwork. It seemed as though her work life and her home life were proving to be equally chaotic.

Just as Chelsea finished the last of her account updates, Stacy appeared in her cubicle entrance. She was wearing grey, summer, suit pants and a blouse. There was a tiny stain on her left shoulder, which Chelsea took to be the remnants of morning mommy-hood, but in actuality it was barely noticeable. Chelsea figured if she had not already been privy to the knowledge of Stacy being a mom, she probably would not have even noticed the stain in the first place. Overall, though, Stacy still seemed put together and rather upbeat for a Friday afternoon. She had been so busy earlier in the day that she had missed their usual Friday lunch, which itself was highly abnormal for Stacy. As a result, this was the first time Stacy had really had a moment to chat with Chelsea all day.

"So, I have a question," Stacy began. "What are you doing tonight?"

"Tonight when? Like for dinner or later?"

"Dinner."

"I have to meet my parents at Maggianos at seven, but that's about it. Why?"

"Maggianos? They want to go all the way into the city for dinner?" Stacy asked. Stacy knew Chelsea enough to know her parents rarely ventured into the city, so a city dinner-date seemed out of place.

"I know right? That's what I thought too, but Mom insisted. She said she had this insatiable craving for Maggianos and that, since a friend who lives in the city would be joining us for dinner, she felt that restaurant would be most appropriate."

"Oh, well, okay then," Stacy finished, smiling.

"Why?" Chelsea asked. "What's going on?"

"Well, our nanny, Vicki, called in sick this morning, so my mom took the kids as a last minute favor so that I wouldn't have to miss work. Apparently, Marcus's latest cooings are the must-see of her bridge club friends, and she said that she would be taking him with her tonight to bridge so that I could have a night off. As it so happens, date night for me isn't an option since Mark is working until nine tonight – they had a shipment come through this morning that needs to go out tomorrow – so I'm on my own. I feel like going out and doing something, so I thought I'd see what you were up to."

"Oh, thanks, hun, that's so awesome of you, but I really can't miss dinner," Chelsea responded, somewhat defeated. She couldn't miss dinner, but the prospect of going out with someone other than family sounded much more uplifting.

"Trust me," she continued, "I would much rather hang out with you than my parents tonight, but," Chelsea finished, "family obligations."

"No, it's cool. I understand. Because work today was so incredibly busy and I couldn't make lunch with you and Danny, I thought I'd try to make it up."

Chelsea thought for a moment before continuing, "You know what? Honestly, Stacy, if you're not doing anything, why don't you come with us tonight? You and I can sit at Maggiano's and have a drink, and then we can all have dinner together. My parents really won't care. I mean, it's not like you haven't met them before."

"They did come to my baby shower," Stacy added.

"Exactly. I mean, I can't tell you which of my mom's friends is going to be there tonight because she won't tell me, but I can't imagine it would be a big deal."

Stacy treaded uneasily, "Well, Chelsea, I don't want to impose. If you're busy, that's okay. I mean, I'm asking last minute –"

"Oh stop," Chelsea responded, cutting off Stacy before she could finish. "Please. It'll be fun! We'll sit and have a glass of wine before they arrive. It's just dinner. Plus, maybe Mom'll be nicer if you're there," Chelsea added laughing.

Stacy chuckled and smiled knowingly in response, as Chelsea had told Stacy about the dinner last week with Vince and her family. Stacy had no desire to be in the middle of a family argument, but wine, dinner, and the city sounded much more promising than sitting around at home, so she agreed. She returned to her desk, and when the end of the work day arrived, she closed up for the day, gathered her things, and the two girls headed off to the city.

The crowd at Maggiano's was a standard, Friday night crowd. Business men in suits who had met women in summer skirts sat at the bar waiting for tables next to young couples just starting out their nights. Families also filled the restaurant, finishing up the last of their lasagnas and spaghetti with meatballs, getting ready to turn over the tables to the later crowds. The air hummed with lively gossip, laughter, and the heavy smell of garlic and marinara sauce.

Chelsea and Stacy arrived around six-thirty, walked in dressed in their work clothes, and felt they fit right in with the rest of the crowd waiting for tables and lounging around the bar. Immediately they headed to the front room, found themselves a small bar table, and ordered two glasses of white wine. Conversation was easy and relaxed. They stayed on fairly neutral topics or discussed work, and the half hour between their arrival and when Chelsea's family was due to arrive passed quickly.

Tina was the first of the party to appear. She entered in khaki capris, flat sandals, and a black tank that hugged her breasts and mid-fifties midsection. Her black hair was curly, but the summer heat had caused the ends to frizz slightly. She seemed frazzled but smiled when she found the girls' table. Chelsea immediately felt there was something she was hiding.

"Hi girls," Tina said, standing at the table. "It's good to see you, Stacy. It's been a while. How long now? Since before the baby I imagine."

"Probably," Stacy returned politely. "Thanks for letting me come."

"Oh, sure, of course. But I hope you don't mind company," Tina said.

"No, not at all."

"Speaking of company," Chelsea began, "Who's joining us tonight?"

"Oh just an old friend, dear, I'm certain you'll remember," her mom responded quickly before clearly working to change the subject. "Have you checked in, yet? We wouldn't want to miss our table."

"Yes, we did already," Chelsea stated. "I wanted to fill Stacy in about your friend except I don't know who it is. Oh, and where is Dad?"

"Your father will be a little late. He had a late night at the office."

Chelsea simply nodded. "Late nights" meant her dad just did not want to come home right away. Chelsea's dad was a dentist and had two other dentists in his practice, so there was no need for him to work late except in emergencies, and those were much less frequent than the "late night appointments" he claimed. But, when Chelsea really thought about it, she could not totally blame her dad. Mom was tough to handle at times, so she could understand why he needed a break every now and again. Apparently, tonight was one of those nights. However, it added to the uncertainty Chelsea already felt in the air since her mother had arrived, but Chelsea decided not to push the subject.

They were directed to their table about fifteen minutes later, and the three of them took a seat and ordered another round of white wine. Stacy and Tina covered pleasantries quickly, asking about work and family. Tina asked how the baby was doing and if the car seat they had bought for Marcus would work when he got bigger. Stacy happily flooded Tina with information about the baby and about being a mother. The car seat, she explained, would be perfect. It was a little tight in the car they currently had, but Stacy mentioned that she and Mark were hoping to buy a new car once they could save up some more money. As a lighthearted joke to end the story, Stacy made note that having a baby really made it difficult to save. Tina saw this as an opening.

"Yes, that is very true," Tina began, smiling, looking at Chelsea. "They certainly take up your money, but that's part of the joy of being a mom! You get to watch them grow and give them the things they need to be happy and successful in doing so. Saving is important, and cars will always be there, but having children is much more worthwhile in the long run."

Stacy smiled and nodded in agreement, commenting that her own mother felt the same way.

"Oh, your mother must be so happy to have a grandchild! You know, that is what you hope for as a parent, to see your children grown, settled, happy, and starting families of their own. Why, just think, you're only twenty-five and have a child! You'll be able to be a grandmother while you're young and able to really enjoy your grandkids. At least you got started early. It can just be such a hard strain on everyone when you wait too long to start a family. You need the energy of youth to keep up with kids these days."

Tina bubbled on with Stacy, but Chelsea would have preferred if her mother had stopped talking. Chelsea knew at what her mom was hinting and could not believe she was choosing to embarrass her this way in front of her co-worker and friend.

Stacy entertained Tina s comments but was intuitive enough to notice the awkwardness thickening in the air. Trying to cut Tina off, Stacy changed the subject to ask what was happening recently with Tina, but that only led to Tina changing the subject to Vince s wedding. Chelsea felt trapped in déjà vu and breathed a heavy sigh of relief when she saw her father enter the dining room in jeans and a striped polo shirt.

Reintroducing himself to Stacy, Tony took a seat alongside Tina, who asked how work went as more of a formality than out of actual interest. Tony then noticed the extra seat at the table, and asked if there were plans for a fifth guest.

"You didn't know Mom invited one of her friends?" Chelsea asked.

"More of a former family friend, dear. Everyone knows him," her mom responded.

"Him?" Chelsea asked, clearly thrown. Chelsea wracked her brain to arrive at a male friend of her mother's. However, instead of responding, her mom simply waved her hand dismissively and moved the conversation forward.

It turned seven-thirty before the question of the missing guest arose for a second time. Again, Tina dismissed the comment, saying that there must just be a hold-up at work or something and switched subjects, but Chelsea caught sight of her mother glimpsing at her watch. Cleary, her mother's friend was later than she had expected, and he was going to miss dinner if he did not arrive soon, as the four of them were already finishing their salads.

Tony turned to Chelsea to ask how school applications were going, and Chelsea again watched her mother roll her eyes at the idea of more schooling. Stacy echoed Tony's interest, and Chelsea explained that she had two more applications left and that it would not be until September or so until she heard something for the January start dates. She had finally narrowed it down to a basic interest in Journalism or Publishing, and she was really hoping for CUNY or the University of Baltimore. If her mom was not on board, at least her dad was supportive. Chelsea assumed that this split in interest would be part of their weekly fighting ritual on Saturday morning.

Tina continued eating her salad quietly until something caught her eye, causing her to sit up about two inches straighter in her chair.

Chelsea, who had been in the middle of taking a sip of her wine, followed her mother's eyes to the entrance of the dinning room and suddenly felt her body go rigid and then numb. Walking through the entryway into the main dining hall was Terry Hussfield, Chelsea's ex-boyfriend of over a year now. The man who had broken her heart after two years of dating was walking – no, strutting – towards some table dressed in jeans and a cocky, navy-blue blazer. He wore a muted, hunter green, button-up shirt underneath the blazer, freshly pressed with the top button undone. His sandy-blond, almost brown hair was swept to the side of his face, just like Chelsea remembered. The sight made her nauseous.

Chelsea could not believe her luck and racked her brain to try to remember if she had recently broken a mirror or crossed paths with a black cat. The odds of running into her ex-boyfriend in the city were slim, but to see him at the same restaurant as she found herself now, with her family nonetheless, was a single girl's definition of reason for suicide.

She watched him walk his stupid, arrogant strut down the middle of the room, and she felt her stomach flip twice. Anger bubbled deep in her chest in a way that felt almost out-of-body. Chelsea was blatantly unaware of the paleness that had overcome her face and was not prepared for how deeply upset the sight of the man who broke her heart could still make her. This was the man who, after two years of dating, said it was over because they were simply moving in different directions, and he needed space to figure out his own life. What there had been to figure out remained a mystery to Chelsea, as nothing about his financial career, condo near the shore, being almost thirty, nor solid 401k seemed like it needed "figuring out," but that was where he had left her: broken hearted, single, and condemned to move back in with her family due to her own lack of financial stability. And, to make matters worse, they had met by way of Charles, because Terry was an old golfing buddy of Brandon's, the middle of the three boys in Charles' family. This had made the break-up even more awkward, because Chelsea knew she was destined to run into Terry down the road at some point. She had just always hoped that "some point" would not turn out to be a moment like the one in which she currently found herself.

The fork in Chelsea's left hand struggled for air as the knuckles in the hand grasping it turned white. Words ran dry as Chelsea's mouth sat agape, trying to form some utterance of disbelief. Terry was not just heading towards any table, he was headed towards her table.

Then her mom stood up. Chelsea's eyes flashed from Terry, who was now a mere ten feet from the table, to her mother. Her own mother *stood* as this lowlife neared them? How dare she?

"Terry!" Tina beamed. "How wonderful to see you. I was starting to wonder if you were even coming at all."

What? Chelsea felt her eyes bulge in furry.

"What the hell is going on?" Chelsea asked. Niceties were simply out of the question. Chelsea's mere shock had bypassed that part of social interactions completely, and she was working in stream-of-consciousness mode. Stacy remained seated, clearly confused, and Tony sat glued to his chair, frowning, staring down at his plate with a crimson-red face.

"Well, hunny, you remember Terry," her mom started and then turned to Stacy. "This is Terry, Chelsea's –"

"*Ex-boyfriend,*" Chelsea scathed. "Would you mind telling me what the hell is going on, Mom?"

"Your mom invited me to dinner," Terry began, seeming to smile either at himself or the situation, Chelsea was not sure which at the moment. Both, however, made Chelsea irate and dizzy.

"Clearly," Chelsea seethed.

"Well, Rachel's wedding is coming up, and I knew that you and Terry had met via the two of them, so I felt that it was only right for you two to make up before the wedding, since you'll be seeing each other there. I thought it would be best to do it sooner rather than later, especially because you made it clear, Chelsea, that you weren't bringing anyone else to the wedding. I know you guys had your differences, but there's no reason you can't move past them. Terry's been doing very well for himself."

Chelsea was so upset that she bypassed the point of yelling and went straight to a calm, harsh, whisper. "*What?*"

"Look, it's about time the two of you started speaking again. I've already spoken with Terry, haven't I, dear?" Tina asked, turning to Terry, acting as though this was in everyone's best interest. "And he agrees that the reasons you two broke up a year ago were silly and petty and that it might be worth getting back on speaking terms and seeing where it might lead."

"Well, it's leading to me going home. That's where it's leading," Chelsea stated, starting to stand. Her mom anxiously motioned to Terry to do something.

"Chelsea," Terry started, "I just want to talk to you."

"Well I don't want to talk to you," Chelsea returned, stopping to look him dead in the eyes.

"Look, your mom's right. We're going to be seeing each other at Rachel's wedding in a month anyway. I'm not dating anyone and, from what I hear, neither are you. Plus," he began, a quick chuckle passing under his breath, "I honestly can't remember now why we broke up at this point. It might at least be worth talking about now or maybe after dinner over drinks?"

Chelsea noticed that people at the tables near her were starting to notice the onset of their quarrel, so she kept her tone as even-tempered as possible, doing her best to throw daggers at Terry visually.

"We broke up because you told me I wasn't what you wanted, remember? I think your exact words were, 'I just don't see you fitting into the direction my life is heading,' or, oh, silly me, did you forget already? I may have to see you in a couple of weeks for the sake of Rachel and the wedding, but don't you dare, even for a second, think that I'm interested in rekindling anything that we had. You put me through Hell. I don't ever plan on going through that again, and, believe me, there's nothing you can say at this point that will change my mind."

Chelsea turned to her mother, "And Mom, let me tell you something. You might be my mother, and I might love you, but don't you dare, again, ever interfere where my love life is concerned. Is that clear? How dare you? This is none of your business. I can't believe you would stoop so low."

"Young lady–" her mom began.

"Don't," Chelsea said firmly, "'Young lady' me." Chelsea motioned to Stacy, signaling they were leaving, and Chelsea gathered her purse while she finished scolding her mother.

"I will not be home when you return tonight. Do not call me. Do not try to get ahold of me. I will come back when I have cooled off and can speak to you with some civility, but right now, I'm leaving."

Stacy had already started walking out awkwardly, leaving without offering to pay for the dinner she had ordered but never eaten. Chelsea met her at the front door after a simple "goodbye" to her father and not even so much as a word to her mother or Terry. Chelsea felt bad leaving her father in that situation. It was clear he had had no idea of the planned set-up, and she was sure the remainder of his night and weekend would be utterly painful, but there was nothing she could do at this point. To say she was even hanging by a thread was a stretch. The river of anger and hate ran so deep inside her she was not sure if she still possessed any human ideals or if she had not been overtaken completely by some other, devil-like emotional state entirely.

Chelsea apologized profusely to Stacy for the horror that the night had become. She was beyond embarrassed by what had transpired and that her friend and co-worker had witnessed such an atrocity. Stacy and Chelsea were work friends, yes, but not close enough for Chelsea to feel okay with Stacy having experienced tonight's dinner. Chelsea truly felt that she would never be able to apologize enough.

Stacy explained that she was simply sorry for what Chelsea had been through and offered up her house to Chelsea for the weekend. Although sincerely appreciative, Chelsea declined, feeling that a house with a baby was not a house she needed to be in at the moment. Chelsea needed space, and she determined the best way to obtain that space was to check herself into a hotel. Her mother would probably call Rachel, Danielle, and all of their relatives, so she wanted a different escape plan. A hotel seemed the most feasible, even though not the most financially sound. Regardless of the money, however, Chelsea just needed an immediate release. She could figure out the rest sometime in the morning.

Chapter 12 - Your Life is Worse Than Mine

"**W**hat the hell happened last night?" Danielle pried, speaking to Chelsea from her cell-phone. Rachel had picked Danielle up first thing that morning and both of them were filled with questions and worry, dying to know what exactly had transpired at the restaurant. It had been months since any newsworthy event had transpired in any of their lives, and, as this was absolutely a newsworthy moment, Rachel and Danielle wanted to visit Chelsea and hear what had happened.

Chelsea sighed, "Don't even get me started."

Chelsea had checked herself into the local Holiday-Inn and had sped over to the gym bright and early that morning to work off the anger she still had lingering inside her from the previous night's events. The mile and a half track-run had done her a lot of good. She could feel the endorphins kicking in, and she did not feel like bypassing her bettering mood by venting about the events that had transpired just yet.

"Well, you're going to have to dish. Rachel and I received frantic phone calls from your mother last night asking if we knew where you were. When we tried calling you, your phone was off. Your mother explained that you had gotten into a fight at the restaurant and stormed off, but she would not say why. Given how often you two seem to fight, we weren't too worried that something had happened to you, per se, because we figured you had just turned off your phone to escape hearing it ring five million times. However, you need to tell us where you are, because we are on our way there right now."

"No, really, guys, it's fine, I don't think I want to –" Chelsea started and then found herself cut off by Rachel's voice in the background telling Danielle to tell Chelsea that she wouldn't put up with any excuses, that they were coming over ASAP, and that she had already bought Chelsea an iced mocha. Chelsea knew her friends well enough to know they would not turn around, and the idea of an iced mocha suddenly sounded more than sublime, so Chelsea relented and gave them directions to the Holiday-Inn.

Chelsea tidied up her hotel room enough for Rachel and Danielle to sit comfortably on the bed or desk chair. She threw her clothes from last night and her workout clothes back into her suitcase and pulled back her hair before the girls arrived. The hotel room was not chilly, but her wet hair made her cold, so Chelsea was glad she had thought to bring a zipped-hoodie with her to throw on over her khaki shorts and tank top.

When Rachel and Danielle arrived, they were in lounge attire as well. Rachel wore jeans and a Juicy Couture, short sleeve, black zip-hoodie with a lace camisole underneath and black summer sandals, and Danielle had on black capris, matching tennis shoes, and a simple pink t-shirt. Chelsea felt relieved that they had not shown up all dressed up, expecting to go out around town. She just did not have the energy at this point, but she was thrilled to see that her friends had brought her favorite morning coffee. A little sugar and caffeine somehow always made the day better.

Eventually Chelsea caught Rachel and Danielle up on the events of the previous night. Danielle shook her head and Rachel gawked in horror. Neither could believe the nerve required for Chelsea's mom to bring Terry to a family dinner, and they could only imagine how irate her father must have been for the entire set-up. They all speculated how the Farrera Saturday morning fight would play out, and they were all equally glad to not have to experience it.

"So what are you going to do now?" Rachel asked.

"What do you mean, what is she going to do now? She's going to move on with her life," Danielle interjected, and then turned to

Chelsea, "You can totally come stay with me for a little while if you want, while you look for a place. We have an extra room."

Chelsea shook her head. "That's nice of you, Danielle, really, but it's not necessary. I'm going to stay here for another week or so and then head home until I figure stuff out."

"And deal with your mother?" Danielle wondered.

"I have to face her eventually," Chelsea countered, and she knew it to be the truth. She could not run away from the inevitable. She'd have to deal with her mother eventually, and now seemed like as good a time as any. Granted "now" meant in a week or so, but there was no use in putting it off more than that. By then she hoped she would have a better idea of what her future direction would be – job interviews or grad school – and that would make the encounter with her mother easier.

"Point," Danielle finished.

Rachel could not help but ask, "What do you even say?" It was a rhetorical question, so the girls just sat in silence for a moment.

Then Rachel, in an attempt to help, offered, "There will be lots of single guys at the wedding. Some guys are coming without dates. You might like them."

Although the offer was gracious and delivered with the best of intentions, Chelsea could not help but laugh at Rachel's comment.

"Thanks, Rachel, but right now I think I'm fine. I don't need any more drama."

"Well, at least you'll be *in* the wedding," Danielle offered, "which means you'll be able to stay super busy."

"Right," Chelsea agreed, but she still could not help feeling like, despite the truth in Danielle's comment, there was suddenly an air of pity in the room. She tried to shake it off as paranoia, but she found herself wondering if her two friends didn't feel the slightest sense of pity for her situation. The idea left a foul aftertaste in her brain, and she needed to move on to avoid lingering in its stench for too long.

Luckily, Rachel changed topics for her, but not in a way that seemed like it was an excited change. In fact, Rachel's tone hinted of uncertainty and loss.

"Well, if it's okay to switch subjects, I have a question for you guys."

"What's going on?" Danielle asked. The girls were fully aware of the prenuptial agreement paperwork Rachel had received a few months back and the mini rollercoaster of emotions that it had caused her. At first, her anger and sense of betrayal were obvious. She practically refused to speak about it for an entire two weeks and had been celibate for equally as long, if not longer, purely out of fury. However, it had not been too hard for Rachel to withhold sex seeing as how Charles had also spent those two weekends golfing in New Hampshire and Virginia respectively. Rachel had stated that he had become more distant and angry with her for not signing the papers immediately. However, that had only caused her anger and hurt to increase, which put off her signing the papers even further. Although the girls had tried talking to her about it, Rachel had made it clear that this part of her life was not up for discussion. Her anger and hurt had just been so great that she had shut herself out from her friends entirely. She wouldn't have even known how to start being a good friend when she felt her life was so off balance and burried in rubble. Long ago she had promised not to allow others to get the best of her, but she had determined that to mean she should face major issues alone so, literally, *no one* could see her pain. She hated showing emotion and chaotic uncertainty to people, and with those she admired and loved, it left her feeling needy. In her mind, adults should be needy.

Therefore, neither Danielle nor Chelsea had had the chance to help Rachel through it. Even Chelsea, who was Rachel's maid-of-honor, had been denied airspace in the conversation, leaving Rachel to deal with her situation on her own.

The last Chelsea and Danielle had heard, though, Rachel had finally, mid-July, signed the papers, giving into the arrangements set forth by Charles' parents. When Rachel finally informed Chelsea and Danielle, she admitted signing the papers simply because she did not have the headspace to try to compromise with his parents this close to the wedding. She had told them that if signing the prenuptial agreement was what his parents needed to feel better about the marriage, then she would oblige. They were, after all, helping her pay for the wedding, so clearly they liked her. She felt that maybe this was more of a formality, and reading too much into the specifics of the agreement was going against the spirit of the marriage. Therefore, she just decided to sign and move forward with everything.

According to the agreement, Rachel had to stay married and loyal to Charles for five years before she would see a penny from a divorce, excluding any wedding or regular gifts she received from him or his family. Then, after the five years, all assets and money would be split sixty-forty, sixty-percent to him, forty-percent to her, and, in addition, Charles was entitled to any property purchased before or after their wedding. It did not seem like the fairest solution, given they were already living together and had been successfully dating for three years, but those were the terms. In the end, and in all honesty, Rachel was doing her best at trying not to care. She did not see a divorce in her future, so what difference did it make that she signed the pre-nup? She had grown up in a house with parents who had a loving and successful marriage, so she had no reason to believe she couldn't have the same thing herself. She had told Chelsea and Danielle that everything, therefore, was fine, but sometimes a "fine" to Rachel was simply her way of telling her friends she didn't want them dealing with an issue.

Consequently, Danielle and Chelsea wondered if Rachel really felt as "fine" with the agreement as she continuously claimed. They wondered if she had not just signed the papers to keep her world as rosy-colored as possible. Rachel had wanted to be married since she was old enough to say the word "wedding," and she had solidified every detail by the time they had all graduated college. Although she had not outwardly admitted it, both girls knew her well enough to know she had been discourage to have not been married right after college. Now that she was so close to the wedding she had always envisioned, now that she had a man who seemed to give her and provide her with everything she had ever wanted and hoped for, now that she was almost a wife, neither Chelsea nor Danielle could see Rachel passing it up for anything, even for a pre-nup that was not necessarily looking out for her best interests. They had tried to explain that to her, but she had wanted no part of it. Chelsea and Danielle could do nothing now but be supportive, even though they secretly wondered if Rachel had done the right thing.

Given Rachel's current questioning tone of voice, however, the girls wondered if her sudden need to switch topics wasn't about said papers.

Rachel continued with her question, clearly annoyed and disappointed, "What do you do when your future mother-in-law is trying to reorder and redo your flower arrangement?"

Chelsea chuckled in relief, suddenly thankful that the issue at hand was nothing pressing, and Rachel quickly glared back at her.

"What's so funny?" Rachel insisted. Evidently, she was taken aback by Chelsea's response.

"No, nothing. I'm just relieved it's not something major," Chelsea explained, reaching for her iced mocha.

"Flowers are major!" Rachel retorted.

"Oh. Right. Major," Chelsea said as she drank her iced mocha.

"She is taking over," Rachel explained. "How do I get her to stop?"

"Well, what is she doing exactly?"

"It's what she's not allowing me to do!" Rachel stated. "Apparently I can't determine what will look good at my own wedding. In fact, not only am I not allowed to order the flowers anymore, but she cancelled my orders and seems to be redoing my entire theme with another company!"

"What do you mean *redoing?*" Chelsea asked. She had been with Rachel months ago when she had settled her flower order for the bouquets, reception centerpieces, and hall decorations. Rachel had had the champagne and white color scheme with black ribbon designed from the start, which meant Chelsea could start to understand how infuriated Rachel had to be if she had really lost control of that area of her wedding.

Rachel's face tinted red as she recounted the story to her friends. "Just what I said," she explained. "Redoing. She claims I consented to turning over the arrangement decisions to her –"

"– which you would never do," Chelsea interjected. "We finalized those decisions months ago!"

"That is exactly what I argued," Rachel continued, "but she said I signed off on it. When I demanded an explanation, she simply stated that the agreement was in writing on an additional sheet of paper in the manila envelope that held the prenuptial agreement. Apparently I had signed it along with the other papers, but how was I supposed to know? It was in the same folder as the prenuptial papers, so why would I have thought that envelope contained papers regarding a totally different topic? That's such bullshit! I told her that that was completely unfair and utterly shitty of her to do – in nicer words, of course – and basically that she tricked me, and I was not okay with it."

"And?" Danielle asked simply.

"And," Rachel said, obviously at a loss, "There's nothing I can do about it, legally or otherwise. Not that I would want to do anything legally. That would only upset them, clearly, and that would be dumb considering I'm marrying into that family. But still, I'm so mad!"

"I would be too," Chelsea agreed.

Danielle waited a moment before asking the question she had rolling around in her brain. She wanted Rachel to calm down before she asked, because, although it was the obvious question to ask, she knew it would upset Rachel. And it did.

115

"What do you mean, did I read the papers?" Rachel angrily asked in return. "You know all the ins and outs of the pre-nup! Of course I read the papers."

"Then how did you miss the one about handing over flower arrangements to your future mother-in-law?" Danielle countered.

"Well, I didn't read *all* of them," Rachel threw back. "There was a lot of legal jargon, so I just browsed the highlighted parts regarding a divorce and to what I would be entitled. There were a lot of papers and a lot of different lines to sign and initial. How was I to know a pre-nup packet contained more than just information regarding the pre-nup?"

"By reading them," Danielle finished. She could not believe Rachel had not looked at the papers more closely. Every part of her being screamed at her friend for her stupidity. She could have avoided this entire mess if she had only listened for half a second to Danielle's advice when she had tried to talk to her back in July. After Rachel had mentioned the prenuptial agreement to Danielle, Danielle had offered to buy Rachel coffee and go over the entire agreement with her but to no avail. Rachel had declined both times Danielle had asked, so Danielle dropped it. Although the situation made Danielle feel slightly sorry for Rachel, she now felt more annoyed than anything, knowing she could have caught this piece of ceremonial fine-print. Danielle was having a hard time finding pity for her friend. It was hard for her to pity someone over something that could have been avoided. Maybe that was the lawyer in her speaking, or maybe it was mere rationale, but either way, Danielle condemned her friend's stupidity more than she felt sympathy for her. She probably would have made a bad bridesmaid, she determined. Better she was simply a guest at this point.

Rachel fumed, "You know, I didn't come here to be criticized, Danielle. I don't appreciate you making light of my problem like it's not a big deal."

"Sorry," Danielle said because it was what one was supposed to say as a friend, but she did not stop there. "I just don't know how you can be so upset over something you could have avoided."

"Like your situation with Paul could be avoided?" Rachel threw back, her words stemming from anger.

"Excuse me?" Danielle returned.

"You heard me," Rachel stated.

"How dare you?" Danielle countered. "You have no idea what we're going through."

"Because you won't talk about it," Rachel responded, crossing her arms at her friend.

"Because you haven't been around," Danielle retorted. "You're so busy with this damn wedding, acting like it's the end-all-be-all of your life that you forgot that your friends have lives and problems, too. Like Chelsea, for example, or did you forget that's the entire reason we came? We didn't come here to talk about you, Rachel. We came here for Chelsea, so how dare you bring up your own issues or even act like you know about mine when you have no idea."

"Stop it," Chelsea interjected, trying to stop the impending argument. "Both of you, just stop. This is crazy."

"What?" Danielle said, now turning towards Chelsea. "You know just as well as I do that Rachel has been nothing but self-absorbed and wedding drunk for the past two months, and that she blocks out every problem she has with Charles because she's too scared to think that her relationship might actually need help."

"Charles and I are fine!"

Danielle chuckled, disbelieving, "Right. Fine. You practically haven't seen your fiancé in two months because he keeps galavanting around with his golf buddies. You don't think that's a little weird? You don't think that it's a little odd that he wants to be away from you this often and this close to the wedding? Weren't you the one that thought he might be having an affair instead of golfing, or did you overlook that as well, just like you're going to overlook your mother-in-law interfering with your wedding because you're too

117

dumb to read the fine print and too scared to turn to her friends for any help or face the problems you might actually have in your own life?"

"Well at least my husband isn't considering moving out of state to get away from me," Rachel threw back, stabbing the verbal dagger as far into Danielle as she could. She refused to be the one with the most fucked up life, and she retaliated the only way she knew how – by redirecting the problem and focusing it on someone else.

"How does it feel, knowing he'd rather take a job promotion than be with you?"

"How dare you?" Danielle's voice turned harsh and jagged. "You've never had to work for anything in your life – mommy and daddy paying for everything, and you're now marrying into even more money. You have no debt, student loans, nor car loans to repay and manage. Your biggest concern is what color car Charles is going to buy you as a wedding present or whether you want large or extra large diamond earrings on your wedding day. You have no idea what I'm going through or what it's like to try to keep a relationship alive while life is working to tear the two of you apart without question or remorse."

"Oh poor you," Rachel mocked. "Poor little Danielle, pretending the big, bad world is out to get her. You act like you have no say in what happens, but really you can't see that you're getting in your own way. You want your own career and independence and yet you're supposedly trying to create this great life with Paul, one that's supposed to work as a cohesive unit. You can't have it all, Danielle. You can't have a career and independence, success and individuality *and* a husband or long-term boyfriend with security and companionship and unified goals. You can't be a team when you're only focused on you. Something somewhere has to give."

"Don't pull that 1950s bullshit with me!" Danielle argued. "I don't want to be a housewife like you're hoping to be. I can still have a career and a husband. Women do it all the time, or have you not looked around at the world lately? Lots of people do it. Your parents do it, for crying out loud, or did you forget that was well? Plus, Paul supports me and what I do. He wants me to succeed just as much as I want him to."

"Oh, sure," Rachel pretended. "Until he realizes you're making more money than he makes, which will make him feel obselete and useless. And don't even try to pull that parent bullshit with me. My mom works because it gives her something to do with her time since Dad works all the time, but her job is not her life. Yours, on the other hand, seems to be your entire reason for being, and that is going to drive him away. You're going to drive him away, just like Chelsea drove away Terry."

Chelsea turned, shocked at her best friend's comment, and instantly scolded Rachel, not caring if she was the maid-of-honor in her wedding or not. "*Excuse me?*"

"What?" Rachel said, her tone unchanged even though she was still facing Danielle.

"What the fuck is that supposed to mean?" Chelsea demanded.

"What, you didn't know?" Rachel insisted. "That wasn't part of the restaurant argument last night between you and Terry?"

"No," Chelsea continued, "And what am I supposed to know, exactly?"

"That that's why Terry left you," Rachel explained very matter-of-factly. "Because you kept talking about wanting to go to grad school and travel and be a writer."

"*So?*"

"So, that's not what Terry wanted. You didn't know that?"

Rachel could not believe Chelsea did not know any of this. She had heard it all from Charles right after Chelsea and Terry's break-up a year ago, so she was certain Terry had laid it all out for Chelsea during the actual break-up.

"Clearly, she didn't know that," Danielle mocked.

"Clearly," Chelsea chimed, sitting back in her chair, crossing her arms, and pressing her lips in fury before contining sarcastically, "Please, enlighten me. How could I have been a better girlfriend?"

Rachel could hear and see the disdain in her friend's voice and tried covering her tracks. She had not meant to upset Chelsea as much as she suddenly realized she had.

"Look, I'm not the one that said it, okay? I figured he told you when you broke up last year. How was I to know you didn't know?"

"Oh, no, please, continue. I'd love to know what the shit-head said about me."

"No," Danielle intervened, "Chelsea, you don't need to know. It doesn't matter. He's an asshole, and whatever he said is of little consequence at this point. It's only going to infuriate you more, and you don't need that."

"No, really," Chelsea countered and then turned to address Rachel, "I want to know. I have to see him in a month anyways, or did you forget you invited him to your wedding? You never go into battle blind, and I won't make that mistake again. Unlike last night, I'd prefer to be ready to face the bastard again, so, please, tell me what he said."

Rachel did not feel like delving into the details. She realized Chelsea was becoming angrier by the second, and since it was not Rachel's fault Terry and Chelsea had broken up, she did not feel like being the messenger. She tried to backtrack as much as possible and switch topics, but Chelsea would not let her, and Danielle sat back to let Rachel dig her own grave on this one. Rachel was left with no other choice than to explain what she knew. In order to save herself as much as possible, lighten the blow she reluctantly knew she was about to throw at her best friend, and diffuse whatever tension she could, she kept the details to just the basics.

She explained to Chelsea that Terry had reached a point in his life where he was ready for his life to move forward, and that meant focusing on his business and his future. He needed to solidify his career and his finances, and he felt he could not do that when Chelsea was still trying to figure out what she wanted to do with her life. He said he needed someone with solid footing and that he did not feel she had that. Even though he had loved her, or at least cared about her greatly, he did not have the time or energy to support her "searching" and still make certain he made it to where he needed to be.

Chelsea and Danielle sat stunned as they soaked in Rachel's story. Unable to wrap her brain around what Rachel was telling her regarding Terry's opinions of her during their relationship, and the fact that Rachel knew more about her own break-up than even she did, Chelsea just sat in silence. Danielle matched Chelsea's silence simply because she was dumbfounded that Rachel had brought this up now, knowing she should have waited for a more appropriate time to fill her in.

After Rachel had finished, there was a silence that hung in the room like a thick London fog. Danielle sat waiting for Chelsea or Rachel to speak, Rachel wondered why Chelsea was being so quiet, and Chelsea squirmed in her chair, refusing to look at either of her friends while speeding through parts of her relationship with Terry, trying to align what she remembered with what she had just heard. Suddenly she found herself wanting to be left alone again, almost as much as she had wanted to be alone the night before. This time, however, her own friends had caused the altercation, and they had been invited into her room intially to undo the stress she had faced the previous night.

Chelsea came to the realization that, lately, everything in her life sucked.

Much to Chelsea's relief, Danielle cut through the silence first, creating a story about how she should probably leave because she had to return home to finish a deposition. Nothing about driving home with Rachel sounded ideal, but today – or at least the latest event of today – needed to end and needed to end as soon as possible. She had contemplated calling a taxi, but she concluded that there were worse things than a 20 minute drive home with her idiot friend. Still, she knew that the sooner she could start the drive back with Rachel to the city, the sooner she could go home and be done with this morning's fiasco. She was wrought with anger over Rachel's comment about her relationship with Paul, and she felt violated by the fact that Rachel's comment had created an unwanted, immediate assessment of the pros and cons of different options in her head. She decided that having a naturally rational and argumentative brain was less than desireable in certain situations, like the one at hand, and going home to be alone might give her the headspace she needed to sort through the information she now had.

Chelsea neither stood to say goodbye nor walked her friends to the door when they turned to leave, gathered their things, and shut the door behind them. She had no qualms with Danielle, but that Rachel had the audacity to repeat those things that Terry had apparently told Charles irritated her because Terry was already an asshole in her mind, and because she could not believe Rachel had kept that information from her for so long.

Rachel, on the other hand, had no idea what to think. In an hour she had gone from angry victim of criticism regarding the pre-nup to bearer of hurt and unwanted news, and she had not been prepared to deal with any part of that. Her life seemed to be throwing more curveballs at her than she could handle.

In fact, everyone's life seemed to be changing. There was a silence in Chelsea's room after her friends left, one mirroring the silence Rachel and Danielle experienced during the car ride home. However, it wasn't necessarily a bad thing. The silence gave them all a moment to think, which was needed seeing how their lives seemed to be fraying at the seams.

Chapter 13 - Direction

When Danielle returned home, Paul was cooking steaks on the grill on their small balcony. He did not hear her enter. She left him to continue cooking in his workout shorts and t-shirt, oblivious to her return home and current state of frustration.

Actually, to say she was frustrated was an understatement. Danielle did not know what she was exactly. Confused? Maybe. Upset? Sure. Distraught? Now there was a good word. Yes, maybe she was more distraught than anything else. And why not? Who wouldn't be distraught after the morning she had just had? Her friend accused her of being selfish and possibly causing the demise of her own relationship. She, the one who always thought about both sides of an argument, she, the one who always tried to be the voice of reason for her friends, now found herself more confused and disturbed than ever. Was she really going to "get in her own way," as Rachel had so bluntly put it, and ruin a relationship that had withstood the test of an already chaotic five years?

Danielle let out a frustrated sigh as she stormed into her bedroom to shower off the morning. She needed a fresh start and a clear head if she was going to talk to Paul about what was bothering her, and she determined today was as good a day as any to talk to him about everything.

When Danielle entered the kitchen, she noticed that Paul had placed the steaks on the counter along with chips and veggie sticks. He was sitting on the couch in the living room in front of the tv and was flipping through channels, apparently looking for something interesting enough to pass the time.

Danielle grabbed herself a steak and some veggie sticks. They served as a decent alternative to actual vegetables when she had no desire to put forth any cooking effort. She filled a glass with water, grabbed some silverware, and headed to the couch to join Paul. They needed to talk.

Much to Danielle's surprise, Paul turned off the television almost immediately after she sat down next to him. He did not turn to face her, nor did he offer up any pre-conversational small talk. Instead, Paul simply stated that there were some things they needed to discuss.

Paul started, "I guess there's really no good way to bring this up."

"The move," Danielle stated knowingly. It was not a question.

"Right. You know I'm leaving for Albany in two weeks, and we haven't discussed this at all. I don't even know what you're thinking or what we're planning on doing. You keep finding some court case to work on every time I bring it up."

Danielle sighed. How was she supposed to explain everything that was running through her head? Ever since she found out his start date at the new branch had been moved up to the end of August, she had forced herself to focus on work so as to not think about the impending move and the uncertainty she felt inside. She was no closer to finding a reasonable solution today than she had been when he first told her on their anniversary.

"I know," she stated. "I only keep putting it off because I don't know what to do, and the whole thing about the date getting pushed up really threw me. I was just grasping the fact that you were leaving around Halloween, and now suddenly it's like you're leaving tomorrow. What's worse is I feel like this is us at graduation all over again: you're leaving, and I won't see you."

"Graduation?" Paul inquired, confused. "Like from college? Is that why you're so upset, because you're thinking about the first time we had to do the long-distance thing? That was so long ago, Danielle."

"And we almost broke up when you finally came to live with me," Danielle finished.

Danielle had moved too fast for Paul to follow. "Wait. Are we talking about the separation part or the reconnecting part?"

"I don't know," Danielle replied, exhausted. "This is why I'm having such a hard time with this. I don't ever know what to think, and my thoughts move so quickly from one point to another that it just makes me tired, and I end up not wanting to deal with it any longer."

"Well, maybe you could walk me through at least part of it, because I'm lost," Paul admitted.

Danielle put down her food and faced Paul. This would require her full attention, and she did not want any distractions while she tried to explain the different arguments in her head.

"Okay," she started. "Bear with me. All of this makes even my head hurt, so let me know if I start to lose you."

Danielle began her explanations and arguments. She started by saying that she felt like this was graduation all over again, and this move meant that they were going to be "commuter dating," having to travel back and forth just to see one another at least once a month. She said she was not naïve enough to think that either of them would be able to find the mountains of time required to make the trip every weekend, so they probably would not see one another as often as they would like. So, the idea of withdrawl – from living with him to seeing him so little – was heartbreaking.

Then, if she were comparing it to graduation, there was the hopeful reunion of finally moving back to be with one another, although, admittedly, she was not sure how or when that would be yet. Plus, the last time they reunited they almost completely fell apart, and she was not so sure she could handle going through that again. She said it seemed like that would be setting them up for a repeat of history, and they both knew how well historical repeats usually ended.

All of that simply meant that it left her with only one other option: one of them had to leave a job, and she could not justify that either. She explained that she loved her job, and that it was not that she wouldn't consider leaving it, but it was so hard for new attorneys to find work anymore that leaving this job without something solid to go to seemed counterproductive. That left Paul to leave his job, which she would never in a million years ask him to do because it was a great opportunity for him. So then, once that argument was made, that only left her back to square one with them doing the long-distance thing indefinitely, and nothing about that sounded like a good idea either.

"I can't come up with a viable solution," she finally stated, "and I hate not knowing what to do, Paul. I'm so good with finding answers and information when it comes to my job, but yet with our lives I'm at a total loss."

"You have a stake in this decision," Paul answered. "You're more emotionally vested in this choice than in the ones you make at work for other people. It makes sense that it would be harder."

"How do people do it?" Danielle finally admitted, looking at Paul with helpless eyes.

"Do what?"

"Make it work? I mean, people get transferred all the time, and couples still find a way to make it work. How do they do it, and if they can do it, why is this so hard for us?"

Paul could see Danielle was starting to break down from the frustration. He rubbed his hand through her hair and against her back, trying to calm her down.

"They make it work because they have to," Paul stated. "They're married or have families and just have to make it work."

"So, what? Are we supposed to get married now to make this work?" Danielle shot back.

Paul laughed, "That's not what I meant. We can still make it work. I was just...answering your question."

Danielle waited before responding. The question in her head was a rhetorical one, and it seemed stupid to even take up airspace with such senselessness, but she still wondered: could they really make it work? This seemed like such an insurmountable obstacle, one that left them with little choices and her with even less hope. She just saw everything spinning out of control, like it was already happening. She could see his bags packed and the apartment empty, the phone calls at first, late at night, saying they missed one another and would make it work, and then the arguments a few months down the road when reality set in and neither could see changing his or her current situation anymore than they could see fixing it now. The arguments were what scared her the most. Arugments led to anger and frustration, anger and frustration led to more fights, and the repeat fighting only led to impending relationship doom: the break-up. She worried that that was where they were headed, but she could not bring herself to say any of it aloud, as though speaking the words brought truth to something that was still only an idea. At least, she hoped it was all only an idea, or better yet, simply an unwarranted worry.

Paul saw the entire thought process play out on Danielle's face. He could not tell the specifics of what she was thinking, only that what she was thinking brought her pain.

"It will be okay," he assured her. "Who knows, maybe in a few months the Albany branch will pick up and I can come back here."

A sigh of disbelief escaped her. Paul was always so optimistic, so hopeful, and as much as she wanted to believe him and wanted to keep her world as uncomplicated as possible, his quick answer did not seem to take enough into consideration.

"Or maybe," he continued, taking her silence as the okay to explore more optimistic possibilities, "you'll be able to find a great firm in Albany to start working for, and you'll come out there to live.

I know it's not top on your list; I know you love it here, but maybe that's how things will work out for a while."

Danielle gave into his attempts and agreed. "Yeah," she said, "maybe." But Paul knew her better than to think she believed him.

"You're not buying it," he responded. Danielle simply pressed her lips together and shook her head. He asked to know what she was thinking, and she considered her own thoughts for a moment before saying anything.

"It's just," she began but then realized she had no concrete way to finish that statement, so she tried another route. "I spent this morning with the girls, and it ended terribly. Rachel has some fucked up idea of what marriage should be, and she'd rather pretend she has the fairytale than face any cracks in her relationship, and poor Chelsea is battling a dilusional mother and crazy ex-boyfriend and yet still finds a way to pull through it all. It's just … how can I be so unhappy when, aside from this inevitable move and the fact that I have no idea what the hell we're going to do about it, we actually have a pretty amazing thing here? I find I'm actually jealous of them. They have direction. They have a shit-ton of problems to face, but they have direction, and it makes me jealous because I feel completely lost. What's wrong with me? Why am I making this so much harder than it should be?"

Paul hugged Danielle close to him and kissed her temple. "Because you're my realist," he explained lovingly. "Because you always find a way to argue every side of a situation, and it's driving you crazy. But that's why I love you, because you don't pretend things are something they're not, and if it weren't for that, we probably wouldn't have made it as far as we have. I love you because you keep us honest, and you always want what's best for us, not just what's best for you or what's best for me, but what's best for both of us. That's why this is so hard for you, because you see every side of every option."

"And I hate it," she admitted, succumbing to her sadness. "I just want it all to work itself out."

"And it will," he said, kissing her again. "It will."

Danielle stayed sad and confused for a few more minutes, and Paul waited for her to say something before breaking the silence himself. He just ran his fingers through her hair and allowed her the space she needed to think and deal with what they had just discussed. She did not appreciate the fact that the problem was still as unresolved as it had been when they started, and she knew they were not done discussing it for that very reason, but she gave herself a few minutes to just exist without complications.

Eventually, they went back to their discussion. She refused to let the day finish without some solution, even if it wasn't the most perfect solution, because at least it would be something, some direction.

Finally, Paul and she decided to leave it open for discussion for the time being but agreed that she would start looking for work in Albany. She did not want to leave her job, and she did not really care for this option, but neither of them wanted him to turn down his job. That did not leave much wiggle-room. If they wanted to stay together, her finding a new job seemed like the only choice. They knew the possibility of her finding a new job quickly was slim, so they would probably have to live apart for a few months. At least if she were looking, though, they could hope to shorten how much time they actually spent apart. Living together had made both of them so happy. Paul loved living with Danielle, and Danielle loved having her best friend with her every day. Neither wanted to elongate their undesired future separation.

Danielle, therefore, would start job hunting. She might have hated the idea, but the idea, at least, was a direction. Inside, though, she still could not help but wonder if it was the right direction.

Chapter 14 - Family

Chelsea sat a table in Starbucks drinking her coffee, contemplating the long awaited talk with her mother she was going to have that evening. It had been almost a week since their blowout, and Chelsea could not spend any more money on hotel rooms if it was not necessary. However, she wanted to be alert and informed for tonight's conversation, so she had asked Vince to join her.

Vince arrived fifteen minutes late, just as Chelsea filled her cup of coffee for a second time. He sat at the table in his work clothes – a button-up, black collared-shirt; dark, well-fitted jeans, and a pair of black, still-shiny, dress shoes. His hair was almost black, neat and short, and sat atop his tanned, rectangularly shaped head. The strong features of his face cut nicely against the skin, and he looked put-together and confident, like a man who knew where he was going in life. He was good at his job of selling alcohol to venders, but he had an air about him that suggested he would be good at everything he did.

Right now, Chelsea really needed him to be good at giving her advice. They were the same age, had grown up together, and he knew her as well as a close cousin could know another family member. She worried about tonight's reunion with her mother, and given that Vince knew her family so well, Chelsea needed not only his opinion on what he foresaw as her best plan of action but also any dirt he could give her on what her mother had been saying. She wanted to arm herself with informational weapons for what she saw as tonight's impending battle.

"So are you going to get to the point, or do I have to bring it up?" Vince asked once Chelsea returned to the table with her coffee. Vince knew that small talk was not the reason for their coffee date.

Chelsea looked up at Vince. "Okay, I actually need help with my mother. I have to see her tonight, and I'm terrified. I feel like I'm walking into the executioner's room without a bargaining plea."

Vince laughed, "Chels, it's just one fight. It's not like there haven't been plenty of those in your day, and, from what I see sitting in front of me, you're still alive. It's not going to be that bad."

"Yeah, but Vince, you weren't there last week. It was awful. She actually *invited* Terry to dinner."

Vince's eyes widened in surprise. "Oh," he admitted but not before laughing, "well that wasn't quite the story I heard. Mom told me Terry just showed up. Figures though, when do I ever get the whole story?"

"Yeah, totally not the whole story. Mom definitely asked Terry to come, and then of course I fucking blew up like Mt. Vesuvius right there in the restaurant and stormed out. Oh my God, Vince, I was so mad."

"Bet that was a fun sight to see."

Chelsea shot him a sarcastic stare and a fake sneer, "Very funny. Ha. Ha."

"Okay, but honestly Chelsea, just go home and talk to your mom. You have to see her eventually."

"But what do I say?" Chelsea whined. She played with the cup in her hand and did not look up at Vince when she spoke. The knots in her stomach were tightening and she suddenly wished she had worn a flowy dress and not the shorts and tank-top currently clinging to her stomach. Her clothes made her feel more constricted, which seemed counterproductive to what she needed to feel in order to deal with what she was going to face after coffee.

Vince gave her a few seconds of space before answering. He did not like seeing Chelsea upset and knew her mother could be a handful. He had never been on the receiving end of Tina's rants, but he grew up in the family and knew as well as anyone how stubborn Tina became when she put her mind to something. Still, it was hard to see his cousin, his twenty-seven year-old cousin, become this distraught over a simple family disagreement.

"Honestly, Chelsea, this is not a big deal."

Chelsea stared up at him with the, "you've got to be kidding," look.

Vince quickly explained, "No, really, it's not. Look, you're twenty-seven, not seventeen, and you have a right to run your own life. Just tell her to butt out for a while. That's what I tell my mom to do when she gets all crazy stupid about wedding stuff. Chels, just chill out and tell people you want to do what you want to do, and they are going to have to learn to deal with it because you're old enough to make your own decisions."

"Oh, right, like that's going to go over well. 'Hey, Mom, butt out'," Chelsea mocked. "Vince, I've been telling her that for the past year, and she still hasn't gotten it."

"Well, then maybe you need to move out," Vince stated very matter-of-factly.

"Maybe," Chelsea agreed, but as she ran through the numbers in her head, she knew she still either needed a better paying job or loans to make that an actual reality.

Vince tried a different approach. "I know you're life's not what you had pictured it would be at this point, but you're doing a good job. You just mentioned you're looking into going back to school, and maybe you should. Get out of here, Chelsea. Go do something with your life. Who gives a shit if you get married tomorrow or not. Shit, I'm getting married tomorrow, practically, and I just want it all to be over already. You girls are crazy with your wedding shit, and I'm looking forward to not having to hear about it twenty-four/seven to be honest. Maybe that's what you need, too. Get out of it all. Go do your wedding duty stuff for your friend, come party at mine the month after, and then get out of here."

Chelsea nodded as he spoke, because what he said made sense. She needed a change. She needed to make it through wedding season with her friends and family and then change up something to break up the monotony of her life.

Then Vince laughed and poked Chelsea's arm and said, "And hey, I have a lot of single friends coming to the wedding. You might start out your new life with a bang, eh?"

Chelsea laughed and pushed back at his arm, "Ew, I'm not talking about that with you!"

Vince shrugged his shoulders and raised his eyebrows knowingly. He did not have to say anything more than what his gesture already said.

"Just saying," he finally finished.

"Yeah, yeah," Chelsea returned. She could use some good sex, plain and simple, and they both knew it. However, that did not fix the mother issue.

"Okay, well," Chelsea began, changing subjects, "aside from worrying about my sex-life, can we worry about tonight and my mother, please?"

"I thought we finished talking about that," Vince stated.

"What did we finish?" Chelsea countered. As far as she remembered they had not solidified any game plan.

"You were going to tell her to back off."

"*Right*," Chelsea replied, "because that's going to work brilliantly. Vince, that's not an answer. You know I can't say that. Can't you give me something? Anything? I appreciate the 'back off' take, but I can't go in there with that as my only option."

"Well, just go in and, I don't know, let her do the talking. Maybe she'll talk herself into an answer."

Vince sipped his coffee and then suddenly perked up. He remembered something.

"Actually," he began, "I don't know if this helps at all, but I think I heard my mom say something about a Dennis or Daniel or something the other day to her."

"Oh my God, you mean that guy from your mom's work? It's like her co-worker's nephew or whatever."

"Yeah, she was talking about working on getting a hold of him with a date."

"Oh, Jesus," Chelsea replied. She rememered her mom bringing up some guy that Vince's mom knew, but she did not think her mom had actually been serious, especially after the Terry incident. Chelsea had just figured Terry had been her mom's ultimate goal, that the other guy was just a ruse. Maybe, though, her mom was just aiming for anything, and since Terry failed she went back to plan B?

"Damn," Chelsea said. "Yeah, she had mentioned some guy by that name or whatever a few months ago as a potential date for Rachel's wedding, but I told her no. I guess she still hasn't dropped it, but at least I know. Thanks. Better I know that before I return home than have her bring it up unexpectedly."

Vince just seemed confused by the whole thing. "Yeah, sure. Whatever. I don't know what I did, but if it helped, then great."

"Yeah, no, it did. Thanks."

Vince moved his hands slightly as though to say, "Don't worry about it," and then he looked at his watch.

"Well, I should probably be going. I told Elena I'd bring home wine for dinner, and it's almost six-thirty. I think she wants to cook with it or something."

"Oh, fun."

Vince just shrugged. Both of them stood and walked towards the doors. Chelsea thanked him again for his help. Vince told her not to mention it and that she should really stop worrying so much about her parents' opinions. They'll always be there, and they'll always have opinions. At some point, he reminded her, she needed to start doing what was best for her and make it work. He told her he didn't feel he did anything more than point out the obvious but wished her the best of luck regardless. Chelsea hugged him goodbye and then headed to her car to go home and face her own reality.

Her mom was sitting at the dinner table in the kitchen, finishing up a bottle of merlot and reading the latest People magazine. Her curly black hair was pulled back with a clip, and she wore black capris and a coral colored, basic, crew-neck t-shirt. Tony sat in the next room, the living room, with a glass of wine as he flipped through channels on the tv, his bare feet propped up on the coffee table in front of him. They did not hear the front door open, as Chelsea received no response from them when she entered. After taking a few steps into the house, though, Chelsea wondered if their silence wasn't silent anger as opposed to what she initially determined to be sheer oblivion.

Chelsea stood at the base of the stairs for five seconds, questioning her need to enter the war-zone. She knew she could walk up the stairs and face them another day, like during their usual Saturday morning argument fest and not have to deal with any of it tonight. Unfortunately, her conscience weighed in, pointing out that slowly stripping off the bandaid was always more painful than just ripping it off all at once. Facing her parents now would be the quick, rip-off version rather than prolongued torture.

Chelsea headed for the kitchen. The smell of pasta sauce lingered in the air, and Chelsea could see remnant pieces of Italian bread on the cutting board on the counter. Unless they had packaged some up in containers that were hidden away in the fridge, they had left none for her. Chelsea was simply glad her nerves and her previous cups of coffee filled up her stomach enough to suffice for the night.

Taking a deep breath, Chelsea walked towards her mother. She could see her sitting at the dinner table and her father just a few feet away in the next room, beyond the kitchen's half-wall partition.

"Hi, Mom, Dad," she started, "I'm home."

When neither of her parents responded to her initial greeting, she tried again. Tony kept watching tv, which Chelsea had a hard time deciphering as a sign of indifference or just sheer deafness.

Tina, on the other hand, slowly put down her glass of wine and spoke without looking up from her magazine.

"Are you staying, or are you running off again?" she asked coldly.

Chelsea stood momentarily on unsteady ground, not sure how to respond. It seemed like more of a rhetorical question than anything else, and Chelsea had not been prepared for rhetorical questions nor her mother's sudden coldness. She had been prepared for blazing swords and the onset of argumentative paragraphs. Therefore, as she went to respond, she did so cautiously.

"No, I'm here now," she stated.

Her mom simply nodded her head, and Chelsea stood statuesque, unsure of what to do.

Her mom turned the page to her magazine before continuing, "Well, I didn't save you dinner. I stopped doing that the day after you ran off; I figured there was no point in wasting food for someone who clearly didn't want to enjoy it."

When Chelsea did not respond, due to her preocupation with understanding the awkwardness in the room, her mom continued unabashed, "You know, you have no idea what I go through to try to make your life easier and make you happy. I don't appreciate you acting like a rebellious teenager. You're twenty-seven for Christ's sake; it's time you stopped acting like a child and grew up. You can't just go running off everytime something doesn't work out."

Chelsea swallowed slowly so as not to snap back at her mother. The fight was about to start. Chelsea moved closer to the dinner table so she was not talking to her mom from a distance.

"Mom, I didn't run off like a twelve-year-old. I moved out briefly. There's a difference. And, yes, I am twenty-seven, and I would appreciate it if you recognized that as well. I couldn't believe what transpired at the restaurant, that you would go behind my back like that. What you did at the restaurant was hurtful and contemptuous."

"Contemptuous?" her mom raged. "Behind your back?"

There was a heated silence before Tina officially put down the magazine. "Now listen here, signorina, I will not have such blasphemous words thrown at me in my own house."

"I help pay the bills!" Chelsea threw in quickly, trying to find some ground to stand on in this verbal onslaught.

"It is still *casa mia*, and you may stay so long as you understand that. I do not run a hotel. You cannot just come and go as you please. If that's what you want, then move out." Her mom continued to sit at the table, the added emphasis of standing apparently not yet needed. Her words were forceful enough that the gesture would have been overkill.

Chelsea tried counting to ten quickly in her head. Her tenant status was not what she was here to discuss nor did she want to talk of such things any longer.

"Mom, I'm here to talk about Terry and the weddings, okay?" she stated, trying to direct the topic of conversation. Vince may have suggested allowing Tina run her own thoughts in a circle, but if the circle was going to include Chelsea's living or not living at home, then that was not a circle Chelsea wanted to visit yet, at least, not until she knew something definitive about school or a job.

"Well you can forget about Terry. He didn't even bother staying for dinner after you ran off."

Her mom picked up the magazine again and flipped through it rapidly, not focusing on any page but rather trying to give her hands and her mind something else to do. She mumbled to herself something about him being ungrateful after she had gone through the trouble of inviting him, and she did so under her breath in a manner that suggested she did not want Chelsea to hear. Chelsea heard anyway, and although she did not say anything, she shook her head and wanted to say, "Told you so." Her mother had been dumb to invite him, entertaining the fleeting idea that they had any chance of reconnecting, and, although Chelsea enjoyed seeing her mom disappointed by the man Chelsea already hated, she knew better than to rub it in.

However, Tina's muddled cursing about Terry had apparently been for her ears only, as she returned to normal volume saying, "I think you've lost your chance with him."

With Tina still focused on flipping her magazine pages, Chelsea's face scrunched up in disbelief. What an idiot, she thought. She could not believe her mother. One second she was cursing the man, and then the next she acted like it was Chelsea's fault, that Chelsea had ruined her own chances. Did she not understand that when it came to Terry, Chelsea did not even *want* another chance?

Chelsea suddenly could do nothing but shake her head at her mother's delusions and restate the obvious. "I don't want another chance with him, Mom. I can't believe that, a year after we broke up, you still act like I am the one who fucked things up. How am I to blame, here?"

"Women are always blamed. That's a fact of life, like it or not, and I was trying to help you save face."

"*What?*" Chelsea gasped, looking at her mother in disbelief.

"What?" her mom retorted, not understanding her daughter's surprise.

"How the hell do you figure *we* are the ones who are always blamed?"

Tina, taking a large sip of wine, turned calmly to her daughter. Clearly, her daughter had missed this part of growing up, and Tina only felt pity at the present moment, which caused her to address her daughter very calmly and in a teacherly manner.

"Chelsea," she began, "there is just something you have to understand. Like it or not, society isn't as progressive as you want to believe it is. Women still carry certain burdens when it comes to relationships and the men in their lives. I know you think that I was trying to intervene unfairly, but I was only trying to help. I was trying to give you a second chance or a respectable way out, but the way you stormed off only made you look worse."

The single laugh that escaped Chelsea's lips resonated through the house. She did not have to say the words to convey the sentiment that she thought her mom was officially off her rocker.

"Fine, you don't believe me?" Tina countered. "Let me explain. You see, you ran out of the restaurant. You threw a fit, and you ran out. That action alone made you look like you're hot-headed and irrational, and, even if it was a warranted reaction, people start to wonder what happened and then feel bad for the person left at the scene. In this case, it was a boy your own age and your family. Maybe you felt you had a right to run off, and maybe you could have done so calmly and under the radar, but the way you did it made only you look bad."

Chelsea glared at her mother. "So what? So I look bad to people I don't know. What difference does that make?"

"Appearances are everything, Chelsea. You don't know who was in that restaurant, or who those people know, or who you might or might not run into again in the future, and you can't just go blowing up anywhere you want."

"Okay, Mom, whatever. That's one example. That doesn't mean women are always blamed. That's a hugely loaded statement to make."

"No? You don't think so?" Tina challenged again.

"No," Chelsea dared, "I don't."

"Okay. Fine. If a guy is beating up his girlfriend, what do you think?"

"The guy's an asshole."

"And what if he does it again?"

"Well, he's still an asshole, but then she's just an idiot for not leaving."

"So she's an idiot?" Tina repeated.

"Yeah," Chelsea stated. "She's an idiot. If you go back to the person after he hit you, you're just dumb."

"See?" Tina noted. "See what just happened? You focused on the girl in that situation and how she should have done things differently."

"What? Ma, oh my God. That's so different. He was hitting her and she went back. Plus, come on, it's theoretical and like worst case scenario."

"Is it?" Tina prodded. Chelsea just stared at her mom like she was dumb and beating a dead horse at this point.

"Fine. What about your friends?" her mom said, changing scenarios.

"What about my friends, Mom?"

"You've mentioned before about Rachel and Charles, how he's gone all the time, and how she's always upset."

"Yeah, because she's being idealistic and wants this perfect, white-fence and puppies relationship."

"So?"

"So," Chelsea explained, "she just sets herself up for disappointment."

"Well, what about Charles?"

"What about Charles? He's either really just busy or hanging out with his friends, which, you know, whatever. It's a little excessive, but that's kind of how he's always been: 'semi' around. But, if he really is cheating on her then he's retarded, and she needs to get out. Why?"

"Did you not just hear yourself?" her mom wondered.

Chelsea just stared back, confused.

Tina continued, "Chelsea, you just said that Charles has always been this way and it's Rachel's fault if she sets herself up for disappointment."

"So?"

"So, why didn't you say it's Charles' fault for disappointing Rachel?"

"Well, I mean, Charles is being dumb, obviously, but Rachel lives in la-la Rachel-land which sometimes has very little connection to reality."

"So, what you're saying is Rachel is at fault if there are problems."

"No, not completely," Chelsea fought, her thoughts speeding through her head.

After a few moments of thinking, Chelsea finally responded, "Okay, maybe a little. That doesn't make it the woman's fault all the time, though."

"No, I didn't say it *was* the woman's fault. I'm just saying that that's the way it's *perceived*."

Chelsea just stared back at her mother, waiting for her to make a real point.

"Okay, well what about Danielle and Paul?" her mom asked, changing scenarios.

"What about them?" Chelsea retorted. She did not like this game.

"What's going on with them?"

"Mom, whatever you're getting at, it's not working."

"Come on, Chelsea. Just talk to me. I'm not judging."

"You always judge!" Chelsea countered.

"Humor me," she responded.

Chelsea rolled her eyes before continuing, "Fine. Danielle and Paul aren't doing so well. Paul's leaving next week for a work transfer, and Danielle doesn't know what to do. Clearly, she loves him; I mean, it's been five years, but she also loves her job and neither wants to leave it nor wants to leave it without something lined up in Albany."

Tina asked her next question calmly, "And what do you think?"

"What do I think about what?" Chelsea responded, hints of attitude lingering on the words.

"Just what I said. What do you think about it?"

"I don't know. It's her life, not mine, but sometimes I worry for her. The last time they had a long-period, long-distance thing it almost broke them, and sometimes I think maybe they need it again to see if they'll last. Other times I think that a job is a job, and you can have one here or somewhere else. I know it's not as easy to find one anymore, but he is moving because of a job, so clearly he has one, and part of me thinks she's being dumb for not moving too. You don't just find people that you connect with that well just anywhere or that easily. Plus, five years is a really long time to be together, and I think she either needs to decide he's right for her or break it off. He clearly wants to marry her, but sometimes she stands in her own way, and eventually, if it keeps up, it's going to be what drives them apart."

Her mom sat for a moment before responding, sipping her wine and letting the words settle in the air. When she spoke, she asked a very simple question, a question that ran as the apparent theme of the night's conversation.

"And who do you see as the problem in that whole situation?"

Chelsea knew exactly what her mother was implying, yet, as much as she tried to pretend her mother was being stupid and dumb and forcing ancient social beliefs onto present day society, Chelsea could not help but feel that Danielle was ultimately causing her own problems. The thought made Chelsea's stomach curdle. Fighting it as much as she could, she found she could not fight reality completely. Yes, it was true that Paul did not have to take the job, but in the long run, for their relationship, his promotion was not a bad thing, and her being stubborn in accepting the reality of that might cause more problems. There was no answer yet, but Chelsea already found herself agreeing with what Rachel had said a week ago in her hotel room: Danielle was standing in her own way. But did that mean she was the one people wanted to blame? If so, that meant given all the scenarios above, her mother was right: women were blamed, like it or not.

And Chelsea absolutely did not like it.

Tina could read her daughter's entire thought process on her face. Chelsea did not have to say a word for her mom to know exactly what was churning up in her mind. She stood to move closer to her daughter. Lovingly, she put a hand on Chelsea's arm.

"I know," she soothed. "I didn't say it was fair."

Much to Tina's surprise, Chelsea yanked her arm away from her mother and glared back at her in anger.

"This is bullshit!" Chelsea cursed. "No, absolutely not. I don't believe it. I'm not going to sit here and pretend that being a girl somehow denotes automatic blame status. That might have worked for you growing up, but that's not how it's going to work for me, Mom, and I'm not going to condemn my friends to it either. You think you're helping, but you're so confused in your own relationship and worldly ideals that you blind yourself."

Chelsea backed away from her mother.

"No," she continued. "I won't do it. I'm not going to blame myself like I somehow did something wrong. Standing up for yourself is not wrong, Mom. Wanting things for yourself isn't wrong!"

"I'm not saying you're wrong, Chelsea!" her mom cut in, "You're just not seeing the whole picture."

"Yours isn't the whole picture either, Mom!" Chelsea countered.

"But it's the one that's going to get you back into a relatioship," her mom finished.

"*O my God*!" Chelsea moaned, turning away from her mother. "Is that really all you think about?"

"I think about what's best for you." Annoyance and hurt pride seeped into her mom's voice.

"You're not a martyr, Mom, and I'm not an old maid!" Chelsea returned.

"Not yet, no, but I intend to see to it you're not thought of as such for the upcoming weddings."

"Oh, Jesus, Mom, what are you planning? No dates, Mom. Honestly."

Her mom stood her ground verbally and physically, "You do not always know what's best for you. I have invited a date for you to

Rachel's wedding. You can determine what to do with him there, but I will not have you be a source of gossip," she paused, "or blame."

Chelsea shook herself in anger and unabated frustration. She let out a scream somwhere between a growl and an under-her-breath shout. Having nothing else to say to her mother, she stormed out of the room. They lived in two different worlds that held no bridge for common communication, and Chelsea finally saw her life at home as toxic to her sanity. Although still uncertain of her next life move, she concluded with some finality that a move was not only needed but unavoidable. It was only two more weeks until Rachel's wedding, and after that she would look into moving.

Two weeks, she thought. That's manageable.

At the conclusion of Rachel's wedding she would make her decision. Move and work or move and go to graduate school. Both were better options than staying, but neither aided in her forced blind date. If Vince were right, Dennis or Daniel or D-something would be at Rachel's wedding, and from what she remembered, he was a guy with crazy-ex-girlfriend baggage. Clearly, just what she needed.

She rolled her eyes and shut her bedroom door. This had the potential to be a very long two weeks.

Chapter 15 - Work

Phones rang as Chelsea swung the door open to work on Friday morning. Fighting had taken so much out of Chelsea the night before that she accidentally overslept, so she now found herself running into the office fifteen minutes late and to the phone on her desk screaming her name. Sprinting to her desk, in heels and her pinstriped skirt, she plopped into her chair, threw her handbag under her desk, and turned on her bluetooth headset.

"Hobson Bank and Trust, Chelsea speaking, how may I help you?" she breathed into the phone as lightly as possible, trying to prohibit the sound of heavy breathing and exhaustion from slipping into her voice.

The caller coughed multiple times on the other end of the phone line and between phrases.

"Chelsea? It's David."

Immediately, Chelsea's heart flew into overdrive, pounding hard against her chest in undeniable anger at the inevitable Fate.

David coughed again on the other end of the phone line, "I can't make it to work today."

Normally, Chelsea would have done her best to hold her tongue, but she had no patience left, and David found himself on the wrong end of Chelsea's exhaustion. She allowed herself to tell David exactly what she was thinking.

"David," she nearly shouted into the phone, but lowered her tone enough to remain undetected by those semi-close to her, "I don't really care what you have to do right now to get into work, but you better get yourself over here today."

"I'm sick, and I can't come in," he managed weakly.

Chelsea prepped herself mentally for the battle she assumed she would lose but needed to fight nonetheless.

"You're always sick, David. Always. This is nothing new, and I'm tired of trying to pick up all the slack. You can't just conveniently decide to be sick every Friday. That's not how this works. Either get in here and soon or you can call Pat yourself and tell him you're not coming in today. I'm not dealing with this anymore."

Without skipping a beat, David countered Chelsea's complaint, "I can't help that I'm sick, and I'm not coming to the office if I am. I'm going to the doctor today to get meds, and you can tell Pat I'll bring in proof on Monday."

"David!" Chelsea half pleaded, but she knew she was losing.

He coughed again, acting as though his world was over and the cough was making him somehow weary. He said, "I'll see you Monday," and then hung up the phone before Chelsea could argue further.

Clicking off her bluetooth headset, Chelsea simply sat and stared off into nothingness for a few moments, trying to comprehend how she was going to get through today, yet again, on her own. She chalked this up to one more reason why she needed a new job, and silently thanked the gods that it was Friday. Only one more day – an eight hour chunk of time to be exact – and then it would be the weekend, and she would have two days to just recenter herself.

Pulling the hair tie from her head, she took down her ponytail to give her brain more space to think. Last night, upon going to sleep, she had hoped to just coast through today, with her brain in "off" mode. Unfortunately, between running late and David calling off work, today quickly proved to be just the opposite. Chelsea counted up all the things she would now have to do, since David was going to be absent: check his caseload files so she could communicate with his clients, tell Pat that David was going to be absent from work *again*, and then get on with her regular Friday work. Lunch with Danny and Stacy might not be an option, which turned Chelsea's already unsettling thoughts even more pessimistic. A break around lunch would probably have been welcomed, yet she did not have time to dwell on the what-ifs; she had work to do.

Stacy knocked on Chelsea's cubical wall at ten minutes to noon. It was time for their group lunch, and Stacy was coming to collect Chelsea like she usually did. She wore dress capris, flat, strappy sandals, and a light blue, short sleeve, button up top. In her left hand, as always, hung the oversized coffee mug.

"Hey, Stacy," Chelsea said flatly.

"Hey," Stacy said, matching Chelsea's flatness.

Chelsea turned to look at Stacy and made mention of how life-saving a large cup of coffee would be right at the moment before allowing Stacy to continue. Stacy laughed quickly and then spoke, wanting to get out what she needed to say before she chickened out of saying it.

"I can't go to lunch today," Stacy said as normally as possible.

Chelsea looked up at Stacy with questioning eyes. It was not like Stacy to pass up a group lunch, at least definitely not in such a remorseful and worried manner. She usually enjoyed catching up with Danny about their latest suburban adventure, asking about Rachel's weddings, and filling everyone in on baby Marcus. In fact, given last Friday night's abrupt end, Stacy had been asking Chelsea all week about when she was going to talk to her mother. Chelsea had assumed that Stacy would want to know that she had spoken with her mother last night, but if lunch was out of the picture, then the information exchange would be abruptly halted as well.

"Have lots of work?" Chelsea asked, starting with a relatively neutral subject, even though Chelsea knew by Stacy's voice that she was not choosing to stay back because of work.

"Well, yeah, sure. I mean, there's always work to do, but," Stacy started but then chose not to finish. Stacy's avoidance did not go unnoticed.

"But what, Stacy? What's wrong?"

"I just can't go," Stacy finished. "I can't afford it this week."

Chelsea nodded and took a moment to pause before responding. She knew full well what being on a budget was like, and given Stacy and Mark's fight a few months back about finances, Chelsea knew this money concern was not out of the blue. Instead, Chelsea simply commented that she thought staying in for lunch sounded like a good option. The three of them could go and just eat together in the break room for a change.

Stacy smiled sympathetically, a gesture of gratitude for Chelsea's flexibility. They agreed to meet around twelve-fifteen, allowing Chelsea enough time to wrap up what she was doing, grab some food close by, and meet Danny and her in the break room. Even though it was not at a local restaurant, Friday lunch would still take place, and none of them could argue with doing it cheaply.

Chelsea returned around a quarter after twelve with a Subway sandwich in tow, a healthy and relatively inexpensive option, which pleased both her wallet and her waistline.

Upon entering the breakroom, she found Danny and Stacy already seated and midway into their lunches. Danny, sitting at the far end of the table in his black slacks, black leather shoes, crimson button-up shirt, and steel-framed glasses, took another bite of his turkey, cheese, and lettuce sandwich. Stacy, who sat to his left at the four person table, turned over a spoonful of homemade tuna salad onto a wheat cracker before putting the bite-sized cracker into her mouth. The scenario was homemade lunches at their best, and it almost reminded Chelsea of when she used to bring brown bag lunches to high school and eat around the cafeteria tables with her friends. The differnce was that now her friends were dressed in business attire and had houses, families, apartments, and lives to run once five-thirty hit.

When was it again that she became an adult?

She shook her head at the thought and joined her friends at the table. There was no point in entertaining unanswerable questions when her life already presented her with enough situations to keep her brain occupied.

"Oh, Subway!" Stacy stated approvingly. "Which kind did you get?"

"Just one with chicken," Chelsea responded, "and cheese and veggies, but no sauce. I have two more weeks until Rachel's wedding, and I have to be sure I look good in my dress."

Stacy's eyes widened, and she nodded in agreement at Chelsea's comment, unable to utter agreeing words at present due to the bite of tuna fish cracker in her mouth.

Danny laughed under his breath and shook his head.

"Girls," he said. "You're always so worried about the littlest things."

Chelsea returned, "Hey, just because you don't have to stand in front of hundreds of people in a dress, doesn't mean I don't. It requires a certain amount of work and shrinking of the waistline."

Danny smiled and raised his eyebrows, unsure of how to respond. He had plenty of experience in the, "Don't mess with girls and their appearances," department, as some of his previous girlfriends had been quite a handful in that area. He had learned to keep his mouth shut, and he simply nodded at their overly critical nature.

"Perks of being a guy, I guess," Danny did manage to say, winking at Chelsea as a playful return jab, sneaking in the last words. Chelsea simply half smiled and shook her head at him.

Then Stacy sat up quickly and turned to face Chelsea.

"Speaking of guys," she began eagerly, "what ever happened with the incident at the restaurant? How did the conversation with your mother work out?"

Danny simply sat silently as Chelsea filled in Stacy with the cliff-notes version of the event. Although she knew that Stacy wanted the details, Chelsea was exhausted from overdiscussing the entire situation and simply returned with only the most pertinent of details, enough to fill in the gaps and give the basic overview. Luckily, Stacy seemed contented with the given explanation and sympathized with Chelsea, commenting that parents, although they mean well, can sometimes interfere in places they shouldn't.

Taking note of Stacy's comment and her given money tightness, Chelsea asked if everything with Stacy's mother was okay. A head bobble and a moment of silence followed before Stacy indulged her friend's question with an answer.

"It is what it always is," Stacy said. "I love her, and I know she means well, but she almost gave Mark and me an ultimatum the other week."

"Ultimatum?" Danny asked. In all the discussions they had had about Stacy's family, her mother never seemed the type to dish out such a severe consequence. In fact, Stacy always commented on how her mother loved and wanted to be an active role in their lives as well as baby Marcus'. Additionally sometimes, although the babysitting situation had become a bit of a burden back in May, she would actually ask to keep baby Marcus for an evening to show him off to her friends or just allow Mark and Stacy a "couple's" night. Now, an ultimatum seemed incongruent to her normal demeanor.

Stacy finished another bite of her tuna salad and then started wiping off her fresh peach as she spoke. "We were looking for a babysitter, as you both know, because Mom said she wouldn't be able to take care of the baby forever, nor could we really expect her to. I mean, she has her own life, and this isn't her baby to raise, so, you know, fine, I get that. However, she agreed to help us out until Mark and I could fine a suitable babysitter, which, don't get me wrong, we are very appreciative of, especially considering it's not easy to find a good sitter.

"Well," she explained, "we had found Gloria, this twenty-two year old college graduate who was home for the summer but still looking for work, and she came with lots of years of nannying from when she was in high school and college. She seemed good for

Marcus, and, in July was actually very helpful. Then, however, she got a job as she had hoped and, I mean, how can I blame her? She needs a job just like the rest of us, and Mark and I can't compete with that kind of salary, so Mom had to help out again because we were, yet again, without a sitter."

Chelsea and Danny looked on, wondering where the ultimatum was due to fall into the story because nothing yet seemed overly extreme.

Stacy continued, "Again, Mom was helpful but constantly saying that we needed to find a new sitter. However, this time, she started to make perpetual comments about how we needed to find a *reliable* sitter, someone who would *stick around*, which, said once or twice is fine. But, guys, she said it every time she came over and every time she left. In fact, this past week, she sat in on two of our sitter interviews because she no longer trusts us to find someone dependable."

Chelsea made a face that looked like she had just had another one of her fights with her mother. She told Stacy that that must be awful and that she knew what it was like to have an overbearing mother. However, she did ask what exactly the ultimatum was, as it was still not clear.

Stacy shook her head, noting that she was almost at that point.

"Well," she said, "here's what Mom dropped on me this morning when she came over. She said that I had to find a sitter by the end of next week or I would have to start paying her money to compensate for her time and gas. Okay, after my initial shock, that didn't seem too bad, however, she said that if it came to that she would take over babysitter hunting and/or enroll Marcus in a daycare."

The last part of that sentence was when Stacy looked like she had just seen a ghost. She looked distraught and almost sick, and, much to her surprise, Danny and Chelsea simply sat silently and exchanged glances of confusion. Neither knew how to respond, and Stacy, noticing her friends' silence, interrupted their stares to re-explain.

"Daycare!" she shouted in disbelief. "Can you believe it? She wants to put baby Marcus in *daycare!*"

Stacy just sat silently for a moment, rolling the now-cleaned peach around in her hand. Chelsea and Danny exchanged glances, wondering if that was supposed to be the pinnacle of the story.

"Is that the ultimatum?" Danny finally asked. It was probably better that Danny asked rather than Chelsea, although Chelsea had the same question. The question would be more tolerated coming from Danny than from Chelsea, as Danny was a man, and Stacy would probably be more forgiving in his lack of understanding.

Stacy looked at Danny, half shocked and half in pity. "Danny! Of course that's the ultimatum. I mean, can you believe it? That's like the worst possible thing she could have ever suggested. I mean, she's hinted at it before, but never with such finality, and she really means it too, which is the worst part. I mean, can you imagine putting your kid into daycare?"

Stacy clearly and momentarily forgot the makeup of her audience. Chelsea and Danny simply stared silently in response.

Finally, Stacy stepped in to explain, "It's daycare guys. It's expensive and they don't even pay attention to the kids. There are five hundred of them in one place and only like two adults. I mean, how is poor little Marcus ever going to get attention or care if no one even pays attention to him?"

"I don't think there are really that many kids," Chelsea offered, trying to reel Stacy back into reality.

"Did you go to daycare?" Stacy shot back. Obvioulsy, this was still really rubbing Stacy the wrong way.

"Well, no," Chelsea started slowly, but was thusly interrupted.

"See?" Stacy argued.

"But I know lots of people who did," Chelsea offered. "My best friend Danielle being one of them."

"Yeah, but that was back when people still stayed at home so there were fewer kids in daycare," Stacy argued back.

Danny and Chelsea exchanged confused glances once again. Both mentally noted that Stacy was having a much harder time processing this daycare concept than they both would have ever imagined. She was a mommy. She knew mommy things, and daycare just seemed to be another reality of the mommy-world, so how she could find herself in such a tizzy was a mystery to both of them.

"Okay, Stacy," Danny said, "I think you're missing the point. You should be happy that you even have daycare as an option. I mean, if you can find a sitter, great, but daycares are much better now than they used to be. My cousin put her baby in daycare years ago, and she's dong just fine. She's in gradeschool or something now and totally a normal kid."

"Okay, so like *one* example," Stacy commented, putting up a fight but giving away in her voice that she was warming to the idea. Chelsea couldn't believe Danny's one story could calm Stacy so much, but then again, Stacy trusted Danny.

"Of many," Danny finished. "It's really not that bad, Stacy."

"Yeah, and who knows, maybe your mom will still want to see baby Marcus so you'll only be taking him to daycare a few days out of the week instead of every day," Chelsea offered, trying to be part of the conversation, even though she felt supremely underqualified to do so.

"Plus," she continued, "maybe you'll find someone just as wonderful as Gloria in a few weeks, and you can take him out of daycare completely."

Stacy nodded quietly, taking a bite of her peach. Admittedly, she had not considered that angle, and now that her friends were talking her through it, the entire situation seemed less dire than it had this morning.

She took in a breath before speaking again, "You're probably right, and I would absolutely rather have a sitter than hand him over to a room full of other people and strange kids, but maybe it will only be temporary. It's just, neither option is cheap and Mark and I just had this long talk about finances the other night and how we're running a pretty tight ship, and Mom's comment this morning just kind of came out of the blue. I guess it's been stirring and boiling in my head all morning more than it should have been. Thanks, guys. I guess I'm just stressed. You're probably both right, and I'm probably making a way bigger deal out of this than it needs to be."

"Yeah, hunny, it's definitely not an ultimatum," Chelsea concluded. "You'll be okay, and in a month you'll probably have it all figured out."

Then Danny joked, "and if not, Chelsea can babysit Marcus when you bring him to work."

Everyone laughed, and Chelsea shook her head at Danny.

"Yeah, that would probably *not* be the best idea," Chelsea commented.

"No? No late night and weekend babysittings for Aunt Chelsea?" Stacy cooed.

Chelsea tried to laugh lightly but the idea made her stomach turn.

"No, Stacy, probably not. Not that you'd even want me to with all the weddings coming up. I won't be around much, and I'm not the best with kids, so, I'd make a really bad babysitter."

"Oh, that's right, you have wedding duty soon," Stacy returned. "At least you won't have to worry about Terry being your date."

"True, but I know Mom has something up her sleeve as I've apparently already been spoken for, thanks to her," Chelsea explained, rolling her eyes once. "I'm just hoping to avoid him for as long as possible that night."

"Date, too, huh?" Danny said offhandedly, but not without both girls picking up on it.

"Uh oh," Stacy prodded. "Don't tell me Mr. Player suddenly has a date."

"Not the way you're thinking," he corrected. "This is not my doing. My dad can't go with my Mom because he's leaving town for work for a few weeks, so Mom said she's dragging me with her to an event over Labor Day Weekend."

"Where?" Stacy asked excitedly.

"Who knows," Danny said. "I really don't care. It's for someone my family knows. I just know I'm getting free drinks to hang out with Mom."

"Sounds nice. Older women," Chelsea smiled.

"Oh well, "Danny laughed, "and I guess some my age, too. Mom said she knew at least one girl who'd be there who's about my age."

"Oh! Fun! Do you know her?" Stacy asked.

"Don't know. Mom said she's nice, around my age, and works in customer service or something with customers. I figure, she's either a saint and super social or really cynical because she gets to listen to people complain all the time," Danny explained, laughing at his analysis at the end.

"I just hope she's not too homely or something," he added.

"Oh, stop," Stacy said. "I think it's nice of you to go. And who knows, when there are drinks involved, people always tend to be fun."

"Because they're drunk," Chelsea noted, smiling.

"Well, I just know I enjoy drinking, and I figure if she's at least somewhat attractive and single, the odds are at least pretty good," Danny explained. Chelsea laughed. Stacy seemed slightly disturbed.

"Well, may we both be so lucky, then," Chelsea commented.

Stacy interjected, "You two are incorrigible. I just hope you guys are nice to your dates."

"I will be," Danny said. "I'm not a total jerk."

"Very true," Chelsea noted. "I'm just really hoping I don't even have to run into mine. Nothing about the description of 'a crazy ex' sounded pleasing."

"Mm," Danny noted, "good luck with him."

Chelsea let out a singular laugh and said, "Thanks."

The three friends finished their lunches and then returned for the last few hours of work. Stacy seemed calmer now that she had released the story of daycare, Danny apparently had his own date night to face in September, and Chelsea was pleased to know it was not only her family who felt the need to control the lives of their adult children.

Suddenly, Chelsea wanted to kick herself for not thinking of Danny sooner as a date to the wedding. She did not necessarily feel any particular way about him, but he was single and, with him as her date, she could have avoided the whole "blind date" situation she now faced. Too bad it had not occurred to her sooner, because it was not a bad idea. However, she knew she could not suggest it now, as her mother would throw a conniption fit if she tried to back out of what her mother had already arranged, but it would have been a much easier way to pass the night. She did enjoy Danny's company, and he was almost kind of cute sometimes, especially with his steel rimmed glasses.

Damn, she thought. If only I had been smarter a few months back.

After lunch, Chelsea plopped herself in front of her desk and looked at her inbox. Thirteen new emails flooded her screen, five from Candice, the owner of Bouquets R Us, two from her boss, and the rest from a variety of other clients. Well, at least she would stay busy the rest of the day. She could worry about her life later.

Chapter 16 - Broken

It was the last week of August, and Danielle sat on her bed, crosslegged, playing with her hands. The house was silent, save Paul's box shuffling in the kitchen. Danielle could not bring herself to help. She could see the clock tick away the seconds, mocking her frustration and counting down the time before Paul's inevitable leaving, but she could not move herself from the middle of the bed. Instead she sat planted on the comforter, as though if she somehow just stayed put, time would eventually stop, and Paul would not have to leave. She knew that, logically, that did not make any sense, but the screaming chaos inside her head was met with a heavy heart and worry, and the emotional combination immobilized her. Paul would have to finish moving boxes on his own.

Paul had spent most of the weekend packing boxes and shipping what could be shipped in the company-paid moving van on Sunday. His company had scheduled him to be at work on Wednesday morning, allowing him all of Monday and Tuesday to get settled into his apartment and finalize any moving hassles that needed to be addressed. Since he was not in the deepest hurry to leave Danielle, Paul had driven out with the moving van on Sunday and returned home Sunday night to be with her until he left again Tuesday evening. She had taken both days off work to be with him. However, both of them had worked on the couch on their laptops and phones these last two days, doing more work related activities than initially intended.

Unfortunately, that just meant that now, at 5:48 p.m. on Tuesday evening, Danielle was even less ready for Paul to leave, feeling that she had somehow been deprived of the quality time they were supposed to have had in the last forty-eight hours. She silently cursed herself for being so work focused and not realizing what a precious gift the last two days had been. How was it a court case had taken precedence over spending time with Paul when he was due to permanently leave today?

Permanently leave. That was another issue. There had been no resolving of what the two of them were going to do about their lives and relationship. In fact, neither had brought it up at all in the last forty-eight hours. Danielle had thought about mentioning it but instead distracted herself with work or a movie with Paul. Now she found herself with more unanswered questions than possible solutions, and the questions only amplified her worry. She had been unsuccessful in locating full-time work in Albany, and none of the partners or associates at her current firm had any immediate or strong connections to any attorneys there. That left her on her own, which was not sufficient enough to solidify her moving anywhere other than Boston.

And that just meant she and Paul were no closer to finding a solution to their long-distance relationship problem than before.

Danielle rang out her hands, closed her eyes, and tried to shake away her frustration. It was not helping either that different "what-if" scenarios were also running, unchecked, through her head, encompassing everything from, "What if she moved out to be with him albeit not having work?" to, "What if they broke up three months down the road?" Potential arguments, crying, phone calls, and agony played before her, and she did not know how to cease their playback. She could go help Paul with boxes, but she feared that seeing the house so empty would only fuel her bemoaning thoughts. Sitting on the bed and not moving, therefore, made her feel like she at least held control over something, even if it was only momentary at best.

The floors creaked below Paul's feet as he passed through the hallway. The uneven sound of the floorboards led her to believe that he was carrying something, and the thud of a box against the floor and grunting by Paul relayed that whatever he was carrying was heavy. Still, Danielle did not move.

Footsteps moved faster. They headed towards the bedroom door.

"Are you going to come help?" Paul finally asked, standing in the doorframe, but Danielle refused to look at him. She just kept staring at the space in front of her.

The absense of a response irritated Paul. To him, Danielle's perpetual seated position was just a form of pouting, and pouting was not helping. Pouting was avoiding, and whether she wanted to face it or not, he had to leave soon, and her avoidance was the opposite of what he needed.

"Danielle, I don't know what you want, but sitting on the bed isn't helping."

Danielle shook her head. She knew she should be assisting in the move, but she could not bring herself to budge.

"I don't want you to go," she simply replied, looking at her hands.

"Don't do this, Danielle," Paul returned. "You've been fine for the last two days. Don't *now* choose to get all emotional on me. You know I have to go, and I would appreciate it if you would help me with a few things. That box of clothing is really heavy, and it would be nice if you could help me take it outside."

"I know. *I know*," Danielle said, but still did not move.

Paul's aggrevation was being pushed to a breaking point. "Well, if you know, then why don't you come help?"

"Don't yell at me," Danielle responded, finally looking at up Paul with angry eyes.

"Oh my God, Danielle. Stop being dramatic. I'm not yelling. You, however, are pouting, and it isn't doing either of us any good."

Danielle scrunched her eyebrows together in anger and frustration.

"I'm not being dramatic," she finally stated.

Paul rolled his eyes. Deciding to not respond, he simply turned and walked back down the hallway.

His lack of response prompted Danielle's movement from her spot on the bed and full exit from the bedroom.

"Now where are you going?" she insisted.

"Where do you think I'm going?" he chided, not turning around to look at her.

She inhaled anger before answering, "Hey smartass, don't act like I'm not allowed to be upset."

"Jesus, Danielle," he finally stated, stopping, throwing up his hands. "What do you want from me? I can't win with you. I have to leave, and you don't want me to go. I get it, but I still have to go. You're attitude and reluctance to help me isn't doing anything but annoying both of us."

"I'm allowed to be upset!" she retorted.

"I get it!" he responded, stopping at the box he had left near the front door, "You're upset! Fine, be upset. Just be upset *and* help!"

"How is this not bothering you?" she demanded.

Slumping his shoulders towards the box he had just bent down to lift, Paul placed his hands on the edges of the box. He succumbed to what he realized would be an argumentative discussion that would prohibit him from getting any more work done for the time being.

"I don't have a choice, Danielle," he said evenly. "I have a job I am starting in the morning – a job you knew about months ago."

"I know," she repsonded, elongating the last part of the phrase enough to turn it into an almost whine.

"Well if you know," he began, but Danielle cut him off before he could finish.

"I know," she retorted, "but you don't even seem the least bit upset! How is this not bothering you!"

Paul stood up straight, sighing and forgetting about the box at his feet for the moment. "It's not bothering me, because it didn't seem to be bothering you. You've been fine these last two days. In fact, you've been more than fine. You've been so busy doing work I almost thought you had forgotten that I was leaving."

"Forgotten?" she gasped. "How could I forget that you're leaving me?"

"I'm not leaving you!" Paul almost cried.

"But you're going to Albany, and I don't know when I'm going to see you again," she complained.

"You can come out this weekend." Paul responded. That seemed like the logical response.

Danielle crossed her arms and raised her eyebrows in a way that made Paul realize he had just stepped into a trap. "Rachel's wedding's this weekend, or did you forget already?"

Paul sighed again and then closed his eyes, this time because he knew more inevitable fighting was about to unleash itself as the result of his response.

"You forgot!" Danielle cried. "But you promised you would come!"

"I can't," Paul responded, shrugging. "It's my first week at the office and I already know I'm going to be working this weekend as a result. They gave me these last two days off so I could move, but because I stayed here there's a list of things I'm going to have to do this weekend."

"*You're not coming?*" Danielle cried, almost screaching in her response.

Paul could see it in her face that everything had just shattered around her.

"I can't go to this wedding alone. You can't *not* come to this wedding. It's Rachel's wedding. You promised you would be there."

"I'm sorry, Danielle. I can't. I can't make it."

"But you promised!" she cried.

"There's nothing I can do, Danielle. I have to work."

"*All weekend?*" she demanded.

"I don't know, hunny. But even if it's not *all* weekend, the drive alone is too long that I can't promise to make it."

Danielle broke down crying, "Oh my God, Paul. What the hell is happening to us?"

Danielle's sudden crying startled Paul. Granted they were arguing, but this was not such a monumentous obstacle that it would have warranted crying, at least not by Paul's standards.

"What do you mean, 'What's happening to us'? What's wrong, Danielle? Why are you crying?" Paul did not know whether to be concerned or confused.

"Just what I said," she muttered between now steady sobs. "What's happening to us? Look at us, Paul, just look at us. You're leaving again, and I have no idea what we're supposed to do about *us*. This is like the worst déjà vu ever."

"What are you talking about?" Paul asked, requiring some help to get back aboard the Danielle-thought-process train.

"I don't want you to go," Danielle managed, finally, staring at Paul with pleading eyes. "I don't want us to break again like we did all those years ago. I don't want to lose you."

"You're not losing me, and we're not breaking. I'm going to Albany, Danielle, not China. I'll still talk to you all the time and see you. Calm down."

Danielle just cried quietly where she stood. She wanted to scream out *I love you; don't go. Stay with me, and we'll figure it out. I can't lose you again, and I can't go through what we went through all those years ago just to make it work. I can't. Please don't go*, but she couldn't. She just stood immobilized again by fear.

Paul stepped closer and held her shoulders. He could see she was hurting inside, but he truly did not know how to find her in her thoughts. She looked lost, and he did not know how to help. He answered the only way he knew how and said what he thought she wanted to hear.

"Come with me," he said.

She looked him square in the eyes, her face aching in a way that suggested the words had somehow torn her in two.

"I mean it," he continued, hoping his reassurance was the glue she needed to piece herself back together. "Come with me. We can figure it out in Albany. I don't care that you don't have a job there yet. We'll be fine for a while, and we'll be together. We'll just make it work. Come with me."

But everything Danielle knew was working against her. Years of experience and practice had told her that rash decision-making led to disaster, and if she left now just because it hurt to see him go, that would fall under the "rash decision-making" category. Discipline and logic were safe, and emotional moments made for poor decisions. That had been her training. That is what she had learned in three years of lawschool. In fact, that was her job. That is how she defined herself. To go against that would defy everything she had come to believe about the world and understand about herself.

However, nothing about this moment was rational. It did not make any sense to her that she could be so frozen by fear outwardly and yet be screaming inwardly, that her heart could hurt as much as it did just to see him leave yet still beat perfectly enough for her to survive. She could not comprehend how every part of her wanted to cling to him and be with him despite all the rustling in her brain over the pros and cons of her choosing to either stay in Boston or agree to move to Albany. How was it she could fast forward through so many scenarios in her head, so many weeks and months out into the future and only have passed over mere seconds of reality? What part of any of that made sense?

But while Danielle's brain slaved over scenarios, silence was all that Paul heard. Silence and the panic look behind her eyes were the answers that Paul understood. Her response to his answer had been silence, and silence, to Paul, was a "no." She did not want to come with him to Albany.

Denied, Paul released his hands from Danielle's shoulders. He reached down for his keys and then lifted the heavy box of clothing up off the ground, holding onto the only tangible thing he had left at the moment, broken from Danielle's silent rejection. He could only offer so much, only push so far, and only wait so long. If she wanted to stay in Boston, then she would, and he knew changing her mind was as futile as praying for rain in the desert. Her silence had been his answer. He could not make her come, and he could not pretend any longer. His work was now in Albany, but he had hoped his life would not have had to be left behind in Boston. Yet, here he was, grasping the last bit of his stuff and walking away from the last five years of his life.

He paused at the elevator to look back at Danielle, wanting her to be by his side, wanting her to choose him, choose *them*. But there she stood, crying in the doorway, unmoved and unchanged from when he had released her from his grasp.

The doors to the elevator closed behind him, and he closed his eyes and sighed. He knew he could only do so much. Eventually she had to make up her own mind.

On the other end of the closing elevator doors, Danielle gasped in pain. Inside she screamed *Wait!* and in her mind she ran after him, but in reality she stood immobilized, a statue in her now very empty apartment.

Suddenly, she crumbled to the ground and continued to cry from a place deep in her heart.

Chapter 17 - One Day Left

Rachel's house was a frenzied mess of receipts, shoes, boxed gifts, and the rustlings of people. It was the Friday before the wedding, the day of the rehearsal, and, of course, Rachel was running late. Her parents and her in-laws were consolidating gifts, Charles was packing his suitcase in his room and away from the women in the front hall, and Rachel was running between finishing up her hair and makeup in the bathroom and talking to the reception hall's event coordinator over last minute head counts and minor detail specifications. In fact, Rachel was so distracted and preoccupied with everything that even the littlest tasks seemed challenging. Putting on shoes, for example, was a struggle as the silver strap did not seem to want to maneuver itself around Rachel's left heel properly. Things were clearly chaotic.

Suddenly, Rachel realized that these next two days were going to be nothing short of a whirlwind of a wedding blur. She quickly thanked the wedding gods for photographers and bridesmaids, as they would help her throughout the day and ensure she could reflect on the anticipated perfection in the days to come. She even found herself momentarily relieved that her mother-in-law had taken the reigns on the flower arrangements, because it was one less thing she would have to manage on a day that was supposd to be her personal celebration of perfection and womanly success. She also secretly and quickly prayed that the flowers were not completely hideous. Her mother-in-law had never fully appreciated her choice of color scheme, and she feared her new flowers would somehow be speckled purple or pink or something. However, she also no longer had to worry about making that phone call, so after a quick silent prayer to the flower gods, the thoughts of flowers evaporated from her mind.

She had more immediate obstacles to tackle, like the rehearsal dinner and tonight's singledom.

Charles had agreed to stay in a hotel room the night before the wedding in order to keep with the tradition of not seeing the bride before the ceremony. Rachel had refused to stay at her parent's place as all of the hair, nail, and makeup appointments were within only a few miles of their place in the city. She had insisted she needed her own bed and to not have to rummage through a suitcase in order to ensure everything worked smoothly on her wedding day, so Charles had relinquished himself to a hotel. He was finishing up the last bits of packing when his parents called from the front hall saying it was time to leave. He sauntered into the bathroom to relay the message to Rachel, who was still curling her hair.

Charles returned to the front hall with a message that Rachel would still be a while, and Rachel's parents agreed to stay behind and take her to the church themselves if Charles and his parents wanted to head over and get things started. Rachel seemed oblivious to the conversation taking place down the long hallway. However, when she heard the front door close she bolted out of the bathroom, almost pulling her blond hair out with the hot curling iron, and yanked the chord out of the socket instead of laying the curling iron on the marble counter top.

"Where are they going?" she demanded.

Her mother casually looked at her daughter's frantic face and responded, "They've headed to the church. Come on, hunny, we need to get going."

"But I'm not ready!" Rachel cried, wide-eyed and pointing to her currect state of dress. She had barely applied her makeup, let alone finshed curling her hair.

"Well, then, you need to finish quickly. We were supposed to be there ten minutes ago."

Rachel's sigh could have been heard by the neighbors if the door had been even the slightest bit ajar. Her parents' insistence on keeping to the schedule was neither helping to calm her nor allowing her to enjoy the moment.

"Stop rushing me. This is my wedding."

"Rehearsal dinner," her dad started, but his wife shot him a look that prevented him from continuing with his clarification.

"Well, then, go without me," Rachel replied, shaking her hands and the curling iron in the air as she ran back into the bathroom.

"Rachel, we're leaving in five minutes. You need to be ready," her mother finished, calling after her calmly but with finality. Being late did not uphold any of the standards she had taught her daughter.

Rachel, feeling her mom's invisible push to keep to the schedule, threw the curling iron into the basket under the sink, put on only one more quick swipe of lipstick, and ran to grab a black cartigan from the closet as she feared her sleeveless dress might not be warm-enough in the air-conditioned restaurant later that evening. In her rushed momentum, she dropped the cartigan from the hanger onto a pile of Charles' boxer shorts. As she yanked it off the pile, she heard a light scraping on the floor. Not knowing what it might be, she bent down for a closer look. A single Trojan condom sat inside the sole of one of Charles' shoes.

Confused, Rachel stopped. She stared at the condom for a moment and then slowly bent down to pick it up. The green square read, "Twisted Pleasure," and Rachel moved her eyes slowly from the shoe to the pile of boxers, her hand reaching out slowly and automatically to sift through the boxers that were still on the shelf. There was nothing else there, just boxers. No box. No receipt. No other single squares. Just boxers. Rachel twisted her own brain to think about anything other than the "What?" that kept passing through her head.

"Let's go, Rachel," Rachel's mom shouted from the hallway, shaking Rachel back to reality. Rachel slipped the condom into her bra for safe keeping until she could figure out what to do with it. She and Charles and never used that kind of condom before, although they did use them semi-frequently since she only half-trusted birth control. However, they were more of an "Ultra Thin" kind of a couple. Were these new for their honeymoon? But why would there have only been one? And why would it have been in between boxers?

"Rachel!" This time it was her father. It was safe to assume her parents were losing patience when her father chimed in. Rachel closed the closet doors and half pretended to run down the hallway. She was not about to mess up her hair now, just to be a few minutes faster, but she also knew they probably did need to leave.

Rachel tapped her fingers against her purse as she and her parents walked out to the car. Twisted Pleasure?

The church bells chimed six when Rachel and her parents finally arrived. They were a half hour late, and everyone was already inside practicing the line up and walk down the aisle. The men already stood at the alter, Charles' eldest brother, his Best Man and first in line, was followed by the second brother and the rest of Charles' friends. The women entered in reverse order. Chelsea, the Maid of Honor, was last.

While waiting in the hall to practice the procession, Rachel leaned into Chelsea.

"Can I ask you something?" she whispered.

Chelsea glanced to her right, turning her ear towards Rachel without fully turning her head.

"Yeah, Rach, what's up?"

Rachel took notice that there was still another bridesmaid ahead of Chelsea and decided to ask lightly, "How, um, how was everything before I got here?"

"Fine," Chelsea replied confused but happy to oblige. "Everything was great. I'm just glad you're here because we need you to finish practicing."

"Right," Rachel stated, nodding her head once and playing with the ribbons of her practice bouquet, backing off from Chelsea and back into line.

A few pauses later, Lauren started down the aisle. Rachel glanced around to ensure it was just Chelsea and her now and leaned back into Chelsea's right ear.

"Okay, that really wasn't my question."

Chelsea turned her head again towards Rachel. "Okay?"

"What do you do when, um," Rachel started, "well, um, how do you," but she fumbled over how to say what she wanted to say correctly. She quickly reached down the left side of her bra and pulled out the condom, taping Chelsea on the right shoulder with it's corner.

Feeling the scratching tap, Chelsea's eyes looked downward towards her shoulder and eyed the green square. Upon seeing it, she let out a small giggle.

"What is that, Rach?" Chelsea chuckled, "I don't have any use for it, but thank you."

Rachel shook her head quickly, "No, Chelsea. I found – I – they were in Charles' boxers."

Chelsea laughed a little harder, "I bet they were."

Chelsea noticed the spacing between her and the bridesmaid in front of her and started her slow walk down the aisle, laughing under her breath at the green condom square.

Rachel did a double take in trying to say something to Chelsea and then realized Chelsea was already halfway to the first pew, and therefore Rachel had lost her chance to explain. She clearly had not communicated her concern well enough to Chelsea because Chelsea's reaction was the opposite of what she had intended. Her failure to communicate her concern clearly just created more angst.

Normally she dealt with her own issues privately, but this one was becoming too big for her to keep to herself.

Taking a deep breath, she quickly put the condom back in her bra and then straightened her hair and bouquet before her own practice walk down the aisle.

They'd have to talk after the rehearsal.

The Ruth Chris steakhouse in downtown Boston bustled with activity when the wedding party arrived for their rehearsal dinner. They had a reserved section in the back corner, and they entered to find wine bottles awaiting them.

Rachel, greatly relieved the rehearsal at the church had gone smoothly and trouble free, looked forward to a nice dinner before retreating back to her own bed for as much sleep as she could muster. Initially she had intended on a long bath and glass of champagne prior to bed to end what she had foreseen as an evening of perfection, but now her head swarmed with wedding plans and condom questions. Although some of the stress was now abated, as she had finished with the church portion of the rehearsal, much remained. She wondered if she would even get much sleep at all, given her current worries.

Seeing an opportunity to steal away to the bathroom with Chelsea to talk, Rachel leaned over to Chelsea and asked if she would come with her. She needed to clear her head.

"You okay?" Chelsea asked on their way to the ladies' room. Rachel seemed distant, which confused Chelsea greatly. So much momentum had been building for this day that Chelsea had almost completely expected Rachel to be in full-on Rachel mode for the next forty-eight hours. Instead, she seemed to be merely going through the motions, which was clearly not the normal demeanor for Chelsea's best friend.

"I don't know," Rachel stated, making note that they were not the only two in the bathroom at the moment and postponed the condom question. She smiled lightly instead and said, "Just a lot going on."

"Definitely," Chelsea nodded. "But this is what you've been wanting for so long! It's going to be beautiful, Rachel. Don't worry. It'll work out fine."

Rachel pretended to apply more lipstick while the other woman in the bathroom finished drying her hands before leaving. She eyed the doorway for a moment to ensure no one else was about to enter.

Chelsea took note of Rachel's sideways glance. When she asked what was wrong, Rachel took one more cautionary sideways glance and then proceeded to pull out the green condom square again. Laughing again, Chelsea asked point-blank what on earth Rachel was doing hiding a condom in her bra.

"I found it," Rachel stated.

Chelsea scrunched her face slightly. "Ew. Then throw it away."

Rachel shook her head quickly, "No, Chelsea, not like that. I found it in one of Charles' shoes. In my haste earlier I'd dropped my cartigan on his pile of boxers. When I grabbed it I heard this scraping noise. It must have fallen out of his boxers and caused the noise because I found this in his shoe."

"And?" Chelsea asked.

"And," Rachel insisted, "I've never seen these before, Chels. We don't use," she started, making a face as she glanced down at the writing on the condom, "'Twisted Pleasure.' Ever."

Staring back blankly, Chelsea suddenly understood why Rachel was so upset.

"Oh," Chelsea started and then stopped. A different condom threw up red flags and thoughts of another woman, but how did Chelsea say that to her friend who was less than twenty-four hours from being married?

Playing it safe, Chelsea started, "I don't know what to tell you, Rach. I mean, do you and Charles even use condoms?"

"Well, yeah, usually," Rachel responded. "I don't want to get pregnant yet."

Shrugging, Chelsea tried to stay away from her worst fear and responded, "Well, then maybe that's why you found them. Maybe he picked up a different box this time?"

Rachel retorted in disbelief, "After three years, he's now picking out a different kind?"

Suddenly the door to the bathroom swung open and Rachel scrambled to put the condom away in her purse before it was noticed by the new bathroom visitor.

Chelsea lowered her voice and responded as generically as possible, wondering, "They've always been the same?"

Rachel's frustrations echoed in her stance and voice, even though she tried to conceal them now that a stranger had entered their conversation.

"Well, no, not *always*, but not," she finished glancing down at her purse intending for her eyes to say "those" for her.

Chelsea understood but had no helpful response. She had no intention of telling her friend right now that the answer could be another woman.

"I don't know, Rach. I mean, it could be a surprise for tomorrow?"

"Wouldn't there have been more then?" Rachel inquired, cutting her off.

"Maybe there are? Maybe that one just fell out?" Chelsea offered meakly, but both she and Rachel knew that that was not what Rachel was thinking either. Although Rachel had wanted to shake it off and go home to the champagne and a bubble bath evening she had planned for herself, the thought of the red wine and late night from a few months prior stained her brain. She remembered his phone being off and him sneaking home only after she'd fallen asleep. Were these two somehow connected? Was Charles seeing another woman, or was this her mind playing tricks on her?

Rachel shook her head at Chelsea's comment. "Maybe," was all she replied. She wanted so badly to be married. She had always wanted it, to have her own family and complete what she saw as the female symbol of success. She loved Charles so much and loved the life they were making with one another that she wondered if this doubt was nothing more than self-sabotage. People did that, right? Created notions of things that weren't there at all? Maybe she was afraid she was finally going to be happy, and this was her mind's way of defending itself?

But the more she thought through that logic, the stupider it seemed. That was not logic at all. That was a pre-wedding meltdown, and she was not about to break down this close to her wedding.

She looked at herself squarely through the bathroom's mirror. She set her shoulders and decided right there that she was going to go back out to the dinner party and not think about it. She was not going to sabotage herself less than twenty-four hours before her own wedding. Chelsea was right. They were just a surprise for the wedding night and honeymoon, and one had simply fallen out. It was that simple, or, well, she was going to be sure it stayed that simple.

Chelsea could see the thought process unfolding on Rachel's face and knew instantly that she was recentering herself for wedding mode. Although she did not know how exactly to react to what Rachel had said, she knew she felt an inkling of sadness for her best friend. That was a lot to handle so close to a wedding, and she knew Rachel's determination to be married out-ranked many other factors. Rachel had been looking forward to this day since before they scrapbooked those pictures together in college, and she knew that in Rachel's mind, twenty-seven was starting to border on "old." Chelsea feared that if Rachel's doubts did hold any water that they would be dried up by the mere fact that Rachel did not want to wait any longer to be a wife. Right or wrong, Rachel's mind was made up and she would work to forget the entire condom conversation.

Chelsea felt her phone vibrate in her purse. She pulled it out and noticed a text from Danielle, but she decided she would respond to it later. She had not heard from Danielle all week, and knowing that Paul had left only days before made her wonder just how Danielle had been holding up. The text of, "Call me later?" was as uninformative as Danielle's silence all week had been, but she would have to wait until after dinner to call.

Turning around, Rachel smiled at Chelsea and motioned to the door, just as another person entered the bathroom. Rachel clutched her purse securely, walking out of the bathroom in front of Chelsea, her eyes set on her new goal. Condom away and hoping to be forgotten, the night was now wide open for steak, family, and one last night of being a "Ms."

Chapter 18 – Old Fires Rising

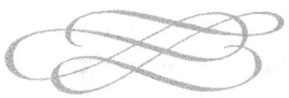

As Chelsea said goodbye to Rachel for the evening, she got in her car and reached for her phone and dialed Danielle's number. The night was winding down, and she hoped Danielle would be awake. It was almost 10.00 p.m., and she was hoping Danielle would pick up the phone.

Much to her delight, Danielle answered almost immediately. In fact, Danielle had spent so much of her night stewing, alone, on her porch, that she was relieved that Chelsea's phone call momentarily saved her from her own internal battle.

"Hi!" Chelsea stated, smiling, relieved she had not waited too long to return her friend's phone call. The drive home was the perfect opportunity to talk to Danielle.

Danielle was equally relieved, although somewhat less smiley, and her emotional state came through in her tone.

Chelsea inquired, "What's up?"

Danielle shook her head and replied, "Nothing." She wanted to know how the rehearsal dinner had gone before bringing to light her own frustrations. Delving into detail, Chelsea brought Danielle up to speed on the ins and outs of the wedding and how things were looking for tomorrow. She even divulged the story of the green condom square, to which Danielle pleasantly found herself laughing for the first time all week.

"That is sad though," Danielle finally admitted, after her laughter ceased. "But I don't know if it surprises me. That girl wants so badly to be married. She always has, and she now has a man who can provide her with a comfortable life, money, and the things she'd always talked about. I can't see her giving it up for something that's only suspicion."

"Well, would you?" Chelsea inquired, playing devil's advocate. "Would you call it off when there's no hard evidence to go on other than suspicion, or would you do what she's doing?"

Danielle paused, blankly shaking her head, "I don't know. I don't know what I would do, but I'm not Rachel. She and I do things differently, and I'm also not in her position. I mean, I don't know what Charles is doing or not doing, but I know Paul's not cheating on me."

Chelsea smiled knowingly and sympathetically, "But he left this week, didn't he?"

Danielle tapped her finger on her beer bottle and nodded, "Yup. Tuesday night. Been gone since."

"How are you doing?"

Danielle let out a long sigh, "I don't know. I'm a mess right now. I'm on like my third beer, I've been sitting here on the porch, and I can't stop fidgeting or thinking."

"Have you talked to him at all?"

"Kind of?" Danielle answered, although she sort of posed the question to herself. "He called when he arrived in Albany on Tuesday night, but we got into a fight before he left, and as much as we may want to talk to one another, it's really awkward. I don't know what to say, and I think he's in the same boat."

"Fight? What happened?"

"He left, and I stayed. That's about what happened. I was an emotional wreck, and he didn't think I had a right to be."

Chelsea laughed, disbelieving, "What did he think, you were going to be cheering him off? Of course you were upset."

Danielle sighed again, "That's what I said, but he said I had been so even-keeled all week that my sudden emotional upheaval was both unforeseen and unnecessary. But, I think he was more frustrated that I didn't go with him."

"I didn't know you were thinking about going," Chelsea admitted. "You had mentioned looking for work out there, but that was about as far as it ever went."

Danielle took another sip of beer before continuing, "And it was. I asked around briefly, but when no one at the firm had any real or immediate connections to anyone in Albany, I stopped. I wasn't going to push for leads that didn't exist, and I became so tied up in the case we were working on that it was suddenly the end of August, and I was still at square one. I wasn't going to up and move when I had nowhere to go."

"Did you tell him that?" Chelsea wondered.

"Eh, kinda."

"Meaning?"

"Meaning no. I didn't really tell him much. We never really talked about it because talking about something with no answers became more of a frustration than a productive conversation, so we just didn't talk about it."

Chelsea could see why Danielle was so frustrated. She had backed herself into a corner without an escape route. Of course she was not going to leave for Albany without a job, but it seemed she had also not really given herself a chance to find one either.

Feeling badly for her friend, Chelsea said she was sorry and then stopped. She was at a loss for what else to say.

Danielle took over the silence, "I just don't know what to do. I still don't know why he got so mad, and it's bothering me Everything is so awkward as a result."

Suddenly, Chelsea found herself confused.

"Wait," she asked, "was he the only one mad?"

"Well, I mean," Danielle explained, "he was definitely mad at me."

"What about you? I thought you just said you were frustrated, too?"

"Well, yeah, I mean, I was a mess. I still am, but I'm more annoyed that he's mad at me. I don't seriously know what he was so mad about or what he wanted me to have done. He was the one that left."

Chelsea started to say something and then stopped herself in her tracks. She actually found herself becoming frustrated with her friend. How was it Danielle could not see that the source of Paul's frustration was partially Danielle? Of course he was mad. Shit, Chelsea herself would have been mad, too. Actually, Chelsea was starting to get mad just from Danielle's last comment. Danielle clearly did not see how she was standing in her own way.

Instantly, and with that last thought, Chelsea nearly slammed on her brakes in digust. She quickly pulled onto a side street and parked momentarily so as to prevent herself from causing an accident.

Oh my God, she thought.

Instantly her brain sifted through past conversations. Both Rachel and her mother flowed through her head like a foggy poison. Despite how unwanted some of their comments in the past had been, they were the ones now pushing themselves to the forefront of Chelsea's mind. Their words echoed, and Chelsea could not help but realize they rang true. Danielle, as Rachel had pointed out so bluntly that one morning in the hotel room, was standing in her own damn way. She could not help but feel that Danielle held blame for her current situation as a result. Then she thought of her mother, and it was the opinion of her mother, the truth of that opinion, that burned Chelsea the most. She hated that she found herself agreeing with her mother.

Damnit, Mom, Chelsea thought. She did not like the idea of agreeing with a viewpoint she saw as completely backwards, but she also could not run from the realization that she felt it fit so perfectly into the situation Danielle faced. Danielle had so many options, but she refused to take or even seemingly consider them. Maybe she currently did not have the perfect job lined up, but maybe she could have found *something* in Albany. Instead she had nothing to go to in Albany, and she used that excuse as her entire reason for staying. Sure Albany wasn't Boston, but maybe Albany could end up being great because that was where her life was now, or, well, at least the other half of her life. Nothing was perfect all the time, and Danielle was kidding herself if she thought she could have it all, all the time.

Danielle realized that Chelsea's silence on the other end of the phone probably was not a pause for good thoughts. When she inquired as to what Chelsea was thinking, Chelsea tried to tread slowly. She was relieved Danielle had finally called and felt comfortable talking to her. She did not want to end communications yet by causing Danielle to become defensive, but she also could not bring herself to sit by idly while Danielle pretended she was the victim.

"It's just," Chelsea started, "look, Danielle, I know you're really upset. I know. I can hear it in your voice, and I think I would be too if I were in your shoes. Your boyfriend just left indefinitely, and you feel like you're at a dead end with nowhere to go from here."

"I know, right?" Danielle agreed.

"It's just," Chelsea sighed, "I feel like you created your own dead-end, Danielle."

There was a brief pause on the other end of the phone before Danielle responded, "What do you mean, 'created my own dead-end'?"

"Danielle, I had this really awkward conversation with my mom a few weeks back or so, after she pulled Terry into an attempted blind dinner date. Do you remember that?"

"Yeah," Danielle responded, no idea where Chelsea was going with her story.

"When I went back to the house the week after that fiasco, she gave me this disappointed lecture about women and society, etc, etc. Did I ever tell you about that?" Chelsea asked, half hoping she would not have to explain further. The idea alone made her head hurt, but now, having to possibly explain how she saw her mother's theories playing out in Danielle's life made her almost nauseated. It would just be easier if Danielle already knew the story.

But she didn't. Her "no" response made Chelsea readjust and breathe in slowly to calm her nerves before relaying to her friend information she had initially loathed. She had already dealt with one friend's dilemma today. It seemed to be her day for interventions, and Danielle was just next on the list.

"Okay, well, do you remember when you guys came over to my hotel room and the three of us ended up fighting over stuff that Rachel said about you and Paul."

"I try not to remember that, thank you," Danielle retorted.

"All right, but bear with me for a minute, okay?"

The silence on the other end of the phone was enough of an agreement to keep Chelsea going.

"Well, I was stunned that Rachel said what she said to you about how you're getting in your own way. I know she tends to deflect issues away from her. However, she's not usually so blunt, and it shocked me that she said that to you, point-blank. I tried to forget about it, but when I went home my mom hit me with one of her, 'life lessons in being a woman,' talks. She kept saying how she was disappointed in me that I had caused such a scene at the restaurant because it made me look like the bad guy whether that had been my intention or not. She went on to to say that even beyond the restaurant incident, women in society tend to be blamed for things that happen to them."

"I don't –" Danielle started but was cut-off by Chelsea before she could finish her thought.

"Just, let me finish. Anyway, I thought my mother was crazy, like straight nutso, and I dismissed her rantings as old-fashioned and archaic. There was no way that what she was stating was anywhere close to being right. That would be absurd. Did she not remember the feminist movement? Honestly…but I'm starting to think, now, that maybe she wasn't all wrong either."

Danielle sat on the other end of the phone wondering what any of this had to do with her. "What are you trying to say, Chelsea?"

"I'm just saying that I know you love what you do, Danielle. I do. You have worked so hard to get your degree, and you're a great lawyer. But if you had such a difficult time seeing Paul leave, maybe you love Paul more than you'd like to admit."

"Of course I love Paul," Danielle agreed. "That was never the issue."

"Then why are you still here?" Chelsea questioned. "If you love him that much and you've been together this long, why are you still here in Boston? I'm not saying that Rachel or my mom are always right, but maybe with this they are. Maybe you are standing in your own way, Danielle. Maybe, this time, you choose Paul. Putting up a wall that only lets you choose your career might not be the answer this time. I hate that they might be right about this, but you only have yourself to blame if you really want to be with Paul and you're not."

Silence. The receiver on both ends screamed with endless silence. Chelsea dared not say more at the moment as she knew her words probably needed to settle, and Danielle tapped her beer against the table in annoyance.

You've got to be kidding, Danielle thought. I'm here calling my friend because I'm an emotional mess, and she turns around and tells me I'm to blame for it?

The hand around the phone tightened as Danielle tried to siphon her anger away from her mouth so as to not blow up at her friend, but it only half worked.

"Are you kidding me, Chelsea?" Danielle threw through the phone. "I called because I needed your help, not because I wanted to be scolded, and yet here we are. You're telling me I'm the idiot to blame for the mess I'm in."

Chelsea, understanding her friend's anger, said calmly, "Danielle, I'm not here to scold you. I was just trying to help. I don't like seeing you upset, but I don't want you to put yourself into a bind that's not necessary. Don't get mad at me."

"What do you want from me, Chels? I don't know what to do; I'm a mess, and I'm heading to a wedding tomorrow *alone*, having never thought I would be in this position."

Chelsea shook her head, "I don't know. I don't know what to –" and then Chelsea stopped herself. She had an idea. She would call Stacy from work and see if she could get herself to the wedding tomorrow to be Danielle's "date." Stacy could use a night out, Danielle liked her the few times they'd met in the past, and Chelsea would also not have to deal with her scary blind date alone! It would be perfect, so long as she could finagle actually getting Stacy there.

"You sure Paul's not coming back tomorrow?" Chelsea asked.

Danielle half laughed, "Yeah. Not at all."

"Okay, well, don't worry. I'll see you tomorrow at the wedding, and we'll have a great time. You'll see."

The girls said their goodbyes. Chelsea headed home to get what little sleep she could manage before waking early in the morning to phone Stacy. Danielle inhaled the last of her beer before retiring for the night and possibly crying herself to sleep for the fourth night in a row. She was still in a daze from what Chelsea had said, and she wanted to sleep it off and start fresh in the morning. She still could not believe Chelsea had pointed the finger back at her, suggesting that all she faced she had somehow brought on herself. It was absurd, and she refused to deal with it at the moment. Instead she would sleep and revisit it all tomorrow.

She needed a plan, but right now it was just better to sleep. She would worry about a plan tomorrow.

Chapter 19 - To a Wedding We Go

Chelsea rose early Saturday morning, having not slept well for fear she would oversleep and miss her alarm. She lazily threw on a pair of linen shorts, a burgundy tank and a short sleeve camisole before heading downstairs to call Stacy. She wanted to put in the request for Stacy to come to the wedding before she was in full Maid of Honor mode, and she had to be at Rachel's by 8:00 a.m. Luckily, since she was getting her hair, makeup, and nails done with the rest of the bridal party today, she was able to forego all the necessary morning primping she would normally do.

It was nearly 7:30 a.m. when she finally made her way downstairs. Her mother had already made a pot of coffee, and both she and Tony were sitting watching the morning news. Chelsea was surprised the fighting ritual had not yet begun, and she just prayed she would be out of the house before it was in full swing.

Tina noticed Chelsea enter and did not miss a beat before speaking to her daugther.

"You have a lot going on today," she mentioned.

"Yup," Chelsea returned, staying as positive as possible, searching for her phone. She needed to call Stacy soon to ensure she had enough time to find a sitter or alternate baby-watching options if she was going to be able to come to the wedding today, or at least the reception if nothing else.

"Don't forget deodorant and perfume. It's hot out there, and we don't need you smelling badly since you'll be on the go all day," her mom stated.

Chelsea rolled her eyes and dialed Stacy's number. The voicemail picked up and Chelsea headed towards the counter to grab a banana while leaving a message, hoping the noise would drown out her voice a tinge because she really did not want her mother to start asking questions. Chelsea told Stacy to call her back when she had a moment and that she was inviting her to the wedding as her date and hoped she could make it. She fibbed, not wanting to divulge all the details of Paul and Danielle over voicemail. She figured there would be an extra seat regardless of whose date Stacy was, so she might as well let Stacy think she was her date for now.

"What are you doing? You already have a date," her mom insisted sternly after eavesdropping on the conversation.

Chelsea's eyes widened in annoyance for she did not have the patience for her mother at that moment. Plus, she realized she had to leave now if she wanted to reach Rachel's in time, so she picked up her pace in the house.

"Mom, whatever. I know. Don't worry about it," Chelsea responded.

"Don't 'whatever' me, young lady. I worked hard to get you this date, and I will not have you embarrass me."

"Mom!" Chelsea responded defensively, spit-firing the cliff note version to her mother. "Oh my God, it's not for me, okay? Paul can't make it to the wedding so I'm trying to get Stacy there to help keep Danielle company since I'll be with the bridal party all day. Calm down."

"Paul can't come?" Her mother's concern had suddenly switched gears. "Did something happen with them?"

Chelsea took a bite of her banana before responding. "No. He's moved to Albany for work and can't make this weekend. Danielle's having a hard time with it."

"She didn't go with him?" she wondered.

"No."

"No, like not yet, no? Or no, like not at all, no?"

"Like, just no. She doesn't know what she wants or what she should do yet. She's just having a hard time with it," Chelsea answered, taking another bite of the banana, hoping the last statement would end the conversation.

"That girl's going to ruin the best thing she ever had," her mom stated, turning back around in her chair to watch the TV. "Just wait. She's too stubborn to realize she's standing in her own way."

Flashbacks from last night's conversation and Rachel's attacking words from weeks ago flashed in Chelsea's mind, and she shook her head to dismiss them. She would not let her mother get the best of her today as she needed to remain positive in order to make it through this marathon of a day successfully.

"Well, just don't you forget about your date tonight," her mom reiterated. "He's a nice boy."

Chelsea heard her phone beep and saw a text from Stacy asking what Chelsea wanted. Chelsea dismissed her mom with a simple, "Okay, Mom," while she typed back the basic details to Stacy, hoping Stacy would be able to make coming to the wedding work. Upon hitting the send button, Chelsea checked the clock, saw it was 7:41 a.m., and then went into overdrive mode. She needed to leave, and she needed to leave now.

Inhaling the last of the banana, she grabbed the phone in the hand with the banana peel and used her other hand to grab her purse from the counter. She threw open the door to the garbage can to throw away the banana peel, and in her haste simultaneously tossed in her phone. Cursing under her breath, Chelsea put her purse on the counter to dive into the garbage for her phone, which had unfortunately made its way towards the bottom of the can. Moving aside crumbs and boxes and half eaten sandwiches, Chelsea made a face of disgust, disbelieving that she could be wrist deep in garbage before 8:00 a.m.

That's a really bad metaphor, she thought. This better be the only "garbage" I have to sift through today.

Finding her phone, she grabbed it and then let the pile of garbage fall back where it had been originally. As she did so, the flutter of something with a deep blue color against a white corner caught her eye. Looking more closely, she saw the letters CUNY and realized it was a letter from CUNY Graduate School.

The graduate school? she wondered. But why would it be in the garbage?

Diving a little further into the muck, she pulled out what ended up being four torn pieces of an envelope with paper inside. And, as it turned out, it wasn't a small envelope either. The pieces aligned themselves into a large, 8.5"x11" envelope and included a decent stack of papers hiding within.

Rage boiled inside Chelsea's chest. Without even realizing it, she blurted out the words "Mom" and "What" before she caught herself and made herself be quiet again.

Not fully turning around, her mother simply shouted back at Chelsea, asking what she wanted. Chelsea responded with a mere, "Nothing," and proceeded to stuff the paper squares in her purse. She would look at them later. Alone. Without her mother.

She said goodbye to her family and bolted out the door. Her father responded simply, and her mother shouted something about meeting her date somewhere, but Chelsea had stopped listening. She had places to be.

Rachel awaited her friend outside her condo building. The early morning sun kissed her skin, and she felt a warm hug from the morning air. She was adorned in diamond and pearl earrings, a pearl necklace, oversized Gucci sunglasses, and a basic, back-zip, blue linen dress. In her left hand she held a small, Vera Bradley, blue paisley duffle carrying her jewelry for the wedding, shoes, makeup for touch-ups, and lingerie for the night. Her left hand clutched one of the two large Tumi suitcases she had packed. This one held clothes for the honeymoon, and the one not with her held a combination of Charles and her clothes. That one was already on its way to the hotel. Everything was in order, and Rachel was smiling. Today was the day, and so far it was perfect.

"You look like you're in a good mood today!" Chelsea chimed, pulling up to Rachel and unlocking the doors.

Rachel lifted the suitcase into Chelsea's back seat and then climbed into the passenger side of the car, cooing lightly about how she was so excited for today and ready to start being married. She also thanked Chelsea for picking her up. They had worked through so many of the nuts and bolts for this wedding together that Rachel couldn't imagine starting such a monumental day with any other friend.

Chelsea could not help but notice how Rachel's spirits had genuinely changed overnight. She was happier, not as a mere formality or front, but genuinely happier. Upon inquiry, Rachel explained that when she had returned home, she had found a bouquet of two dozen red roses waiting for her on her doorstep with a note attached. It had been from Charles professing how, "excited he was to start their lives together," which Rachel said in a manner suggesting that those had been the exact words he had used. When Rachel took Chelsea's simple nod as a sign of disbelief, she pulled the tiny card out from her purse to show as evidence. On the card were the typed words, "Looking forward to tomorrow. I love you and will see you in the morning. Love, Charles." Chelsea smiled, noting the difference in words from the card to Rachel's recollection of the card, and then shook away her critique and congratulated her friend.

At least it was a genuine gesture on his part, Chelsea thought. She understood why Rachel's concerns had been assuaged, at least for now, and was sincerely glad to know her friend could move on with today untainted by worry. Chelsea, despite her remaining skepticism, vowed to be supportive.

Rachel also made mention that the flowers were from a company she'd never heard of before, something like the Toys R Us store, but she couldn't remember.

"Bouquets R Us?" Chelsea asked curiously.

"Yeah, I think that was it," Rachel said off-handedly. "I'd never heard of them before."

Chelsea laughed, "I work with them. They're a relatively new start-up company that we funded a year back, and they have been the neediest start-up I've ever handled, banking wise. The owner's nice though, just a handful."

Then Chelsea added, "I had no idea Charles knew them."

"Yeah, don't know," Rachel said. "Maybe that's the new flower company or something his mom went with."

"Wait, you don't know who's bringing the flowers?" Chelsea wondered, shocked. It was not like Rachel to skip such a large detail, even if she had relinquishedcommand of the flower rrangements to her mother-in-law.

Rachel threw Chelsea a look and a half laugh, "Please. After that bullshit with the pre-nup, I gave up on the flowers. Charles' mom can take care of it. I just had better not have pink and purple everywhere. If I do, I'll throw a fit. Otherwise, I don't really care."

"Wow," Chelsea responded, thoroughly impressed, "I'm proud of you."

"Yeah, well, it bothered me for a while, but then I realized that if your parents can drive you as crazy as they do, and you can find a way to get through it, then I'll find a way to get through this flower ordeal," Rachel stated, smiling at Chelsea and searching for her lipstick in her duffle.

"Oh, but could we grab coffee though?" Rachel inquired almost instantly after finding her lipstick. "There's a Drive-Thru Starbucks around the corner, and I could really go for some coffee."

"Sure," Chelsea responded, thankful Rachel changed subjects. "Do you want food, too?"

"No," Rachel said, sending Chelsea a look that suggested Chelsea had clearly missed something. "I have a dress to fit into. I don't need food."

Chelsea raised her eye brows as if to say, "Oh, of course; silly, me," and then mentioned that Rachel should go into Chelsea's purse and pull out some money while they pulled into the Starbucks' Drive-Thru.

Grabbing Chelsea's purse, Rachel's hand searched for a wallet but instead came upon torn scraps of paper. Pulling one of the scraps out of the purse, Rachel asked Chelsea what exactly she was doing with torn paper.

Chelsea, shaking her head and breathing deeply, explained to Rachel that she had found the envelope and paper scraps ripped up and submerged in the garbage can this morning. She had pulled them out in a fury, seething at the fact that her mother could be so heartless in throwing something away that was clearly not hers to throw away.

"But you've been waiting for these university responses for weeks now," Rachel noted, baffled.

"Exactly," Chelsea agreed. That fact just made the situation worse. "So I stole them back without telling her. I'll look at it later."

"But it looks official, Chels. This might be an acceptance letter or something."

"I agree. But I didn't have time to check."

As though she had just given Rachel the "Go Ahead," Rachel determined to solve the graduate school mystery while Chelsea took care of the coffee orders. How exciting it would be to uncover her friend's acceptance to graduate school. Rachel was already having a great morning, so why not keep the pace going and hopefully share good news with a friend? Plus, Rachel loved feeling needed, and helping Chlesea unravel this mystery gave her purpose and allowed her to fulfill that desire to be needed.

Once the envelope was arranged correctly, Rachel tore back the envelope itself to reveal the papers below it. Scanning quickly, she looked for a clue, a word that would explain the meaning of the letter without having to read every last word. Then, as quickly as she had started skimming the papers, the aftertaste of resentment coated her gut, flashbacks of the prenuptial agreement fiasco entering her mind. Maybe skimming was not the best idea. She refocused her attention back to the top of the paper and read the document completely and aloud.

"Dear Chelsea," Rachel began, putting on the most official voice she could muster, "Thank you for applying to the CUNY Graduate School of Journalism. After reviewing your application and portfolio, we are pleased to inform you that you have been accepted."

Rachel stopped reading. A smile of pride passed over her face, and her voice echoed her smile. She stared at Chelsea, who sat stunned in the driver's seat, her hands holding cups of coffee in mid-air. Her wide eyes met Rachel's, and both passed unspoken words of disbelief and joy to the other. Instantly, and almost fumbling the cups and spilling the coffee all over her car, Chelsea threw Rachel's cup into her hand and leaned over the console to get a better look at the torn pieces of paper that held the words Chelsea had been waiting for for weeks.

Chelsea let out a small squeal of victory, covering her mouth, and then pointed to the letter. "Oh my God. I'm accepted. Oh my God! Rachel, I'm going to CUNY!"

Horns of anger sounded from the cars behind Chelsea as Chelsea held up the line to the drive-thru pick-up window.

"Oh, shit," Chelsea said, shaking herself back to reality, placing her iced mocha coffee cup in its cup holder and putting the car back into drive. Once moving forward, she again let out a squeal of victory. She was accepted. She was going to CUNY in January.

"Chelsea, I'm so happy for you!" Rachel chimed. "We are both having such an amazing day! You're going to CUNY, and I'm getting married!"

"Yeah," Chelsea agreed, smiling widely at the latest knews. Then she started laughing, "Now I just have to tell my mother."

Stacy arrived at the wedding twenty minutes before the ceremony was due to begin. She was dressed in a short, sleeveless, brown linen dress and cute ballet flats. Her strawberry blond hair was pulled back in a quick ponytail, and a large, brown diaper bag was slung over her left shoulder. In her arms, in miniature khaki pants and a white shirt, slept baby Marcus. Stacy had not been able to find a sitter.

Chelsea met Stacy at the door. Chelsea's hair was pulled back into a braided chignon with a silver rhinestone clip along the right side which sat tucked away in the braid. She had bare feet at the moment, but adorning her body was a sky-blue, floor-length, silk dress with a low v-neck front and a long, silk bow that tied in the back. Her taned, olive skin stood out nicely against the richness of the sky-blue, and the subtle silver necklace around her neck was the perfect accent to the neckline of the dress.

Stacy looked at Chelsea and shook her head, "You look beautiful!"

Chelsea smiled and hugged Stacy, "Thanks, you do too. And thank you so much for coming!"

Stacy smiled back at Chelsea, "Thanks for the invite! I'm so sorry I couldn't find a sitter, though. It's Labor Day Weekend, and I was having the hardest time making any headway in that department."

"Oh, it's okay, Stacy. I mean, technically it's a 'no guest under 18' wedding, but whatever. I'm really not that worried about it, and if someone gives you shit for it, tell them to come talk to me," Chelsea finished, smiling at the last part of her statement.

Stacy, eased by Chelsea's insistance that having Marcus was okay, relaxed. She was happy to help Chelsea out, and, quite frankly, happy to get away from her mother for the afternoon and also not have to spend any more money on nannies. She and Mark had been unlucky at finding a full-time childcare provider, and since her mother had been hassling them about one for so long, they now paid her mother a full-time nanny income as a result, instead of putting Marcus in daycare. Stacy abhorred the idea of daycare but had additionally promised her mother that if they could not find a sitter by the end of September that Stacy would either look into working part-time or really look more closely at daycare. This had assuaged her mother enough to nanny on a full-time basis for the time being, but both knew it was not a permanent fix.

Today, though, Stacy was on her own and fine with things being that way. She was just glad she was not having to pay someone today to watch her son and that her having Marcus at the wedding was not a huge inconvenience.

Leading Stacy through the church lobby, Chelsea asked how work had been on Friday, since she had taken off to be with Rachel for the rehearsal.

"Fine. Busy. David was in, but I think that was on the mere technicality that he knew you had no chance of showing up and therefore couldn't leave the department to completely fend for itself," Stacy explained, to which Chelsea shook her head.

Stacy continued, "He was as lazy as usual, and you guys were crazy busy yesterday. I don't know if this means anything, but you got so many calls from this company called Bouquets R Us that they ended up forwarding me the calls."

Chelsea looked at Stacy, confused, "Why? I mean, they're always really needy, but what did they want?"

"I don't really know the whole story, but the woman said something about looking into another loan."

"Oh God," Chelsea started, but then stopped and looked at Stacy. "Who called?"

Stacy, feeling like she may have added more stress to Chelsea's day inserted, "I mean, I don't want to take up your time."

"No, it's fine," Chelsea replied. "Tell me."

"It was the owner, and she wants the loan for new stores, I think," Stacy stated. "But, I don't know if that means anything or not."

Chelsea thought for a moment before responding. It did make sense. Charles' mother had pull with a number of different societies in the area, and if she was using them for her son's wedding, it would only make sense that she would recommend them to others. Maybe Candice was looking to expand. That, however, just meant more hand-holding on Chelsea's part come work on Tuesday.

Oh well, Chelsea thought, no time to worry about it now.

Thanking Stacy once more for coming, Chelsea pointed to Danielle in the fifth pew on the bride's side and told Stacy that Danielle had a seat waiting for her. Chelsea had already told Danielle to expect Stacy, and although frustrated at first that Chelsea even hinted that Danielle could not handle today by herself, Danielle had secretly been relieved to have someone to sit with all day. She was still stewing over last night's conversation, but the last thing she really wanted was to be sitting alone all day. Stacy, even with the baby, would be a welcomed companion.

Once Stacy was on her way down the aisle, Chelsea ran back to the girls' dressing room to put on shoes and help Rachel tie up last minute ends before the ceremony started. Thoughts of Bouquets R Us raced around Chelsea's brain, but she did her best to push them aside for now. If she really wanted to spin through "what ifs," she'd have the entire ceremony to do so as she would be stuck at the alter on flower duty for the next thirty minutes or so. However, now was not the time.

Once back in the dressing room, Chelsea threw on her shoes and helped Rachel and her mother perfect the placement of the veil. Rachel beamed, and the mermaid-turned-ballgown dress hugged Rachel's body effortlessly. She looked beautiful, and even Chelsea could not help but smile.

"Oh, Rachel, you look amazing," Chelsea stated.

"I better!" Rachel chimed, smiling and accepting the white rose bouquet Chelsea handed her. "I wonder if he'll cry."

Chelsea shook her head and shrugged her shoulders. Then she laughed, "Do you really want your husband crying on your wedding day?"

"Once I start reading my vows, he'd better!" Rachel responded, glowing and grinning from ear to ear, as though the thought of seeing Charles cry was, itself, funny. Then, as she thought of Charles crying, she stopped laughing and continued more seriously, "That is, assuming I can get through them."

Chelsea pulled up next to Rachel and grasped her forearm in confidence. "You'll be great."

Rachel leaned over and hugged her best friend. She felt so loved.

"Ready?" Chelsea finally asked as the other bridesmaids headed out of the dressing room. It was both a serious and rhetorical question.

Rachel took in a deep breath, grasped her bouquet securely, and smiled, "More than you know."

Chapter 20 - Dinner and a Disaster

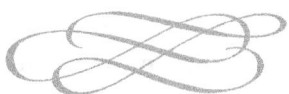

After the wedding, the party moved to the Langham Boston, which buzzed with activity. The hotel's Wilson Ballroom sounded with laughter and music as Rachel and Charles' reception started. The beautiful white, black, and sky blue, five tiered cake sat on a grand entrance table on the right side of the doorway. The tables were covered in a beautiful, white, linen tablecloth and adorned with white cushioned chairs and white napkins. A skinny, black vase sat in the middle of the table with white roses inside, and it was surrounded by a small amount of blue glass pebbles. Elegant was an understatement. The atmosphere in the ballroom was perfect, and even Rachel had to compliment her mother-in-law for the flower arrangements. Despite her initial frustration and worry, the company she had chosen to do the final arrangements had done a truly supurb job.

Inside the buzzing hall, guests were mingling and gathering around the open bars. They waited for dinner and to finally retire to their assigned tables. The wedding party was the last to arrive, the signal to the guests that it was time to be seated. Chelsea was thankful she had a reserved seat at the head table. Not wanting to leave her friends alone all night, as they sat at the same table as her parents, Chelsea knew she had to at least make an appearance. She determined, however, that that could wait just a little longer.

Rachel oozed with joy and was completely ennamored with everything that was occuring around her. Things could not have been more perfect if she had hand-designed the day herself. She had made it through her vows successfully, and, despite Charles' non-crying reaction, she felt the ceremony had been flawless. She had even changed from her church dress into her reception gown, and the response she was receiving from people's "oohs" and "aahs" only widened her already expansive smile.

Yes, she thought, she had absolutely made the right decision in buying two dresses. This was more memorable and exactly the reaction she had wanted on her wedding day. Two dresses, two looks, one perfect day.

Looking over at her husband, her heart lightened a little more. She was now married. She was now Mrs. Charles Waterford II, and she was now successfully able to check one more thing off of her Life Checklist. All the worrying, effort, running around, and even the issue over the flowers, had been worth it because she was so happy.

Next on the list? The honeymoon and keys to a beautiful new car. Kids could be discussed at a later date. She was finally married and wanted to enjoy her husband and their new life fully before partaking in another and more serious long-term adventure. Plus, everything today was so perfect that she wanted to keep it that way for as long as possible: just the two of them in complete harmony. Nothing could ruin her day now.

As for Danielle, the entire experience of the day was taking its toll. Having considered forgoing the wedding entirely, Danielle now kicked herself for such an idea. This was one of her best friends, and to not be in attendance to show support would have been the coward's way out, and Danielle was no coward. She defended and argued with the best of them, so to think a little event like a wedding could scare her, shook her. Clearly, her life's alignment was off, and she was determined to get it back on track as soon as possible. She just wished her emotions could get out of her way.

Ever since Paul had left on Tuesday, Danielle had been an emotional wreck, crying every night and hoping that each night's conversation with him would be somehow less awkward. But they were not. The pain caused by his leaving and her refusal to do anything but stay in Boston was apparent, and neither she nor Paul knew how to work around the mess yet. With their conversations becoming ever more brief, Danielle felt a little part of her would permanently die if the situation was not corrected quickly.

As a result, that same small part of her was thankful Chelsea had gone out of her way to invite Stacy as a last minute "date." After their conversation the night before, Danielle had not known how to approach today, but she found herself relieved to have someone around her. She may have been angry with Chelsea initially for what she said, but Danielle was starting to think that maybe Chelsea was right, even though the truth hurt. Luckily, she had a caring friend who had enabled her to go through today with the buddy system, and she could not have asked for a better "buddy." Even the baby was less annoying than Danielle initially imagined having a baby at a wedding could be. She found Stacy refreshing and upbeat, something Danielle needed at the moment.

In talking with Stacy, Danielle quickly realized that Stacy was clearly in love with her husband and family. Danielle found herself soothed, persuaded by the idea that something like love and partnership held immense value. Stacy even discussed how the layoffs and tight money situations had been so devastating that she and Mark had discussed divorce at one point but had pulled through it okay. They had some scuffs and bruises, a few arguments here and there, and a doubting moment or two, but Stacy explained that she was so in love with her husband that she just knew they would make it through their problems somehow. Plus, life had its own unique and perpetual set of problems. Problems never really went away; they just changed. Therefore, in Stacy's mind, as long as she had found someone with whom to wade through the problematic stages, enjoying and loving each other's company along the way was better than going at it alone. The latter only seemed like it would add to an already difficult situation, especially if the two people truly loved one another.

Danielle found Stacy's argument to be very valid, and she discovered she was listening to Stacy intently. Stacy's perspective was at least one worth entertaining.

After that conversation, Danielle looked up at Rachel and Charles and noted how happy and glowing Rachel was. She was marrying a man she loved and admired, and, despite all the problems they had had and the doubt Danielle sometimes felt about the strength of Rachel and Charles' relationship, Rachel still chose Charles over everything else. While watching them, Danielle suddenly started to wonder if maybe she should have chosen Paul.

With a glass of wine in hand and dinner and toasts finally completed, Chelsea made her way over to the table where her parents were sitting with Danielle and Stacy. She was in a good place, the love and happiness of the wedding osmosising its way into her bones. Admittedly, events like these were tough on Chelsea as she knew she was as single as they came now. She could have easily become depressed knowing that a year prior she had seemed close to a wedding of her own, but she had things today for which to be excited. As a result, she was allowing those things to fill her heart and her head. Plus, she simply refused to be upset. She had a drink. She had her friends. She was in a semi-attractive, sky-blue bridesmaids dress, and she had her acceptance letter to CUNY. Yes, she had definite reason to be happy.

At the same time, however, she did have to tell her parents about CUNY. Weighing her options between telling them now versus telling them later, Chelsea sipped at her wine and decided that unless it came up, she could afford to wait until later.

"Hello everyone," Chelsea chimed, kissing her dad's cheek and quickly kissing her mother's before Tina was able to respond.

Chelsea then moved to another table to grab a chair and pulled up between Stacy and Danielle.

While Chelsea moved to grab a seat, her mom made no hesitation in introducing Chelsea's blind date.

"Chelsea, this is Darren," her mom stated, motioning to the man to her right. Chelsea leaned over and shook hands with Darren to be polite, nodding and smiling like she knew she should, but also instantly knowing she had no attraction to the man. She, however, refused to be rude or give her mother an inch in the way of potential criticism, so she smiled and played along as best she could. She could also feel Danielle squeeze her knee and glance sideways at her in sympathy. Clearly, Danielle was on the same wavelength as Chelsea.

"Nice to meet you," Chelsea said finally.

Darren was seated next to her mom in khakis and a bright green shirt. Unfortunately, Darren's stocky build was not complimented by the shirt's green coloring. It was not that Darren was fat, but he looked like an ex-line backer or shot-putter, and the shirt and coloring were just off for his body type. Darren's hands were also rough, an aspect which, when Chelsea shook his hand, surprised her. She assumed his job was in the business field. Therefore, why he had rough hands was unbeknownced to her and strike two in her attraction book. He also had that crazy-ex girlfriend scenario brewing in his past, which made strike three, but, again, Chelsea played nicely.

"So, Mom says you work with," Chelsea started, hoping Darren would finish the sentence for her.

"Welding," Darren interjected, his voice even and bordering on monotone. He brushed his hand through his short, dusty brown hair in nervousness. He, too, knew this was a blind date and was also trying to be as polite as possible.

Noticing Chelsea's clearly confused look, however, Darren continued, "I used to work in business until I got laid off a few months back and needed a job. A buddy of mine got into welding, and I've been apprenticing for awhile, if you will."

"Interesting," Chelsea stated, nodding and then looking over at her mother who was fixated on everything Darren was saying like it was papal gold.

"Isn't that great, Chelsea?" her mom asked. "He has ambition and drive."

Chelsea smiled as nicely as she could, wishing she could have rolled her eyes instead. "Mm hmm."

"Not dating anyone?" Danielle asked, hoping to help Chelsea and back the guy into a corner over the crazy ex-girlfriend.

"Nah, not right now," Darren said. "Dated a girl for a while, but it didn't work out."

Well that was easy, Chelsea thought. He brought it up himself.

"Really?" Chelsea wondered as lightly as possible, like it was the first time she'd heard he was single, "What happened?"

Darren threw down some wine to settle himself before responding. He smacked his lips together and said, "She was a partier. I told her we couldn't have kids if she was out drinking and smoking all the time. Apparently she wanted to keep partying, so we had to end it."

Chelsea, Danielle, and Stacy all looked at one another, confused. That was not the explanation they had been expecting.

"That's horrible, Darren," Chelsea's mom offered. "To think a woman would do such a thing, and especially with a man who wants kids!"

"Tina," Chelsea's dad scolded, intent on silencing her before she made a mockery out of the situation. He was already furious with the whole blind date situation and had been silent through dinner as a result. Now, however, he just wanted to get through the wedding and get home. His wife's antics were not high on his patience list.

"Oh don't, 'Tina' me," Tina said turning to her husband and then back to Darren, "How many kids did you want?"

"Four eventually," Darren offered. "With someone who don't smoke."

Danielle cringed at "don't smoke." Poor English grated on her attorney nerve.

"Four," Chelsea said, looking as pale as a ghost and drinking the rest of the wine in her glass. "Wow."

"How many do you want, dear?" Tina asked, now posing the question to Chelsea.

Holding back the disbelieving laugh, Chelsea simply stated, "Don't yet."

Her mom, smiling and trying to cover for Chelsea's response, said, "Well, of course not *yet*. I know you want to be married first."

"Yeah, no," Chelsea said, very calmly and matter of factly, refusing to give in to any other "women are blamed" scenarios, said, "I want to finish grad school first."

A smug smile passed over Chelsea's face, and her mom instantly turned as red as a turnip.

Darren, on the other hand, asked a follow-up question about which school and program she found interesting, as any respectful gentleman should do. Chelsea, almost feeling sorry for Darren now, finally found herself loosening up to the man who had to deal with her mother for the entire night.

"CUNY," Chelsea replied happily, only to see her mother's redden even further.

"Aw, nice," Darren said. "New York's great. I got cousins up near there. Great city. Good for you."

Smiling genuinely this time, Chelsea thanked Darren and agreed that she, too, was excited for a new start in January.

Her mom, unhappy with the news she had just heard, asked Chelsea simply if she could speak with her for a moment. Although Chelsea tried to finagle her way out of the impending meeting, she could not. Telling Darren it was a pleasure meeting him, she felt a quick squeeze of her hand in confidence from Danielle. Chelsea then followed her mother out the doors to a quiet place in the hotel's hallway.

"What do you think you're doing?" she bellowed quietly, trying to contain the rage she felt inside.

"What?" Chelsea answered back, trying to play the, "I don't know what you're talking about," card.

"Don't 'what' me. How dare you embarrass me that way!"

"Embarrass you?" Chelsea could not believe what she was hearing. She did not even throw a fit or cause a scene this time, and she had still embarrassed her mother.

"I can't win, can I?" Chelsea asked.

"What are you talking about? There's no 'winning' here, but how dare you make me look like a fool in front of our guest."

"He asked me a question, Mom. I was being polite."

Her mother, refusing to relinquish the upper hand in the conversation, quickly added, "And there will be no going to CUNY. Is that clear?"

"I'm sorry?" Chelsea replied. "I don't think you have a say in that, Mom."

"You live in my house!" she roared softly.

"Yeah, and you look at and throw away *my* mail?" Chelsea returned, pulling out the scraps of paper from her purse to show her mother. Tina shook in anger at what Chelsea was holding. She had thrown that horrid envelope away just the night before and stuffed it far down in the garbage to ensure Chelsea would not accidentally see it. How could she have found it?

"You know that's a felony, right?" Chelsea asked smugly, knowing her mother knew she was in the wrong.

"How did you get that?" Tina hissed.

"How did I get that? What do you mean *how*, Mom? The question isn't how but why did I have to go digging through the garbage to get it? The question I should be asking is why *didn't* I get this when it first arrived?"

Her mom shook her head in anger, "You don't know what you want. I was pushing you in the right direction."

"By, what, sending me on a blind wedding date with *him?*" Chelsea asked, mouth agape, pointing back in the direction of the ballroom. "Do you even know me, Mom? How the hell could you have ever figured I would have wanted *that?*"

"You don't know what you want," her mother simply said again.

"Oh, and you do?" Chelsea countered.

"I know what's best for you. I'm your mother."

"Mom, listen to yourself," Chelsea pleaded. "What are you hoping to do by controlling my life?"

"You're messing with Fate by trying to enhance your career and scouring the country for answers in the wrong places."

Chelsea almost laughed. She actually felt sorry for her mother. Her mom was clearly reaching for something she could not obtain, and she was trying to manage a life that was not her own. It was out of pity that Chelsea gathered up the torn scraps of paper in her hand and held them up to her mother.

"Fate?" Chelsea started, "How do you know what my Fate is if you keep messing with it, Mom? This is Fate. This letter is my Fate."

"You don't know what you're talking about," her mother scathed.

"Mom!" Chelsea nearly shouted, closing her eyes in annoyance. "I'm going to tell you this once. Do *not* mess with my stuff, and it's time you backed out of my life."

Pointing back to the reception hall, Chelsea said, "I may not be gettting married, and I may not be living the life you imagined right now, but this is what it is."

Her mom tried to say something, but Chelsea just shook her head once to quiet her. In her annoyance and anger, Chelsea started feeling tears pool in her eyes and her confidence fall from her voice.

"I'm going to CUNY, Mom. I'm getting a loan. I'm going to New York, and I'm leaving to pursue a new life for myself. The sooner you can accept that, the better off we will both be."

Leaving her mother stupified, Chelsea gathered the papers in her hands. Walking back through the doors of the ballroom, she put the pieces back in her purse and tried to sniffle back the tears that were falling lightly down her face. Frustration had gotten the best of her, and she wanted to wipe away the tears before reaching her table. This was not how today was supposed to have gone. She was not supposed to be crying at her friend's wedding, but then again, people were not supposed to have crazy mothers either.

Shaking her head, she wiped the last tear away as she approached her table, but before she reached it a booming voice sounded from the ballroom's entryway.

"Don't walk away from me," Tina shouted as she covered the ground at a galloping pace.

Chelsea stopped in her tracks. She sighed loudly and closed her eyes, tilting her head towards the ceiling and slouching her shoulders in defeat. She wanted this to be over. However, just as she went to turn around and face her mother, another voice boomed, but this time, it came from a place in front of her.

"Tina Farrera!"

It was her dad.

Opening her eyes in shock, Chelsea saw that immediately ahead of her stood her father. The man who had stayed so quiet all through dinner despite his anger was now standing bolt-upright, at his seat. He pulled at his napkin, which was clutched tightly between two white-knuckled hands.

In fear of moving, Chelsea simply glanced over her shoulder at her mother, who had also stopped in her tracks. Clearly, such a display by Tony was shocking to both the Farrera women.

But Tony did not say another word. He did not have to. He did not need to shout across the room or make speeches. His mere presence and forceful display said everything he needed it to say. He was serious. He was mad, and he meant business. This time, it was he who would not be embarrassed in public, and his wife had pushed the last boundary.

As Tina moved silently back to the table, she did not glance at her daughter. She simply moved around her and sat next to her husband, who returned to his seat. Neither spoke, neither looked at the other, but both knew perfectly well that they were both enfuriated and fed up with tonight's behavior. Chelsea wondered if their traditional Saturday morning fighting wouldn't continue into Sunday morning due to the events of the night, and she was silently happy to have a hotel room at the Langham and not have to wake up at the house with them in the morning.

Chelsea closed her eyes and wiped away the small pool of water draining from them. She shook her head in disbelief at how such a happy occasion could bring out the worst in people. And for her, after such moments of chaos, she found she needed a moment of solitude. She headed back to the table to grab her purse and then find a quieter space to recooperate.

Looking back at the table, Chelsea saw Darren's chair empty. He must have disappeared sometime during the fighting, and, given her family's latest display, she knew it safe to assume that he probably would not return for the duration of the evening. Something inside her sighed in relief for not having to play hostess anymore to a date she had not wanted in the first place.

Chelsea headed out towards the bathroom to try to clear her head of the events that had just ensued. She left her friends at the table and would catch them up on everything when she returned. Unfortunately, on her way out of the ballroom, an unwelcomed presence caught her eye. Heading away from the bar with a full drink in hand was Terry, the last man she wanted to see. When he saw her, Terry simply laughed once and shook his head at Chelsea. Chelsea wanted to scream and retreat into herself all at the same time. She bounded out of the ballroom as fast as she possibly could. She wanted to disappear from this escalating nightmare.

Chelsea, therefore, felt greatly relieved when she found the bathroom empty. She approached the sink, set her purse on the counter with both hands, leaned onto it, bowed her head, and started crying. There was a constant stream of water cascading down her face, and her breathing was unsteady. The emotional toll of the day had proven to be too much. Chelsea could not help but feel weak and very much alone. She was humiliated. She had just been scolded by a certifiably insane woman who was determined to control her life; she had been the center of a very public display of anger back in the ballroom, which had brought nothing but unnecessary attention to her by the people around her; and she had just been laughed at and mocked, nonverbally, by her completely horrendous ex-boyfriend who had also, as it happened, broken her heart a year ago. She may have enjoyed portraying herself as this "with it" and "together," strong woman, but right now she felt anything but strong.

And so she cried over a sink. She cried out all the frustrations and hurt that she had not only just experienced but also the ones that she had held inside over the past few months. She cried for a life she was so desperately trying to achieve but somehow always felt she was just two steps behind. She cried because she was single, and, despite what she might say otherwise, she really did not want to be. And she cried for the acceptance letter that was the hope she needed but had almost missed because of her own mother.

Yes, Chelsea thought, I am a mess.

She sniffled back a few more tears and adjusted herself back into a standing position. She needed to regain her composure. Then, just as Chelsea looked up to reach for a hand towel to wipe away the water and water marks from her face, she saw Danielle and Stacy enter, baby Marcus in tow. Chelsea looked at them through the mirror and her face gave away everything she was thinking. Stacy stayed a few paces behind Danielle, and Danielle moved up to Chelsea to give her a hug.

"Oh Chelsea," Danielle said, releasing Chelsea from the hug. "I'm so sorry."

Danielle placed herself a few feet away from Chelsea to give Chelsea some room, and Stacy stayed a few feet further behind Danielle.

"It's okay," Chelsea said aloud, trying to smile. "Just a rough few minutes."

"I assumed that once your dad got mad, things were probably pretty serious," Danielle stated. "I've never seen him like that."

"Yeah, right?" Chelsea stated rhetorically. "That's not exactly normal public behavior for him. However, with something like that," Chelsea said, referring to the prior moment in the banquet hall, "that's usually a sign he's reached his absolute limit. Let's just say I'm glad I don't have to be there in the morning to hear them hash it out."

"I agree," Danielle said.

"Well, I thought you handled yourself well," Stacy added lightly, feeling that given what could have happened, Chelsea had kept herself very composed.

Chelsea looked over at Stacy and smiled before shaking her head sympathetically, "Oh gosh, Stacy. I'm so embarrassed. That's the second time now I've dragged you into a family fiasco."

"No, really. It's okay," Stacy returned. "I'm happy to be here. I'm actually having a really good time. Marcus has been really great, and Danielle and I have gotten along well. It's nice actually."

"I just –" Chelsea started but was instantly cut off by Stacy.

"Really. It's fine," Stacy smiled. "How are you doing, though?"

"Eh," Chelsea replied, wiping a few more tears off her face. "I've been better. It was just a lot. It didn't help that I ran into Terry on my way out, and he actually laughed at me."

"Yeah," Danielle started uneasily. "We saw that. That's actually why we came over. We assumed your mom probably did a number on you, but we knew that the Terry incident was probably a breaking point for you."

"It's just not fair," Chelsea said. "I wasn't ready for that. I mean, I knew he was going to be here, but his timing couldn't have been any worse."

Then Chelsea snickered, "He probably planned it that way too, the bastard. Just my luck."

"Forget him," Danielle said. "He's not worth your time. And let me tell you something, you don't need any more bastards in your life."

Chelsea nodded in agreement.

"But you're going to CUNY?" Stacy asked, looking over at Danielle. "Danielle said something about you getting accepted."

Chelsea looked quizzically at Danielle, "You know?"

Danielle smiled and shook her head at Chelsea, "What do you mean? Of course I know! You don't think Rachel would keep something so monumental to herself, do you? She bragged about how she helped you put the envelope back together. She was quite proud of herself, actually, and ecstatic for you, making note of how perfect the day was turning out with such good news so early!"

Danielle's statement made Chelsea genuinely laugh, "Yeah, that sounds like Rachel."

"Chelsea that's wonderful!" Stacy beamed. "When do you start?"

"January," Chelsea responded, finally feeling her initially devastated spirits lift. "I, um, have to be moved into New York City by then, and then it's basically a two year program."

"So you're going?" Stacy wondered.

"Yeah," Chelsa admitted. "I'm ready for something new, and I think diving into the program head-on is the perfect way to go."

"Yay," Stacy chimed in agreement. "That's wonderful! We'll miss you, but I'm so excited for you."

"Thanks, Stacy. I'll miss you too, but I think I'm finally ready to do this, and that's really exciting."

"Agreed. Go after what you want," Stacy said.

Starting to finally feel hints of her old self again, Chelsea stood up a little straighter and adjusted her hair and dress in the mirror. She was glad to no longer be crying and agreed with Stacy's last comment that it was time to turn the tables. Chelsea decided that that meant it was time to help Danielle.

"Speaking of going after what you want," Chelsea finally said as the three girls headed out of the bathroom and down the hallway towards the ballroom. "What do you think you're going to do, Danielle."

"Hey, come on now," Danielle answered. "Not fair."

"Why?" Chelsea asked. "You guys helped me. Now it's my turn to help you."

Baby Marcus started crying and the girls stopped to see what Stacy wanted to do.

"Oh man," Stacy said. "I think he's awake again which means he's probably hungry. You know what, guys, I'm gonna go grab his bottle and then go feed him somewhere a little quieter. I'll catch up with you in a bit, assuming I can get him to go back to sleep."

"Do you need help?" Chelsea offered.

"No, no. It's fine. I knew he had to wake up at some point. I'll just be a little bit. Excuse me."

Stacy took baby Marcus and headed back to the ballroom for his things, leaving the two girls alone in the hallway to talk privately.

"So?" Chelsea asked, redirecting the focus back onto Danielle.

"Chelsea I don't know. Don't ask me."

"Last night you were an absolute wreck, Danielle. You came to my aide just now; I'm here to be your aide because, if I know you, you still aren't satisfied with things."

Danielle stopped walking and leaned against the wall to her immediate left.

"Honestly?" she asked, to which she received a tilted head and raised eyebrow response from Chelsea.

"Okay. Honestly I sat in church today and watched Rachel marry Charles despite all the issues they've been having, and I found that I was actually jealous. I don't know if I'm completely sold on the Charles isn't cheating thing, but, regardless, I was actually jealous. How is it she gets to be so happy, and I'm a wreck inside?"

Chelsea waited to see if Danielle was finished, but Danielle continued.

"And then Stacy, who, by the way, is adorable and thank you so much for inviting her because it was nice not to be alone, but then

Stacy sat next to me and talked about how she and her husband are still together despite rumors of divorce just a few years ago, and, I mean, look at her. She's so happy."

"Yeah," Chelsea agreed, "that she is."

"I just, I don't know, Chels. I think I really messed up this time."

Chelsea treaded cautiously and asked if Danielle had called Paul at all.

"Of course I called," Danielle replied, and then allowed the disappointment to enter her voice. "But he didn't answer. I don't know; I think he's mad at me. I called right before dinner, but he didn't pick up. I know he's not working, not at six at night anyway, and his not answering makes me die just a little more. I mean, I think he probably just doesn't know what to say either, but I hate this. We're at this really, horribly awkward stalemate."

Feeling forced to ask the inevitable, Chelsea asked if it was over, which only made Danielle start crying. Chelsea tried to apologize and pulled out a piece of paper towel she had stuffed away in her purse from the bathroom to hand to Danielle.

Now it was Danielle's turn to feel embarrassed.

"God, I hope not," Danielle said. "I don't want it to be."

"Do you love him?" Chelsea asked. Danielle simply nodded.

"Danielle," Chelsea stated, leaning against the wall next to Danielle to put them on even territory. "I just spent the last ten minutes crying in the bathroom because my mother's an idiot and refuses to let me choose my own path in life. You've always had the freedom to choose. You chose to come to law school here. You chose to date Paul long-distance for a really long time until Paul chose to follow you here to Boston. Now Paul's in Albany, and from the way it sounds, it was a good choice for him."

"And it was," Danielle interrupted.

"But until now, Danielle, he's followed you. He moved to Boston, what, three or four years ago now? And he did that because he wanted to be with you. If you think this move was a good choice for him, then maybe, this time, it's time for you to choose him.

Follow him. Why ruin something that works so well if you don't have to? And you guys work *so* well. Why throw that away? For what, a job?" Chelsea asked, posing the hard question to Danielle that she knew Danielle needed.

"But I like my job," Danielle rebutted.

"But you *love* Paul," Chelsea countered, and Danielle could not repsond. Emotionally it was a great argument. Logically, it made Danielle's head hurt.

Chelsea pushed away from the wall. "Look, tonight's been crazy. Let's go back to the reception, cheer on Rachel some more, do some crazy dancing, and we'll figure it out in the morning."

Without saying a word, Danielle pushed away from the wall, and both she and Chelsea made their way back to the reception hall. Danielle's head fired arguments at itself between leaving and staying, but suddenly the reasons for leaving starting holding more power than before. Maybe it was what Chelsea had just said. Maybe it was the result of being accompanied by Stacy all day, or maybe it was a combination of both. Regardless of the reasoning, Danielle suddenly found herself pulled towards the idea of leaving because she was tired of hurting. She had a five year investment in Paul, and she loved him. Maybe that was enough.

Chelsea walked next to Danielle and thought through her own events of the night. She realized she had one amazing work friend in Stacy, and Chelsea made a mental note to put forth more of an effort in bridging that large gap that existed between them when it came to children and parenting issues. She might not know much of anything, but after what Stacy had been through with her family, she was sure she could be more supportive of anything Stacy faced with Mark and baby Marcus in the near future. She just knew she owed Stacy a lot for everything she had done for Danielle and her tonight.

Back at the reception, the night was now fully underway, and the dance floor was crowded. Stacy caught up with the girls and said her goodbyes, having put baby Marcus to sleep and wanting to do the same herself. Both Chelsea and Danielle thanked her for coming and agreed that they had both had a really great time as a result of her being around. They wished her the best of luck with the rest of the weekend.

Danielle joined Chelsea on the dance floor for a few minutes before leaving as well. Her head was now filled with thoughts, and she did not feel the best place to sort them out was on the dance floor. She wanted to go home. She wanted to be somewhere quiet.

Chelsea hugged Danielle goodbye and then returned to the reception to finish the night as a wonderful and proud Maid of Honor with reason for celebration.

Chapter 21 - The Big Night

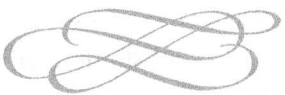

The wedding guests started retreating to their respectful lives as the night continued. Chelsea's parents packed up to leave shortly after Danielle left. Her mom left quietly, not even saying goodbye to her daughter. Her dad, on the other hand, made a point of finding Chelsea before heading home.

"I'm sorry," he apologized, "but I'm very proud of you. You'll do great at CUNY."

Her father's reassurance boosted Chelsea's confidence. She felt contented knowing that at least one of her parents was in her corner, and she was also, therefore, less worried about returning to life at the Farerra house tomorrow afternoon. She was going to CUNY, and her father supported her. Her mother would just have to learn to live with it.

Chelsea successfully avoided Terry for the remainder of the evening. He had left with a blond girl about three-quarters of the way through the reception, and she was just glad to be rid of him. Additionally, Chelsea never saw Darren again that evening. Whether he left after the dinner fight or sometime later during the reception was a mystery, but Chelsea simply knew he was not around. Now, it was just Chelsea, and Chelsea was okay with that.

Sometime around eleven, Rachel and Charles left their own recpetion to head upstairs to the bridal suite. Everything was planned. Champaign, fruit, chocolate, and a large bouquet of flowers awaited the newlywed couple. It was perfect. It was special, and it was everything Rachel could have wanted.

Entering the room, Rachel glowed from a part deep inside her. That college girl she had known a mere five years ago was gleaming with pride from today's events. All those young-girl dreams had come true, even if it was five years later than she would have initially wanted for herself. She had a man she loved, a lifestyle she had always wanted, and a dream car waiting for her after today. Life and today were both working out flawlessly. She felt wrapped in a sense of love and security, and it gave her a new sense of confidence, like she could do more because she was now officially partnered with someone.

Charles poured them each a glass of champagne and met Rachel by the window to admire the view of Boston at night. He had taken off his tuxedo coat and undone a few of the buttons of his shirt in an attempt to unwind and prepare for the night ahead, sans formalwear. Bringing Rachel a matching glass of champagne, Charles admired his wife from behind. He loved the way the reception dress hugged her curves perfectly, but he loved even more that it was coming off soon.

Charles pulled up next to Rachel and handed her the glass.

"Thank you, hunny," Rachel hummed as she took her glass of champagne from her husband. She even felt herself smile a little wider at the thought of the word, "husband." It had a nice ring to it. She was now a wife, and he was now her husband. They were together. Everything was as it should be.

Things will just get better from here, she thought.

Taking a sip, she thought back over the last few months and how foolish she had been to ever worry about another woman. All those nights staying awake and wondering had been in vain. She and Charles were married now. He could have chosen otherwise; he could have foregone the wedding if there had really been someone else, but he had chosen her, and that knowledge alone could not have made her any happier. Plus, she was of the firm belief that, once married, things just got better.

"You seem happy," Charles said, kissing Rachel's exposed shoulder and noting the smile in her eyes.

"I am. So happy," she returned, turning to kiss her husband squarely and passionately. She was exactly where she wanted to be.

Pleased with her response, Charles' hand instantly found its way to the zipper of Rachel's dress and started tugging it downward, pulling Rachel into him. Rachel's body responded immediately, allowing itself to be pulled and caressed by Charles' touch. Within moments the champagne glasses had found their way to the table and Rachel's dress had found its way to the floor. Charles' tuxedo lay strewn along the floor in different pieces making a trail from the window to the king-size bed. Rachel could not believe that after tonight they would not only be married, but that in a few minutes their marriage would also be consumated. What a perfect way to end an amazing day!

Reaching for the pillows, Rachel pulled herself securely into the middle of the bed while Charles reached for a condom. They might be married, but they certainly did not want any little surprises yet. Protection was a must, and Rachel never fully trusted birth control to an extent which would allow Charles and her to forgo the use of a condom. Tonight may have been special, but she did not want it to be *that* special. Someday they would not have to worry about getting pregnant, but that someday was not today.

Pulling himself back up over Rachel, Charles leaned in and kissed her. He ran his strong hands over her breast, and she pulled his shoulders into her. Rachel could feel the heat of his body wave over hers, and she knew she wanted him.

As Charles sat back on his knees, he took the condom in his hands and tore open the small square pouch. Rachel propped herself up on one elbow and went to reach for him when she saw it, the small condom square he held in his hands. She had imagined it would be the playful, green, Twisted Pleasure square she had found buried in their closet, but it was not. In his hands was the small, greyish blue square she knew all too well.

Instantly and instinctively she pulled herself away from him, curling up closer to the pillows. She even let out a tiny squeal of shock.

"Rachel?" Charles asked, noting the strangely odd behavior of his wife and her sudden pull away from him.

"What is *that?*" she asked, pointing to the condom with an expression that suggested he had just brought her the gift of a dead rat or something.

"What is what?" Charles asked, clearly confused.

Suddenly angry, Rachel bolted from the bed and ran over to her purse located on the side table. She had tucked away the green condom square inside it the other day simply out of annoyance. Now, she ripped it out of her purse, threw a pillow in front of her body, and sat on the edge of the bed fuming in anger.

"Then what the hell is this?" she demanded, shaking the green condom square at him, staring him down with eyes ablaze with fury.

Rachel's head screamed. How stupid could she be? She had just married a man whom she was sure was cheating on her. She was suddenly very sure that there must be someone else. Clearly there were other condoms, and, clearly, they were not meant for her. She could not help but feel suddenly broken, like a self-proclaimed idiot, and on her own wedding night no less. How could such a perfect day have gone so incredibly wrong so quickly? This was not how people were supposed to feel on their wedding nights. People were supposed to be happy and in love on their wedding nights, not ready to cry because the condom the husband had just ripped open to put on was the wrong color.

Rachel almost started crying in anger, but she refused to let Charles see her break just yet. He would not get the best of her, not until she had an explanation.

Charles was silent for a moment, which Rachel took to be his attempt to formulate a lie and cover up his trail.

"Damnit, Charles!" Rachel nearly screamed. All the images she had tucked away flooded her brain. The dancing legs of the red wine mocked her, the constant golf outings to other states and the business meetings scheduled last-minute screamed infidelity. And all she could do right now was sit there, naked, covered with a pillow, and watch them play back in her own mind.

Despite her best attempts, the tears spilled from her eyes. She could not help them. She was broken, the splintered shards of her earlier happines now piercing through her. The most perfect day of her life had been ruined, and she feared her own marriage was already beyond redemption. She flipped from feeling stronger and having a greater sense of purpose as a wife to feeling alone and borderline mocked. She could not even begin to consider the prenuptial agreement, because what good did that do if the marriage was never consumated? Plus, it was not like she was supposed to be getting much of anything for the first five years anyway. This was a mess.

Charles sighed aloud. He knew he had been caught, and there was no way around it. It broke his heart to see her crying there on their hotel room bed over something that was so small in size that he never thought to truly give it serious thought. There was nothing else he could do at this point. He had to tell her.

Charles leaned in to put his hand on Rachel, but she recoiled from him. Sitting himself back in place, he started to explain.

"It's not what you think, Rachel," he started slowly.

Bastard, she thought. It's exactly what I think.

Rachel did not respond verbally but merely stared at him with irate and disbelieving watery eyes. Charles knew what he was about to say might take a while to explain.

"Rachel," he sighed deeply, "really, it's not what you're thinking. There is nobody else."

"Bullshit," she snapped.

"No, really," he replied. There was no reason for him to get upset yet, but he understood that she would be testy for a while. "Let me explain, okay?"

Rachel again did not respond. She simply clung more tightly to the pillow against her body, shook her head, and looked up towards the ceiling. She knew she had nowhere else to go, so she might as well let him talk, but she did not think anything he could say could assuage her feeling of betrayal and devastation.

"Look," Charles began, rubbing his hands together and then planting himself securely on the bed to face Rachel, "I'm not cheating on you. I want you to know and remember that, okay? There is no one else, period, but you do know that I am gone a lot. I spend a lot of time away from you, and it's not always what I want. I don't know if this will come as a shock to you or not, because I don't know what you do when I'm gone, but guys, by nature, have to relieve themselves."

Charles paused when he saw Rachel's eyebrows furl, but he did not know if her action was in disbelief or confusion, so he set out to explain himself just to cover his tracks.

"You know," he explained. "Masterbate."

"Damnit, Charles, I know what that means," she seethed. She was annoyed and livid, not stupid.

"Okay," he responded defensively, holding up his hands in peace before continuing. "I wasn't sure and just wanted to clarify."

"Got it."

"Anyway, it can get rather," he began, looking for the right wording, "boring, if you will. After a while the sensation of me is always the same, and I wanted something else to help me out when you're not around."

"So you found someone," she retorted.

"No. Rachel. Listen to me. You're not listening. There is no one else. I bought those condoms because they give me a different feeling when I want to get off and can't be with you."

Rachel looked at him with an expression that oozed with annoyance.

"Oh please," she nearly shouted, "You expect me to believe that you jack-off with a condom on? Do I look like an idiot?"

"No," Charles pleaded, "Rachel you're not listening to what I'm saying."

"I heard you just fine."

"Rachel –"

"Why in the hell would I believe you jack-off to a condom? You guys hate those things! So, what, now you're trying to tell me you're going to consciously pick them up when you're flying solo?"

Charles stared blankly back at her, like he did not understand why she could not grasp what he was saying.

"Yes, that's exactly it. That's exactly what I'm trying to tell you. They're not perfect or ideal all the time, but they're easy, and they work. They're already lubed, and they're easy to clean up. I don't always feel like leaning over the toilet or messing up the towels in my hotel room.

"Plus, this one," he said pointing to the green square now lying next to him, "is just a totally different sensation. That's all. I know how much you love the Ultra Thin ones, and I love using them with you, so I use something else when I'm alone to give me a different sensation. I promise. I'm not hiding anything, Rachel. This one must have just been left over from my last trip and gone unnoticed when I unpacked."

Rachel simply glared at her husband.

"Rachel," Charles stated with emphasis and the even business tonality normally present in his voice, "I love you. There is no one else. Don't be jealous of a condom that is used to help me just get by until I'm back with you again. That's just dumb, and you just told me you're not dumb."

"Do not try to throw that shit back in my face right now."

In a gesture to appease his wife, he reached out to touch her leg and was encouraged when she did not recoil. "I'm sorry, but I'm just saying. Come on, Rachel. You have to know I love you. You're an amazing woman. We just got married, and, besides, look at you. You're beautiful. I'd be stupid not to want to be with you or do anything to jeopardize what we have."

She could feel herself start to cry again. All the days she had spent convincing herself tha the notion of Charles' cheating was crazy had been for naught. She thought of all the TV shows and articles she had scoffed at, thinking how dumb the women must feel when they discover their husbands cheating on them. Now, she was one of those women. She was the dumb one, and she hated the thought. And he dared sit there and act like it's all just a masterbation technique! What was he doing? Was he lying or truly just being an absolute moron? What was she to think? And why did this hurt so much?

She was so confused and agitated that she could not even respond. The sudden roller coaster of emotions that had occurred over the past few minutes was now exiting, unchecked, through her tear ducts.

"Don't cry," he soothed, inching closer to her. "Come here." He pulled her into his shoulder, rubbing his hand down her back. He tried to calm her down as she cried all her emotions out and onto his shoulder.

"It's okay," he assured her. "We're going to be fine. We just got married, Rachel. There's no reason to cry."

The problem, and what Charles did not understand, was that that was exactly why she was crying. The ecstatic / irate exchange of emotions had just occurred within Rachel so quickly that the crying was simply the inevitable aftershock. And, yes, today was her wedding day, and that only escalated the severity of the incident because it made it the worst day possible for such a horrific scene to unfold. Plus, and not that Charles was privy to the information, but Rachel had been sitting on this for so long now that the verbal release alone warranted water works. For all those reasons, there was absolutely reason for her to be crying.

They stayed silent for a while. At first Rachel remained leaning on his shoulder, but Charles eventually excused himself to a shower. He decided to wash off the argument and wedding residue since things had cooled down for the evening anyways. He had kissed her forehead before exiting, reminding her that he loved her.

She, however, remained in bed, clinging to the pillow and leaning against the headboard. She had no gauge of time, and it did not matter to her whether five minutes or forty-five minutes had passed. She simply remained seated, voided, listening to the sounds of the shower fill the airspace around her. Everything that had just transpired suddenly seemed surreal, but the events had burned a hole in her heart, and it still ached. She no longer knew what to believe, but his explanation had seemed so idiodic that she wondered how it could be anything but real. How could someone actually make that up? It seemed all too odd to be a well thought-out lie, but, then again, how was she to know?

She could not, she determined. She could not know the validity of what he had told her other than to know that he was here, they were married, and unless she actually found traces of this "other girl," she almost could do nothing *but* believe him. She had married a man who used a condom to help him masterbate when they were not together. That would have to take some serious getting used to.

The question now was what did she do in the meantime? Did she sever their future plans or continue as though nothing had changed and wait it out to see what surfaced down the road? There was so much to consider, both emotionally and logistically. They were leaving for their honeymoon in the morning, which would be a fiasco to try to get out of now. Plus, part of her just plainly refused to believe that she would spend her honeymoon devastated and closed off to him. It would be emotional, marital suicide. Now that she was married, she knew that first sexual experience needed to be breached, and she had never imagined having to postpone that event.

There was so much to consider that she just sat in silence and let her brain run in overdrive some more. A solution would eventually present itself.

No, she finally thought, after more time had passed. I refuse to let this ruin what I have left of this experience. It may have ruined my mood now, but it will not ruin our week.

Trying to rebuild her composure, Rachel walked over to her suitcase, unpacked the new, white, lace négligé she had purchased for the honeymoon and slipped it on. She did not want to feel exposed, and eliminating the option of being naked for the evening helped with that. Now she could lay in bed knowing she was covered, giving her emotions the sense of being partially protected.

Charles returned from his shower to see his wife lying in bed facing the window. She did not turn over to look at him when he pulled up beside her, but he also knew she was not sleeping by the way she was lying so tightly coiled. He did not know what else to say to convince her that he was being truthful, but he knew well enough to know that leaving her alone right now was the wrong approach, so he pulled up behind her and rubbed her hair.

She started crying again when she felt his hand touch her hair. His touch sparked a subconscious, emotional response. As hard as she tried to keep the tears contained, however, she could not. They fell along her cheeks silently, and it was not until her shoulders shook when she tried to sneak in a breath that Charles realized she was crying again.

He turned her over to face him but noted that she still would not look at him. Normally not one for games or long, drawn-out emotional scenes, he put aside his normal behavioral response as best he could, for he knew that tonight, of all nights, was not the night to be insensitive. He caressed her hair a little longer and kissed her, whispering quietly in her ear that he loved her.

As hard as she tried and no matter how much part of her wanted to stay mad, Rachel started to realize that it was nearly impossible to stay angry when being treated so lovingly, especially because another, bigger part of her wanted tonight to be more perfect than anything. Slowly, she allowed herself to uncoil, giving into his touch and his compassion. She loved him, and she wanted to retreat back into the arms of the man she loved, despite the gaping wound in her heart. Emotions rarely made logical sense, and the dueling battle between wanting and loving him and being angry at and betrayed by him played continuously inside her. She realized she needed to decide which side she would allow to win for the night, and the college girl inside her searching for perfection pulled for the loving

known, actually. Rachel told me at one point, but it clearly didn't /
wanting side to win.

Therefore, when Charles pulled her into him for a deep, slow
kiss, Rachel responded unabated. She really did love him, and
she wanted everything to be perfect on their wedding night. Plus,
she wanted him to know that part of her believed him. She was
still mad and still hurt, but she did not want tonight to forever
be remembered as the night she held out because of a condom
quarrel. Instead, she allowed her arms to find his waist. She held
onto him and permitted him to take the reins for the night. He
did so lovingly and with understood caution. He was relieved that
she had begun to forgive him, accept the truth of the matter, and
understand its utter insignificance. As a thank you to her, he would
make sure tonight was full of love and all about her.

And so it began, their journey together. It may not have been
exactly as she had imagined her wedding night to be, but it was
thoughtful, full of love, what she needed, and a wonderful beginning
to what she hoped would end up being the perfect honeymoon.

Chapter 22 - Big Moves

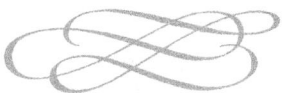

Ⅰt did not take long for Danielle to move herself into a decision upon leaving the wedding, despite how slowly she had moved previously. After Rachel's wedding, Danielle had gone home feeling lonelier and emptier than before. She even felt more broken than the first night after Paul's leaving. Decidedly, she attributed that to her realization of just what their relationship was facing and how much she truly did not want that. She was ill-prepared to confront another long-distance relationship, and the longer Paul was away from her the stronger the desire to be with him became.

As a result, Danielle had returned home from the wedding, cried from a place deep within her gut for a solid half an hour, and then started packing her bag. Just one. She was not leaving permanently, but she was leaving for what was left of the weekend.

It was the best decision she could have made. Leaving at five the next morning, she arrived at his place in just under three hours, and her phone call upon arriving had awakened him. Being told to come to his front door was not what Paul had expected, and he nearly closed the door on her in pure shock. When he finally moved aside to let her in, he made her a cup of coffee and demanded an explanation for such a rash move.

She explained to him that she had been so lonely at the wedding that she just needed to see him. Nearly in tears the entire time she explained it, she stated that the explanation was that simple. She had chosen him.

Still astounded that her emotions had motivated her actions, especially since she always weighed her options so heavily before making a choice, he wondered if maybe she had been partially drunk when she chose to drive off in her car that morning.

When she noted his still puzzled look at seeing her in his Albany apartment, she started re-explaining herself, but he cut her off. It did not matter to him why she had come, he was just thrilled she had come at all. He had anticipated they would have gone much longer before seeing one another as their phone conversations had grown increasingly awkward. Instead, she now sat in front of him. None of their past arguments or awkward phone calls mattered. He had her, and he was determined to keep her. He knew from past experiences that changing her mind was not easy, but while she was in town he would make as compelling an argument as possible for why she should move. Aside from her needing to find a job, he knew he needed to persuade her on why Albany was a great town. Therefore, the first thing on the agenda was a tour of the city. He wanted her to see its unique nature, its ease, and its potential. No, it was not Boston, but it could be a home – their home – and he wanted to show her that.

At Paul's behest, they toured the city and his new office building. It helped that it was a beautiful fall day, and overall, Danielle was impressed. She was still not convinced it was better than Boston nor that she would ever feel that way, but she noted that it was expansive and beautiful in its own right. So long as it was only a temporary move, no longer than a year or two, or with promise of plenty of weekend getaways to the shore, she could see herself living there. It was this final decision that tipped the scale in favor of Paul and even Albany. She could work and live here, so long as there was work to be done. Of that she was now certain.

She returned home Monday night refreshed and hopeful. Her heart finally felt less heavy, and she finally felt as though she had found the strings with which to start mending it. She had chosen Paul, and her decision had been made rationally and with great love and understanding. Simply put, he had moved all those years ago, leaving his home in New York to be with her in Boston, seeking work which was close to her. If he could do that for her, then this time she could do the same for him. Relationships were about give and take, and if she truly wanted this relationship to survive, it was her turn.

Chapter 23 - Tuesday

The Tuesday morning after Labor Day weekend, after the wedding, and after the chaos, life was back to normal. Rachel and Charles were on their honeymoon, Danielle had made up her mind to put serious effort into looking for work in Albany, and work for Chelsea beckoned just like it did any other Tuesday morning.

Chelsea was determined to start the week out correctly, which included arriving on time for work and even with an iced mocha "pick me up" in tow. When she had returned to her house Sunday afternoon, things had already cooled down between her parents, but her mother still purposefully avoided her. Chelsea couldn't say she was surprised or even terribly upset by the lack of interaction with her mother. Chelsea needed to mend herself, too, and seeing as how she had not partaken in any fights with her mother since the wedding, she was only that much more optimistic about her life's new direction.

To make things better, upon arriving at her desk, she found that she had a bouquet of flowers waiting with a note attached. She wasn't sure why she had flowers, so she opened the note immediately hoping for an explanation. The note simply said, "Thank You." There was no signer, no sender, nor mention of its intent. It simply said, "Thank You."

Chelsea stood for a moment and pondered the origin of the flowers. Running her brain through every possible option, Chelsea immediately eliminated certain candidates. Neither of her parents would be thanking her for anything, espcially not her mother, and it was certainly not her co-worker, David. She could not think of any substantial reason why it would have been her boss, since she had not responded to any of her Friday emails or phone calls yet. That left her friends, which seemed feasible but not completely plausible. If it had been one of them, she would have envisioned a more explanatory and elaborate thank-you card.

Letting out a long sigh, Chelsea shook her head once to dismiss the multitude of thoughts running through her head and decided that it was not worth the effort. Instead, she accepted the beautiful gesture as a simple sign of good things to come. She took her seat, started her computer, and opened her mail. Forty-two new emails. Fortyt-two, and all but four of them were from Bouquets R Us. Chelsea laughed to herself. She would at least be busy for the day.

Almost instantly, Danny appeared in her cubicle. He wore tailored, carmel-colored pants, warm brown shoes, a white checkered button up, and his steel rimmed glasses. He was smiling.

"Hey," he said simply.

"Hi, Danny," she responded.

"Survive the weekend?"

Assessing her survival level, she smiled and said, "Yes, and without too many bruises."

He smiled in return and commented that it was good to see her at least laughing about it.

When invited to sit down, Danny actually asked if she had a few minutes to grab coffee with him. When he saw her point to her computer and go to make excuses, he said he already knew she had coffee and clearly a handful of work, but he'd buy her a second one to put in the fridge until lunch. Always a sucker for a free coffee, and determining that a twenty or thirty minute break could not do much damage at this point, she agreed. The two of them headed down the street to the closest Starbucks. Chelsea noted they had not invited Stacy, something very incongruent to Danny's normal behavior. Wondering if there might be a hidden agenda to their coffee, she let him take the lead on their conversation.

"Weekend was nice, yeah?" Danny said, trying to start the conversation as normally as possible.

"Yeah," Chelsea simply replied.

"How was the wedding?" he wondered.

"Crazy," she laughed. "It was great, but it was nuts, not that I would have expected anything less."

"Good," he concluded, pausing the conversation.

Chelsea felt the silence between them teeter on awkward, so she returned the conversational courtesy, "How was your event?"

He laughed and echoed her comment, "Crazy."

"Where did your mom end up taking you?"

"A wedding," he said, smiling to himself sideways.

"You too, huh?" she said and then noticed his sideways smile. "What?"

"No, it was just crazy. I wasn't really there to enjoy myself, you know. I got put to work."

"Work? What does your mother do?" Chelsea wondered.

"Well, it's my sister, actually," Danny stated. "We were there to help her."

"Okay, what does your sister do?" she asked.

"Bothers you," he laughed.

Chelsea searched her brain for a moment and then just stared at Danny.

"Bouquets R Us," he explained. "The flowers and 4,000 emails in your inbox are all from her."

"What?" she asked, merely a subconscious retort for what she was thinking.

He laughed. He had assumed she had no idea. "She's Bouquets R Us. She's the owner."

"Candice Jasper is your sister?"

"Wow," Danny laughed, "no one calls her Candice anymore. We call her Andi, but yes, she's my sister."

Chelsea just stared straight ahead of her as the two of them app-roached Starbucks.

"I take it you had no idea," Danny stated, understanding her silence to be his cue to keep talking.

"Not at all," she replied. "But, I mean, how would I ever have connected a last name like Jasper to yours when yours is Fieldman."

"I know. She kept her last name after her divorce. She already had a home-based decorating and back yard flower business at that point and didn't think changing her name would be good for business."

"That makes sense," Chelsea agreed, pausing to order another venti iced-mocha. If this was how her day was starting, she might need a continual "pick me up" as the day progressed.

"So the flowers on your desk were from her," Danny explain. "I figured she didn't give you any indication or sign her name because she's like that. She's fairly secretive ever since all that stuff happened, so I wanted you to know they were meant for you and from her."

"Oh, yeah, thanks. Of course," Chelsea replied. "But I didn't respond to any of her emails or phone calls yet, so I don't know what she's thanking me for exactly. I mean, I'm happy to help, but I don't know what I did."

Danny looked at her surprised. "The wedding," he stated very matter-of-factly.

"What wedding?" Chelsea asked, "Why would she be thanking me when you helped her?"

He handed Chelsea her iced mocha and led the way outside to the outdoor patio. He assumed, since she didn't already know, that it was probably best he explain outside and away from the crowd of people inside Starbucks.

"She did Rachel and Charles' wedding," he explained.

Chelsea nearly threw her iced mocha clear out of her hands, the news came as such a surprise. Danny lead them over to a table, and they sat down. She was stunned.

"What?" she cried.

"Yes, *that* wedding."

"Wait," she replied, putting her hands up to either stop him from talking or stop her brain from overcrowding itself with memories from the weekend. Taking a moment to breathe, she thought back a little further and then nodded slightly. "Oh, I think I may have known, actually. Rachel told me at one point, but it clearly didn't stick."

Then thinking some more, she became slightly horrified. "Wait, you were there?"

Danny laughed as he could see this was taking Chelsea a while to grasp. "Yes."

"Holy shit."

"What?"

"Like, the whole time?"

"Yes,"

"Oh crap."

"What?" Danny asked again.

"Like, for the reception, too?"

"Yes," he responded. "Which, by the way, was quite funny."

"Oh my God," she said, completely embarrassed.

"What?" he said defensively, "I mean, no offense. It just was. Your dad's pretty scary though."

"Oh shit," she said, her head finally wrapping itself around the fact that her personal life was now completely integrated with her professional life. "I can't believe you saw that."

"Yup. You weren't kidding either when you said your parents could be intense."

Chelsea looked at him like he had just said the sun was yellow. "Duh."

She took a sip of her iced mocha and then added, "I'm so embarrassed that you saw that."

"Don't be," he insisted. "I didn't get the whole back story, but whatever it was seemed quite involved."

"So you don't know? You have no idea what that whole scene was about?"

"Well, I didn't at the time, but Stacy told me this morning. Congrats on CUNY, by the way. That's wonderful."

"Wait, Stacy knew you were there?" Chelsea asked in an almost pleading voice. How the hell could she be so far behind?

"No," he reassured her, "no, she had no idea. That's partly why I didn't invite her to coffee. When we talked this morning, she told me you had been accepted. She seemed really proud of you. Then she said your parents had other opinions. I put the two together and came to the conclusion on my own that that was what the fight was over."

"Oh," Chelsea said.

"Don't worry. This isn't some major co-worker conspiracy," he laughed, seeing relief slowly pass over Chelsea's face. "I wanted to explain the flowers but do it somewhere everyone in the office wouldn't hear."

"Well, thank you," she replied. Then suddenly the mention of flowers made her remember something. She backtracked to something he had said just moments earlier.

"Wait, what do you mean 'ever since all that stuff happened'? You said that when you explained your sister's last name. Ever since what happened?"

"Oh," he responded, standing and pushing in his chair. "Let's head back to work, and I'll explain on the way."

She agreed and followed suit, pushing in her chair and tagging along as he explained.

"It's a long story. I'll try to give you the cliff-note version. However, you have to promise me something."

"Sure, what?"

"You can't tell Rachel," he said firmly.

She looked at him, confused. "Wait, why?"

He stared at her with a serious look on his face. "She doesn't know any of what I'm going to tell you, and Charles' family obviously prefers it that way or you would know all this by now, I'm almost certain of it. Just promise me."

Chelsea weighed her options and quickly decided it was worth keeping the secret. The intertwining of her life just increased exponentially, and she wanted to know more. If that meant keeping a secret from her best friend, clearly one that was already a big secret, she did not see the problem in continuing along the same path.

"As long as it doesn't involve Charles cheating, that's fine," Chelsea finally decided.

"Charles is cheating on her?" Danny said, sounding suddenly concerned.

Chelsea quickly shook her head, "No, he's not. Nevermind. Really. Just tell me."

And so he explained. A little over two years ago Candice's marriage had fallen apart. She and her husband came to irresolvable differences and broke it off. During the divorce she started seeing someone, and when the divorce was finalized they were an item. At least, Danny's family knew they were an item. Apparently, though, and unbeknownst to them, Michelle, the wife of the man Candice was dating, had no idea.

Chelsea scanned her brain quickly. She had heard the name Michelle before and tried intently to place it. Suddenly it clicked.

"Peter?" she screeched. "Charles' brother?"

"Yes," Danny explained, raising his eyebrows knowingly and nodding quickly. Chelsea felt like the wind was suddenly knocked out of her. She knew Rachel had no idea why Charles' brother, Peter, had gotten a divorce. However, it had been the entire reason why Rachel and Charles had signed a prenuptial agreement. Chelsea could not believe what she was hearing.

Danny continued, "Well, clearly Candice and Peter seeing one another made quite a mess of Peter and Michelle's marriage."

"Wait, did she know he was married?" Chelsea suddenly blurted out, curious to know as much information as possible. Danny simply raised his eyebrows knowingly.

"Oh damn," she responded, understanding his gesture.

"Anyways, Michelle clearly filed for divorce, and we all know that marriage ended disasterously. However, when things cooled down, Peter and my sister went back to being serious. They weren't talking weddings or anything, but they were definitely an item.

"At first my family didn't know how to respond, because we liked him initially. My parents were livid, of course, so my sister confided in me instead. I did not know this guy from Adam, but my sister seemed happy. After he returned to her, post-divorce, I decided he was at least serious about her, too.

"It was at that time that she said she wanted to expand her flower store and actually rent space to make it a legitimate business. She said Peter was supportive and willing to put up some of the money. She did not want to ask him for very much. Instead, she wanted me to help back the business.

"You can imagine I debated that for awhile. I don't have money to just throw around, but she really loved what she was doing and believed in it so much that I couldn't turn her down.

"You," he stated, pointing to Chelsea, "know the rest of the business side of it."

"Wait, if you're a backer in her company, why am I just now finding out about it?" she asked suddenly, trying to understand what piece of the puzzle she had missed.

"I didn't want you to know. I told her to keep my name private. I own a percentage, but that's in a separate contract between us, not on the loan papers. Plus, I didn't want to start mixing her business with what you and I do at the office. Why mess with politics if they don't need to get in the way in the first place?"

"True," she answered, seeming assuaged by his explanation.

"However, as Peter and my sister got more involved, Peter's mom started to realize she could not overlook their relationship forever. Now, granted, she keeps how they started dating very private, but she's accepted that they're together. I'm pretty sure she just says they're met through her flower store."

"Ok," Chelsea said.

"Now, with regards to the wedding, Peter's mom decided that she would rather keep the money in the family. That's why they changed flower arrangements and went with my sister."

"Oh," Chelsea responded, dragging out the word as she made the mental connections for herself. "That explains so much. Yeah, Rachel's original florist had no connections to Charles' family. Switching to Bouquets R Us would make more sense, but I don't know why she had to keep it a secret."

"No clue. I just know what my sister and mother tell me, and that's apparently why she got asked to do it. However, because she was asked so close to the wedding, my sister needed help moving, arranging, and organizing everything. I love my sister, but sometimes she's a little more absent-minded than she should be. Instead of hiring more people to help her, she asked all of us to help at the last minute."

"I see," Chelsea stated, now understanding why he and his mom had been at the wedding. Then she suddenly remembered something mentioned during lunch one day before the wedding.

"Wait, I thought you said you were going as your mom's date but also to meet someone."

Danny laughed to himself, "Yeah, you."

"Wait, what?" Chelsea responded automatically. "What the do you mean, 'you'?" Less than a second later Chelsea made the connection for herself.

"Wait, *me*? Are you fucking kidding me? Who the hell," she started, clearly annoyed, but decided just to finish with, "Oh my God."

Danny laughed again, "Yeah, that's why I didn't come bother you during the wedding. You seemed mad enough about being set-up on a blind date by your mother that I didn't think you needed to know Charles' mom had also set you up on one."

"*What?*" Chelsea returned, almost enraged.

"Oh come on," he said, surprised she was being so dramatic. "You know that family. They're *so* about appearances, just like your mom. If someone in the bridal party was single, do you really think Mrs. Waterford would actually let that go unresolved?"

Chelsea half growled to herself in annoyance and then responded, "No. True. Still, that's annoying."

"Well don't let it be. It's over now. I wasn't even going to tell you, but you asked."

"Fine," Chelsea returned, still annoyed.

"Hey, I bought you coffee."

Chelsea looked down at her iced mocha, took another sip, and then smiled lightly. "Yes, you did."

"See, and you're going to CUNY next semester. Tough life, kid," he chided.

The two of them walked for a bit in silence. Then Chelsea wondered, "So that's what you brought me out here to tell me, then, huh? All that stuff about your sister."

"Yeah, kinda," he explained. "I just figured you should know what you helped make happen and a little about the maniac you really do help keep sane with all your email and phone responses. I know you've been working with her for about a year now, and I can't tell you how much she appreciates what you do."

Chelsea simply smiled quietly.

He sipped his iced coffee and then added, "And Stacy was correct when she told you that my sister wants to open a new store. That's exactly what she's stressing about and proabably the content of 95% of those emails you have waiting for you today."

Chelsea laughed, "Thanks for the heads-up."

"Anytime. And, hey, no word to Rachel, right?" he asked, looking for reassurance.

Chelsea held up her hands defensively, "Promise."

"Thanks," he replied, opening the door to their office and allowing her to pass through first.

"Oh, and Chelsea," he said before turning to walk in the opposite direction and towards his desk, "You looked really good in that blue dress."

Chapter 24 - Action

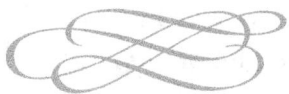

Danielle was back in her office with a mission: find a job in Albany. She insisted, however, in taking the time to properly look for work instead of hastily jumping the gun and moving out to Albany just to move out to Albany. Even though it meant more time apart, Paul had agreed to a deadline of two months to look for work. If after two months no solid leads could be found, she would ask if she could work remotely for a while, move to Albany in the meantime, and hit the pavement in Albany until she found a firm she could join. And this time she had no doubts in her mind that she could achieve her goal of finding work in two months. She had a lot to offer a firm, including the fact that she had been with her current one since she had interned there in lawschool. That sort of devotion and mutual respect was admired, especially in an economy where longevity was not as common as it had once been.

Almost immediately, therefore, Danielle set out to find a new job. Happily, five weeks later, a collegue of hers knew a friend of a friend who taught the Public Law class at Rockefeller College at the University at Albany-Suny. It was a connection, and through him she found a lawfirm that agreed to give her an interview. Ecstatic, Danielle even packed a few more boxes to bring to Paul's place as an affirmative step in showing her belief that this would work, and she would be moving shortly. In accordance with her belief, she was offered a junior attorney position at the firm and started at the beginning of November. She agreed to keep in contact with her current lawfirm, promising to inform them if and when she moved back to Boston. Their relationship ended amicably and with complete, mutual respect.

Now, it the last week of October, and she was packing up the rest of her boxes in preparation for her last drive away from Boston. The boxes lined the entryway of her apartment, and she hoped they would all fit in her car so she would not have to make multiple trips.

Rachel and Chelsea helped.

The three girls packed seventeen boxes, mostly consisting of clothes, shoes, office equipment, and kitchenware. Each of them was properly labeled, well-taped, and stuffed in Danielle's car by Saturday afternoon. It had taken all of Friday night and Saturday morning, but now Danielle's life was neatly packed away and ready to go. Danielle's car had so much in it that she couldn't see anything out of her rear-view mirror, but she did not care. She would at least make it to Albany in one trip, and that was good enough for her.

Once her car was completely packed, the girls decided to go out for a quick bite to eat at Panera before Danielle finally pulled away and drove off to her new life in Albany. It was an emotional time for the girls, but also a happy one, as each of them had new and promising lives in front of them. This would be the last luncheon they would have together for quite some time. Danielle would now be in Albany indefinately, Rachel and Charles had unpacked their wedding gifts and were settled into their condo in downtown Boston, and Chelsea was heading to New York City in a few weeks to apartment hunt before the spring semester at CUNY was underway. They were all certainly on the move.

"I'm so happy for you," Rachel admitted. "You and Paul are such a great couple. I'm glad you made this work."

"Thanks," Danielle admitted openly. She was glad, too. It may have taken her a long time to realize that following Paul did not mean giving up her dream but rather that she was agreeing to *them* working on building *their* dream together. It was a positive and hopeful move, one bounded by mutual respect and appreciation from both sides, and she could not wait to be back with Paul and working towards building their life again. She was, however, admittedly grateful she had found a job. She had told the girls that if she had not found one, this move would have been a thousand times more terrifying.

"Don't be terrified," Chelsea laughed. "It may not be Boston, but Albany's going to be great."

"Whatever," Danielle chided. "You have no right to talk. You're moving to New York City."

Chelsea smiled widely, "Yes. Yes I am. And now that wedding season is over and I survived both your wedding and my cousin's weddings, I am so ready to get out of here and start over!"

"We're coming to visit!" Rachel insisted. "I'm already figuring we have to go Christmas shopping up there together or at least be around for New Years!"

"You're going to spend your first, married New Years Eve with me?" Chelsea wondered playfully.

"Hey," Rachel admitted. "I said together, not just girls."

"You have to watch out for her fine print," Danielle teased, taking a bite of her sandwich. "Ever since she signed that pre-nup she's been putting clauses on all of her statements."

"Not even!" Rachel shot back at Danielle and then looked at Chelsea for support. Chelsea simply shook her head and put up her hands to make the point that she was not getting involved in this argument.

"But yes," Danielle finished, "we will absolutely come visit."

"Good, because I'm going to know a whole lot of nobody here in a few weeks," Chelsea confessed. "I just hope I don't have to rent a place with a creepy roommate."

"Definitely," Rachel agreed quickly.

"Hey, maybe you'll have a really hot guy roommate," Danielle offered.

"And maybe I'll be able to find my own place," Chelsea countered happily. "Come on, this will be like the first time in forever that I'll be able to live on my own. I'm actually rather excited about the idea."

"You should be," Danielle said. "It's nice. Those few months I was alone before Paul came out to live with me initially were really nice. Plus, especially in New York, I bet having your own place would be fun."

"So when are you going apartment hunting?" Rachel wondered.

"Next weekend, actually," Chelsea admitted, but could not keep the smile from creeping up her face. Both girls noticed.

"With?" Rachel asked coyly.

Chelsea realized she'd been caught. "Um, his name is Danny."

"Wait, like bank-boy Danny?" Danielle wondered.

Chelsea nodded, smiling.

"Who's Danny?" Rachel inquired quickly, looking to be caught up as quickly as possible. "And why do I not know about him?"

Chelsea looked to calm everyone down.

"Quit, guys!" she insisted. "It's nothing serious yet. He's someone I work with, and this is so *not* anything right now. He doesn't do the dating thing really, and I'm leaving soon, so it's just fun."

"Well, duh!" Danielle added. "A weekend trip with a boy? Nice going, Chels."

"If he's going apartment hunting with you that's, like, serious," Rachel added, a serious look in her eyes.

"Rach, calm down," Chelsea countered. "It's just a weekend in New York and a few apartments. We're not like *hunting* hunting. I just want to get an idea of what's available, and we thought we'd see the sights in the meantime."

"Mm hmm," Rachel hummed knowingly.

"Well, I think it's great," Danielle finished. "Good for you, Chelsea. I'm glad to see that you're putting yourself back out there."

Chelsea finished her salad and nodded in agreement. "Yes, it is nice. I actually feel alive again and not like I'm suffocating. That's a feeling I haven't had in a really long time, so I have every intention of enjoying it for as long as I can."

"I don't blame you," Danielle stated warmly. "It's a nice feeling, you know?"

Chelsea smiled and just nodded. Rachel also agreed.

"And you and Charles are doing okay?" Danielle wondered as the girls finished their sandwiches. It had been a hectic month and Danielle had not even had time to talk to Rachel since the wedding. Therefore, she had not learned about the condom incident on Rachel's wedding night, nor anything about the honeymoon or post-wedding life for that matter. She had wanted to call, but her first priority had been finding a job.

Rachel answered her question but kept it simple. This was not the time to divulge everything, and, honestly, she didn't want to. Some things were better kept permanent secrets, and the catastrophic condom event was one of them. Since then, though, things had improved. The honeymoon had gone swimmingly. Charles had doted on her all week, which had helped to smooth over any lingering hurt and distress she held. Plus, since returning home, they had fallen back into their routine and spent more weekends together. The last part had helped the most.

Therefore, Rachel kept her response light. "Things have been a lot smoother since the wedding. I'm not stressing over some new little detail all the time, so it's much better. It's not perfect, but we're doing okay."

"Okay?" Chelsea wondered. "Okay" was usually about as good as "Fine" in Rachel's world, so Chelsea worried.

"Yeah, it's good," Rachel returned, "It's not *perfect*, but I'm starting to realize that my idea of marriage was a little too...idealistic."

"What do you mean?" Danielle asked

"Nothing really, just that marriage doesn't fix things, you know? I think I thought getting married would be the thing that made everything start afresh, but it doesn't. When we returned from our honeymoon, we were still...us. We resumed our jobs and the things we did before we got married. I'm really happy, but it took me a while to even myself out and readjust my expectation. I'm learning that things are what they are, and marriage isn't some magical fix-it, or 'restart' button, you know?"

"Well that's good, Rachel," Danielle admitted. "I'm happy for you."

"So no more worries, then?" Chelsea asked, shaking her head subtly. She was referring to the other woman fear that Rachel had had prior to the wedding. Rachel understood.

"No," Rachel said with finality. "He's home more now, and we're getting ready for the holidays, which he's been a really big part in. Things have calmed down, and he is definitely trying to be around more."

Chelsea tugged at Rachel's elbow as an affirmation and hug. Given everything that had transpired before the wedding, she was glad to see things had calmed down at the newlywed's house and that they were at a good place. Rachel had just chalked the whole mess up to pre-wedding stress and realized that things had a way of figuring themselves out when she let them. They were married now, and she had to learn to take things in stride since they'd be together for a long while to come.

Danielle quickly inquired about Stacy, asking Chelsea to tell her one last thank you for her. Chelsea agreed to forward the message the next time she saw Stacy. Chelsea explained that Stacy was now a part-time worker and full-time mommy. They had not been able to find an adequate sitter and were therefore saving money the best way they could. Danielle nodded, understood, and just appreciated Chelsea being able to forward the message whenever she could.

Once finished with their meals, the girls headed outside to say their goodbyes to Danielle. After a hug, smile, and quick wave, Rachel climbed into her brand new, white Lexus, backed out of her parking space and headed home to Charles and the rest of their weekend together.

Danielle piled herself into her own car after giving Chelsea one last long farewell hug. She promised to call soon and honked her horn twice quickly before pulling completely out of the parking lot as she knew Chelsea probably couldn't see her through the boxes in her back seat. Smiling brighting to herself and feeling peaceful for the first time in months, Danielle drove herself and the rest of her life to Paul's apartment in Albany.

Chelsea turned the keys to her car and let out a relieved sigh. As she, too, drove off the lot and headed back to her parents' house, she realized things were finally moving themselves forward. Chelsea could not help but smile at the realization that they were also moving in a full circle. It was five years ago that the same three girls had similarly parted ways after graduation only to end up back together down the road. She wondered if it was only a matter of time before they all ended up back together again in the future.